COLLAPSE

Clash of the Aliens

M. B. WOOD

EBook ISBN: 978-1-68057-023-6
Trade Paperback ISBN: 978-1-68057-021-2

Cover artwork by Michael J. Corales
Kevin J. Anderson, Art Director
Published by
WordFire Press, LLC
PO Box 1840
Monument CO 80132
Kevin J. Anderson & Rebecca Moesta, Publishers

WordFire Press eBook Edition 2019
WordFire Press Trade Paperback Edition 2019
Printed in the USA
Join our WordFire Press Readers Group for
sneak previews, updates, new projects, and giveaways.
Sign up at wordfirepress.com

Created with Vellum

ASHES TO ASHES

One speech triggered a series of events that led to an interstellar war involving three alien species....

THE WHITE HOUSE: AUGUST 8, 1974

"In leaving the presidency, I do so with this prayer: May God's grace be with you in all the days ahead." Richard Nixon's long face, tired and sallow, stared from television sets around the world.

In that instant, the planet's electromagnetic emissions had an element of commonality. Myriad television transmitters all shouted the same message. As the wave front marched forth, its power faded, until barely distinguishable from background radiation.

After traveling interstellar distances, it was like signaling the moon with a flashlight, yet, light years away, there were eyes that saw it....

KUYBYSHEVSKIY, TADZHIKISTAN: MID-21ST CENTURY

"Will they work, Manoucher?" Ibrahim bin Salih wore a white full-length robe of a wealthy Arab. Sweat beaded on his corpulent face.

"They'll work, I swear." Manoucher spoke to Ibrahim in Arabic. He knew his project would turn the tide of the war against the infidel.

"If they do not, many shall seek your head," Ibrahim said. "The Holy Alliance of Jihadists has no more money for you."

Ozone from hot electronics mixed with the sour odor of unwashed bodies and day-old curry. Light from a late afternoon sun pierced cracks in an ill-fitting door. A wheezing air conditioner struggled with the heat from a half dozen technicians and racks of humming electronic equipment.

Manoucher, though an Iranian, favored the drab grays of the Afghanis. He'd just learned the secret purchases of long-range stealth weapons, bio-bombs and harbor-wrecking mines, from Russia and North Korea had ended. The Holy Alliance of Jihadists had used these weapons to visit death upon the homeland of evil, the United States of America. Manoucher spread his hands and shrugged. "Do not these missiles have nuclear warheads?"

"Unless those Russian pigs sold us imitations."

"Please." Manoucher felt a surge of fierce anger. "I've spent too much time in the souk to be cheated by infidel swine. Besides, I checked them myself. All twelve contain nuclear warheads, ten per missile."

"Will your device work?"

"Yes. My only concern is whether the rocket engines are powerful enough to take them to our enemies. I'm sure the nuclear warheads will trigger the lithium-6 deuteride enhancement. They'll be the most powerful bombs ever built."

"Will they kill many?" Ibrahim asked.

Manoucher's contempt for Ibrahim grew. His beloved Alifa

and his three sons had died from a stray American cruise missile. "You worry about *dar al-harb?*" Non-Muslims? "No, these three devices will destroy their communications, so we can fall upon them unseen, to slaughter them like lambs."

"Three devices?" Ibrahim frowned. "Why three? Aren't our enemies in Europe and North America?"

"The East is like the Satan, *dar al-harb*. With one stroke, we shall neutralize both the Chinese and Japanese. Then we won't have to worry about our eastern flank. Forget about the Indians; our Pakistani brothers will take care of them."

"Does the Ayatollah know of this?" Ibrahim's face turned a pale shade of olive-gray.

"That *naqah*." Manoucher used the Arabic word that meant she-camel. "Has no balls. We shall burn out the Great Satan's eyes, cut off his many serpent heads, and bring him to his knees. We must do this so he does not continue to waste the blood of our *mujahedeen* and defile the world with his evil ways. It shall be done."

"It's not your decision to make."

Manoucher bent forward and tapped the keyboard of the computer. *"Shuf."* Look. He pointed to the casualty list on the monitor. "At the rate we sacrifice the pride of Islam, we'll soon have no army."

"I didn't know that." Ibrahim' pudgy hands fidgeted with a string of prayer beads as his eyes wandered. "The Ayatollah says we're winning, that the Russian stealth weapons and bio-bombs have torn the heart out of the Great Satan."

"Yes." Manoucher couldn't stop his lips twisting in contempt. "It's obvious that *naqah* doesn't tell you everything."

"What're you going to do?"

"Today, I begin the attack."

Ibrahim raised his hand and wagged a finger. "You cannot, not without the Ayatollah's blessing—"

"I do not need him to tell me Allah's will. I shall obliterate the capital cities of the Great Satan and his lackeys. And for good measure, those of Russia and China, too."

"Why? They supply us with many of our weapons—"

"Bah. First they take our gold, and now they want all our oil. While they pretend to be neutral, they suck us dry, just like the West. More *dar al-harb*."

"You cannot. Only the great Ayatollah can do this." Ibrahim turned, raised his hand, and called, "Guards, arrest him."

The guards did not move. Their eyes shifted to Manoucher.

"You fool." Manoucher shook his head. He pulled a gun from beneath his flowing robe and fired twice.

Ibrahim staggered and crumpled to the ground.

The technicians stared, silent.

"*Salaam*, Ibrahim. *Insha Allah*." It is Allah's will. Manoucher lowered his head and prayed silently for a moment.

He turned toward the rows of monitors and clapped his hands. "Back to work."

The technicians resumed their tasks without a word.

Manoucher kneeled over Ibrahim's body and searched through his robes. He removed a thin gold chain from around his neck, which held a key. He rose and gestured with his foot at the sprawled body of Ibrahim. "Guards, remove this piece of rubbish."

Manoucher inserted the key into a slot and did the same with the one he took from his pocket. He took a deep breath and turned both keys simultaneously. Red lights began flashing in the electronic module above the computer. His fingers flew over the keyboard as his eyes flicked to the monitors. He felt a smile come as he started the missile launch program.

The covers of three missile silos swung back. Rockets surged from the ground on columns of fire, rising on thunderous smoke clouds. They arced away from each other, inscribing white contrails across a deep blue sky. They climbed higher into the cold blackness of space toward their destinations.

The missile traveling east through the night was the first to reach its destination. At a point three hundred miles above the sacred island of Cheju Do in the Yellow Sea, the device exploded. Its 150-megaton yield created a point of light many times brighter than the sun.

Before its light faded, gamma rays interacted with the air to generate massive electromagnetic pulses. The pulses induced fierce currents in conductors that wrecked the electrical grids from northern Japan to Indonesia and west to the Himalayas.

Electrical spikes overloaded the solid-state electronics controlling the everyday workings of society, fusing them into uselessness. Power pulses overwhelmed communications, power generation equipment, machinery controls, and ignition systems —all electronic systems failed. The infrastructure of several billion people stopped working.

Minutes later, another missile reached a point three hundred miles above Wroclaw, Poland and exploded, swamping Europe with a massive electromagnetic pulse. For a second time, surging currents crashed through electrical grids, wrecking them. Internal combustion engines died, their computer-controlled ignition and fuel injection systems fried. Planes fell from the sky. All communications stopped.

The rocket motor of the third missile hiccupped and stopped. The missile arced down, failing to reach its destination above the heartland of the USA and fell toward the Atlantic Ocean. Its fusing logic recognized the problem and switched to a backup program. The massive fusion bomb exploded one hundred and fifty miles above the ocean, midway between Bermuda and Baltimore. Though much of its energy discharged into the emptiness of the Atlantic, a massive electromagnetic pulse blanketed the eastern seaboard of the United States, wiping out its communications and control networks, paralyzing one-quarter of the US.

High above, gamma ray wave fronts heated communication satellites to the point of vaporization, creating brief flashes of light. Orbital defense systems, navigation satellites, military communication systems flared and died under the blasts of fierce radiation. Only one orbital rail gun, over the Beaufort Sea, escaped the storm of radiation.

The lights went out. The world fell silent.

~

"*Allahu akbar.* The end begins," Manoucher said to no one in particular. He ordered his technicians to begin the process to launch nine missiles, each carrying ten, one-half megaton nuclear bombs, destined for the supine cities of the industrialized world.

~

"Sir, there's a FLASH message on the ELF," the Officer of the Deck called softly to Captain Mapes, referring to the extremely low frequency radio that penetrated the ocean depths.

At thirty-two, Malachi "Ki" Mapes, an African-American from Detroit, was the youngest commander ever of an Ohio class nuclear submarine. After Annapolis, he'd got a doctorate in engineering from MIT.

"Officer of the Deck, I have the con," Ki said.

"Aye, sir. You have the con," the OOD said.

"Helm, come to zero-niner-zero and bring us up to periscope depth. Clear the baffles. Sonar, look sharp."

"Aye, sir," replied the Chief of the Boat from his chair behind the two helmsmen. "Coming to zero-niner-zero, rising to periscope depth."

After completing a spiral turn, the submarine leveled off just below the surface. Its electronic search mast went up, sniffing for searching radar, followed by the search periscope. The Captain made an inspection of the sky and then the surface.

Nothing in sight. Eight-foot waves rolled across the clear blue-green waters of the Arabian Sea under a brassy, cloud-free sky.

The executive officer, Alphonse "Al" Belasario took a turn on the periscope. A former Navy linebacker, he'd graduated from Annapolis six years ago at the top of his class. "All clear."

"Transmit," Ki said.

"Sir," came the voice of the OOD. "There's a message from STRATCOM—"

"Let me have it," Ki said.

The printer in the aft corner of the room buzzed as a sheet of paper emerged. After Ki read it twice, he handed it without a word to his XO, Al Belasario.

TOP SECRET

FROM: CINCSTRAT & POTUS
TO: SSBN 738 MARYLAND
SUBJECT: MISSILE LAUNCH ORDER

AT 0810 ZULU TODAY THREE HOSTILE

1. MISSILES LAUNCHED FROM KUYBYSHEVSKIY, TADZHIKISTAN, 0375438N—0685348E.

2. NINE ADDITIONAL UNOPENED MISSILE SILOS IN THIS COMPLEX. SILO SEPARATION APPROX 500 METERS.

3. SEVERE DAMAGE TO COMMUNICATIONS IN USA, EUROPE, AND JAPAN FROM SEVERAL LARGE, REPEAT, LARGE NUCLEAR EXPLOSIONS.

4. DESTROY THE ABOVE MISSILE SITE—USE EXTREME FORCE: AUTHORIZATION CODE: XZK-CVWQ-BZP35Y.

AS SOON AS POSSIBLE. REPEAT, AS SOON AS POSSIBLE.

Ki took a sharp breath. "Is there more?" he asked.

"Sir, that's it. The radioman reports complete radio silence," the OOD said. "No one's broadcasting anything, not even GPS."

"Sound General Quarters," Ki called. "Have a bird ready to go, a large one." He hesitated. "Mr. Belasario, what kind of spread do we need based upon location, silo separation, and the CEP?" His XO also functioned as the boat's tactician.

Al Belasario's mouth tightened briefly. "Sir, with the uncertainty of the given co-ordinates and the silos spread out over three square kilometers, we should use two Tridents and lay down a grid of fourteen nukes. The 'big ones' oughta be enough to put even those hardened silos out of commission."

"Very well," Ki said. "Prepare number one and two for launch." *Six megatons in that small area*, he thought, *will make one helluva hole*. "Immediately." His voice pitched louder and higher than usual. His stomach lurched as he thought about the message—it was too damn real to be a training exercise. *I hope it's just a drill. Better too much than too little.* Each Trident held seven 400-kiloton MIRV warheads whose individual guidance programs had to be changed for this target.

Ten slow minutes ticked by. The tempo of conversation inside the cramped command center increased, rising above the hum of equipment and the ever-present whisper of air circulating as the officers and crew moved about their tasks. A printer clattered briefly.

Ki glanced at the clock. "Any further communications?"

"Sir," the OOD said. "Radio reports something from NORAD, but it's breaking up. It's coming in on low frequency and it's encrypted. They'll decode it once they get a full sequence."

"Very well," Ki said.

"Number one and two ready for launch," Al said. "Targeted

and fused for maximum ground penetration. Trajectories set for simultaneous time-on-target arrival. Ready, sir."

Ki pulled a key out from inside his shirt. He inserted it into the missile firing control console. "Ready, Mr. Belasario?" They went through the launch codes.

Al Belasario put a similar key in the missile firing control console. "Confirming launch code, sir."

"Commence launch. On my mark, now."

Both keys turned. A row of lights turned red.

"One and two flooded, hatches open."

"Confirm one and two open."

Ki glanced at the OOD. "Any further messages?" He had been waiting for the usual stand down order that came with every firing drill.

The OOD swallowed hard. "No, sir. Radio has not received any further messages." His face was pale. Sweat beaded his forehead.

Ki took a deep breath, stood straight and still. "Launch the birds." *Dear God, it's for real.*

"Activate ignition sequence, now." The weapons officer glanced at the timing counter above his workstation. Thirty seconds ... Numbers ticked off the clock until only zero remained.

The submarine vibrated as though shaken by a giant hand, followed by the rumble of water crashing back into the launch tube. Once again it happened. Silence.

"Closing outer hatches, blowing down launch tubes," said the weapons officer.

Ki felt perspiration trickle down his brow. *Dear Lord,* he thought, *forgive me for releasing such hell upon our world.* "Helm, dive to eight hundred feet. Bring us to one-eight-zero, make turns for twenty knots." It was time to find a deep, dark hole in which to hide, quickly and quietly.

"Aye, Captain. Diving to eight-zero-zero feet. Coming to one-eight-zero degrees, making turns for twenty knots."

"Very well."

"Sir, here's the message from NORAD," the OOD said, face ashen. His hand shook, rattling the sheet of paper.

Ki read the message:

SSBN 738 MARYLAND. AT 0915 ZULU TODAY, NUCLEAR MISSILES LAUNCHED FROM KUYBY-SHEVSKIY, TADZHIKISTAN, 0375438N—0685348E ATTACKED AT LEAST TEN MAJOR US CITIES INCLUDING WASHINGTON DC. DEGREE OF DAMAGE AND CASUALTIES UNKNOWN BUT BELIEVED HIGH, SATELLITE COMMUNICATIONS OUT....

Ki glanced at the clock. It read 0936 ZULU.

A coldness seized his heart and his guts turned. *We were too slow*, he realized. *Our birds were too late. Our world has come to an end.*

RISE OF CHAOS

CLEVELAND, OHIO

A mountain of ice lay heavy on Taylor MacPherson's heart. Though Vivian, his wife, was absent, in his mind's eye he could see her, at the refrigerator, lying in bed next to him. Now Vivian was stuck in Washington after attending a meeting at the Pentagon while seeking work to restart his firm. She hadn't flown home because the nuclear attack had shut down everything. She hadn't answered her cell phone in three days. He prayed for her safe return.

Though Taylor was but thirty, many thought him older, for above his long, angular face with its intensely blue eyes, was a head of prematurely gray hair. He'd closed the doors of his engineering firm when the war disrupted the economy.

The TV screen flashed to a glass and white marble-covered skyscraper. The camera zoomed in on an intersection.

That's new, Taylor thought. He grabbed the remote.

"... This was the scene earlier today at East Ninth Street in Cleveland." The announcer's voice quavered. "The electronic transfer system's paralysis has deepened the financial crisis and the failure of the Fed Wire prevents banks from clearing checks.

The Federal Reserve Governor in Cleveland released all available currency to the local banks. But, bank runs continue."

The screen showed hundreds of people in the plaza before the bank building, pushing and shoving against a blue line of mounted police. Something flew through the air and smashed the large plate glass window next to the bank's entrance. The crowd surged forward. A police horse reared, and an officer swung a billy club. Blood splashed brightly from a blond head. Hands reached up toward the policeman and dragged him from his horse.

A knot formed in Taylor's stomach.

"This took place after the banks suspended payouts on accounts. Earlier, a spokesperson stated the bank had run out of cash. Similar incidents are being reported all around the viewing area." The announcer paused. "We've just obtained these exclusive scenes of the East Coast from WKDA-TV, our affiliate in Pittsburgh, flown in on our own Super-Drone Five."

The screen filled with images of smoking mounds of rubble and shattered buildings. Burned out vehicles littered the open areas.

The knot in Taylor's stomach grew larger. It looked worse than the World Trade Center disaster, much worse.

"This is the Eye-in-the-Sky News from WKDA-TV. From New York to Washington, destruction is beyond belief. There are no apparent survivors in those cities. According to Ham Radio operators, there were nuclear strikes in those areas. The operators reported all communications from Atlanta, Boston, Chicago, Dallas-Fort Worth, Detroit, Houston, Los Angeles, Miami, New York, and San Francisco have ceased. There is no official word on these events."

A stump of an obelisk filled the screen. "This is all that remains of Washington, DC," the voice said. The image switched to a haze-filled valley with several arrow-straight ribbons of still-smoking asphalt with the outline of a plane. "I believe we're looking at Reagan National Airport." The voice rose an octave. "All the aircraft on the ground were destroyed when the District of Columbia was nuked."

"Oh, God." Taylor gasped. "Vivian."

I've gotta talk to someone. He grabbed the phone and touched in the number of his neighbor Alec. *Maybe his ham radio friends can get me better info ... Odd, no answer.* Alec was wheelchair bound and always called when he wanted to go out. *I'd better check on him.* He slipped on a leather jacket and went out.

~

Taylor pushed on the front door of Alec's home. It swung open freely. "Alec? Alec?" he called. The house was silent. Slowly, he walked through the rooms. When he reached the kitchen, Alec was lying face down, motionless, on the floor.

Taylor kneeled and picked up his friend's hand. It was stiff, cold. He rolled Alec over, struggling with his bulk. His face was puffy, bloodied, and gray. Taylor felt with faint hope for a pulse. After several long moments, he gave up. *Why Alec? For what?*

Taylor looked up. All at once his vision came into sharp focus. The ham radio lay on the floor among a litter of books and magazines. He could hear his heart pounding. He tasted bile and fought back the urge to vomit. He staggered to the front door for fresh air. Gunfire rattled in the distance.

A massive cloud of black smoke rose into a blue sky above the bare trees in the direction of downtown Cleveland. Three men in worn construction clothing stood on the next street corner. One yelled and waved a handgun. "Stop. I want your jacket."

Taylor broke into a run. As he turned the corner of the street, a shot cracked. A bullet buzzed over his head like an angry hornet. He ran faster.

After a brief struggle with the key, he got inside his home and slammed and locked the door. The house was quiet; its heavy brick walls muffled outside sounds. He dialed the police, but the line was busy. He couldn't shake the vision of Alec's puffy face.

Something crashed against the front door, then again, louder.

Taylor raced upstairs. He grabbed his Remington 1187 shotgun and loaded it with buckshot. He pulled on a Kevlar bulletproof vest, the one he'd bought after reading accounts of hunters getting shot. He'd felt silly wearing it while hunting. Now it seemed like a good idea. He tiptoed down the stairs.

The pounding continued, echoing through the house. Each strike against the wooden door produced a puff of dust.

Taylor jacked a shell into the chamber. He waited, gun raised, behind the clothes tree by the doorway into the narrow foyer. *I've never shot anyone*, he thought. The very idea made his knees shake. *Maybe they'll go away. Dear God, please make them leave.* A quiver ran through his hand and he gripped the gun more tightly. A splintering crack made him ease a glance. The front door collapsed inward.

A man's unshaven face peered, ferret-like, around the shattered entrance. He pointed a short-barreled revolver at each place he looked.

Taylor froze against the wall and held his breath.

"No one's here. Maybe this isn't the place. Look, it ain't been touched. I bet it's got lots of shit." A long-faced man clad in grubby brown Carhartt work clothes spoke quietly to an older man in worn blue work-pants and a shabby denim jacket. They stepped into the foyer. The long-faced man held a nickel-plated semi-automatic handgun.

Taylor clenched his gun with both hands to keep from shaking.

"You sure? This place is buttoned up tighter'n a crab's ass. I was sure that fucker ran in here."

"Aw, you been smoking too much shit," said the long-faced man. "Let's check it out."

Bastards! Taylor took a deep breath, stepped from behind the clothes tree into the foyer. He pointed his gun and yelled, "freeze."

As two handguns swung up toward him, Taylor fired.

The shotgun blast filled the foyer with noise and smoke. The ferret-faced man crumpled as if in slow motion. Behind him, framing a gaping hole, blood splattered brilliant red on the pale wall.

Taylor pulled the trigger again just as the second man fired.

Pain exploded from the center of Taylor's chest.

The long-faced man staggered and fell, twitching like a deranged cockroach. Blood pulsed from his neck, painting a jagged crimson cross on the beige tile floor.

Taylor bounced off the closet door, slammed into the opposite wall and slid to the floor, his back against the wall. It was as if someone had jumped on his ribs. He tasted the metallic smell of blood and the dry, salty taste of the smokeless gunpowder. It was all he could do to sit, close his eyes, and not move as pain surged through him.

A high-pitched voice called, "Joe? Buddy? Did ya get him?"

Oh, God. Another. Taylor raised his gun.

A young man in a grubby football jacket stepped inside. He froze, Adam's apple bobbing as he looked down at the dead men. He held a handgun loosely, as though not ready to use it.

"Drop your gun and raise your hands." Taylor found each word an effort. His gun's barrel began to waver.

The young man turned with a wide-eyed frightened-deer stare. He swiveled his handgun toward Taylor and raised it as if to aim.

Taylor pulled the trigger.

The young man spun and fell. More blood splattered the wall.

The kick from the shotgun exploded a wave of pain throughout his chest. Nausea swept over him. A blue haze descended as the floor rose up to meet him....

Something cool and hard pressed against Taylor's face as he floated up from a fluid darkness. He opened his eyes to a world askew from floor level. His eyes slid shut. He just wanted to sleep. *If anyone comes, I've had it.* He forced his eyes open. *Must get up. I can't stay here.* As he lifted his head, his skin peeled off the cold tile floor.

As he clawed his way upright, pain repeatedly stabbed him in his chest. Feet unsteady, he reloaded. Each shell clacked home with a familiar, reassuring sound. Silently, he tiptoed to the front door and waited, listening.

In a nearby mountain ash tree, a cardinal sang. Somewhere in the distance a dog barked; sounds of a normal world. Nausea boiled up. He staggered into the bathroom off the foyer, dropped to his knees, and retched into the bowl until nothing more came up.

Later, despite the pain, he dumped the corpses over the edge of the gully behind the house. He watched, drained and detached, as the bodies rolled and slithered down the slope. At the front of his house, he crawled under the bushes to wait, gun ready, watching the driveway. The only sounds were insects' buzzing and sparrows chattering.

It's warm, he thought, *for early April.*

Two hours passed and the shadows lengthened. No one came. Taylor crept back inside the house, stiff and sore as he made his way to the bathroom where he stripped and sponged himself off. He examined the purple bruise the size of a dinner plate on the right side of his chest. *Some ribs might be cracked*, he thought, *but nothing was punctured. I'll live. Thank God for Kevlar.*

Taylor sat on the couch, clutching his shotgun. In spite of the pain, the image of Washington, DC played over and over again, mixed with Vivian's face. His heart ached for her and grief filled his chest like a cold lump. He replayed the past events and knew he couldn't stay here. It wasn't defensible. In spite of his intentions, he fell asleep on the couch.

Noelle Smith's hands shook and her mouth felt dry. As she passed an overweight rent-a-cop guarding the checkout lane in the Mark's superstore, she saw his eyes run over her and focus on her breasts as if she were naked.

Pig, she thought. She grasped her purse to keep the handgun inside from banging around as she strode through the almost-deserted aisles. Her Reeboks squeaked loudly on the plastic-tiled floor. The overhead lights seemed too bright.

I've got *to get Howie's insulin*, she thought. *Those bastards at the Free Clinic wouldn't help him.* Their words came back repeatedly, "All he needs is a shot of insulin—here, take this prescription." *No shit, as if I didn't know that. And that stupid ATM ate my credit card. All I need is a lousy two hundred bucks. It isn't right. I've always paid my bills on time and I'm nowhere near my credit card limit. Thank God for my neighbor. It sure was sweet of Annie to watch my kids.*

"Excuse me." Noelle forced a smile and modulated her voice to sound pleasant. "I came for a prescription."

The round-faced pharmacist behind the counter barely glanced at her. "Name?"

His forehead gleamed as though oiled and a yellow wave of sweat ringed the armpits of his off-white shirt. He punched a button and a counting device rattled pills into a clear plastic vial. Another light on the phone at his elbow joined those already flashing.

"Smith," Noelle said. "Howard Smith."

"One moment, please." He thumbed through a stack of white paper bags on the shelf opposite the counter. The brown jars in the chrome and glass cabinets behind him were almost empty.

Noelle's knees began to shake. *I've got to get this insulin for Howie. I can't let my kid die.*

"That'll be $194.87, cash only," said the pharmacist. "No e-cards, checks, or welfare script. It's company policy until the financial crisis is over." He stared at her and frowned. "Say, weren't you here before?" He extended a hand while withholding the paper bag. He pursed his pudgy lips in an almost pout.

Noelle pulled the gun out, racked it, and aimed it. "Give me the damn prescription," she said, her voice cracking. "And you won't get hurt." The gun felt heavy, enormous.

"Oh." The man's voice rose an octave. His pupils dilated.

"C'mon. Now." Noelle motioned with the gun. Her throat ached, and her knees wobbled. Sweat trickled down her back.

The man paled. He slid the package over the counter, hands shaking, making the bag rustle. "You're m-making a terrible mistake," he said. "I c-can find out who you are."

"Who cares?" Noelle's throat felt scratchy. *You think so? Maybe not.* The busy staff at the Free Clinic had only taken Howie's name and their computers were down. The doctor scribbled a prescription and pushed her out the door. *There're a lot of Smiths in the book and Howie's cell phone isn't on any plan.*

"You'd let my kid die because I don't have cash." She slipped the bag inside her purse and leveled the gun. "Now you know what it's like to fear death."

"P-please." The pharmacist raised his hands. Sweat beaded his brow. "D-don't."

"Turn around." Noelle pointed the gun at his eyes. "Count to one hundred before you move."

The pharmacist faced the cabinets on the rear wall.

"Make like you're looking for something." As she waited, she rocked back on her heels.

The pharmacist began to turn his head.

"I fucking-well said turn around and count to one hundred, you dumb asshole," Noelle said, hand shaking. "Do it, or you're dead." She extended her arm and sighted down the gun's barrel.

The pharmacist sagged as though something gave way. A wet stain spread on his trousers. "P-please, don't kill me."

Noelle smelled urine. "Start counting and don't look until you're finished." She backed away and stuffed the gun into a pocket. At the aisle she turned and almost ran to the exit.

"Stop," a voice cried as Noelle went out the door. From the corner of her eye she saw the guard rise, hand on holstered gun. She sprinted toward her van. She heard a shot, loud and nearby.

She ducked behind a solitary car and glanced back. The visor on the guard's hat reflected the orange-pink light from the high-intensity lamps above. He lumbered onward, head bobbing.

Something inside Noelle snapped. All the frustration and worry about Howie's diabetes, that stupid fucking ATM and shit from snotty bank clerks—it all came to a head. She jerked the gun out and aimed it with both hands, just like in the NRA class. She sighted along its stainless-steel barrel, took a deep breath, and squeezed the trigger.

The gun was louder than she had expected. She flinched, closing her eyes for an instant. A moment later, she peered over the car's hood.

The guard lay unmoving. A dark stain seeped out onto the cracked asphalt from his throat. His gun was still in its holster.

Oh, shit, Noelle thought, *I killed him*. She looked around. The parking lot was quiet, deserted. If anyone had seen it, they weren't showing themselves. *Shit, shit, shit. I've got to get the hell out of here.* Without looking back, she ran to her van.

As her van squealed out of the parking lot, she heard another shot—it was from across the street. She spun the steering wheel and headed toward the freeway.

QUESTIONS, MORE QUESTIONS

MEANWHILE, ON THE DISTANT PLANET CALLED QU'UDA....

This, Bilik Pudjata thought, *is far from the center*.

He stared at the image of the fuel tank of the Egg-that-Flies, which stretched out before him, long and faceted. At the other end, barely visible in the dim starlight, was the bulbous half-asteroid forming the ship's living quarters.

Alone in the cramped compartment next to the propulsion system, away from social contact and with the ship halfway to the Kota star system, he felt like an outcast. For just an instant, a wave of rejection swept over him. It was a brief taste of the insanity that came with societal isolation. Every Qu'uda must belong and this was a taste, just a brief taste, of isolation.

He shivered.

How did I get into this? he thought. *Is it worth it? It was not chance that brought me here to the depths of interstellar space. I had wanted it—no—I'd lusted for it, right from the very start, almost fifteen years ago....*

It was during the time I was female, large with egg, Bilik recalled. *I was monitoring data from the deep space observatory, searching for the aliens when my biocomputer alerted me to a faint signal coming from a nearby star system.*

"Show me." Bilik slid from the wicker-sleeping basket. Her abode, cool and yellow, with the bed-nest its only furniture, seemed stuffy and closed in. Even its moist yellow-green vegetation brought no feeling of refuge. She felt a tingle run from the top of her head crest to the tip of her stubby tail—something was amiss.

"Picture format, maximum amplification," she said.

A holographic image formed, projected before her by tiny subcutaneous fiber optics at each side of her eyes, a direct feed from the biocomputer that nestled beneath the skin of one of her upper limbs.

A snow of static blurred the image. She unsheathed her claws instinctively. Something electric sparked in her egg-heavy body, like the start of the mating-cycle. "Broken Egg." Her mouth filled with a taste like that of dune-drift sand. "What's wrong with this signal? Where's the audio?"

"Listen," the biocomputer's voice said.

A piping squeal filled her ears. Sleeting electronic flotsam coalesced into a shadowy creature with two limbs draped from its upper torso. Its small head had hair and it made animal sounds.

"Egg-sucker." The only creatures that Bilik knew that had hair were mammals. *Ugh*, she thought. *Mammals gave messy live birth and were an evolutionary dead-end.* This creature was ugly, like all dry-land mammalian vermin. It gestured from behind a boxy structure emblazoned with a circular emblem. At one side, a piece of fabric hung limply from a stick.

The creature's appearance filled Bilik with an urge to seek sanctuary in an ancestral swamp, to wriggle deep into its mud until only her nostrils showed.

"Oh, my Egg," she said. "It can't be." She felt the scales in her skin ripple. "It has to be alien."

The image faded into the snow of random noise.

"Location?" she said.

"End-point receptors indicate the source is the Kota system," said the biocomputer.

That was but ten light-years distance.

"Biocomputer, call the Community of Investigators." Bilik paused. "No, wait. Validate the signal's integrity; search for evidence of signal reflection and check for external feed into the observatory."

Before I dare bring this to the attention of the Community of Investigators, she thought, I must be sure that it's not someone just tickling my tail. That meant checking thousands of receptors. *If this is the Hoo-Lii, I must notify the Defenders of Qu'uda, and immediately.* She tried to guess what the Community of Investigators-on-Interstellar Life would want.

"Compare this with known Hoo-Lii signals. Quick, do it now."

As she waited, thoughts nagged at her. *Are they a threat to Qu'uda? Will it affect my hatchling? Will this move me closer to the center, or further away? I want facts within my claws before I talk to the Investigators. Maybe I'm showing too much initiative. I've got my place,* she thought. *And it's far from the center.*

The signals were not band-spread digital, therefore not Hoo-Lii; they were analog with frequency and amplitude modulation.

Egg, she thought. *It's another alien, different, and close. Why did we not see them before? I know we've looked at Kota previously*.

"Biocomputer, compare the Kota and Hoo-Lii star systems."

"Specify parameters."

"Compare spectra and planets in biozone. Compare the historical observations with the latest information received, note anomalies. Visual display."

A holographic listing of the two-star systems appeared: Both had planets within their habitable zones, but they differed in size and amounts of water—not the same.

Now, Bilik thought. *I can call DalChik DuJuga, the Head Investigator, to tell of my discovery.*

~

After Bilik's call, the universal communication link—the Commnet—spread the news planet-wide in less than a day. That set off a great debate and a consensus forming—a quooning—about what she'd discovered and what should be done. Each individual's implanted biocomputer—linked to the Prime Communicator—provided instant access to anyone and all data resources on their world. The volume of communication rose to an all-time high.

Bilik realized these aliens were a dilemma, for there were other aliens, Hoo-Lii, somewhere, out there, too. These aliens, the second species, were close and proof of a habitable planet. She knew their over-crowded world, Qu'uda, needed living space.

~

Over the next six sleep cycles, Bilik became widely known, because consensus makers now called upon her frequently to discuss her discovery. The Qu'uda, in their formal and methodical way, *quooned*. All participated in the decision-making to a greater or lesser degree, depending on their closeness to the center. The exposure to the privileged core made her confidence grow. As a result, she moved closer to the center. It was intoxicating. Her ambitions rose.

~

After the seventh sleep cycle, PiRup, the Prime Communicator, announced; "The aliens may be a threat to Qu'uda. Yet, their planet may offer living space." It was the *quooning*—the consensus garnered from a massive web of bio-computers—which tied their society together, polling them for their opinions.

"Our Defenders must go to Kota, the alien's star system and investigate this planet, to see if it is habitable." His words echoed and reflected the hopes of a crowded world. "We must continue to search for the other aliens, the Hoo-Lii."

We're going to make contact with the aliens, Bilik thought. *I want to be a part of it. I must be.*

"We shall build an interstellar spacecraft, strong and large enough to protect itself from attack," said Mata ChaLik BuMaru, speaker for the Defenders-of-Qu'uda. His voice resonated with the harsh tonalities of one who came from the continent of Ma. "We shall investigate the alien's planet in the Kota star system."

It was then Bilik vowed to be on that ship. *Why not? I now have the status that just might make it possible.*

"Bilik Pudjata." Mata ChaLik BuMaru's holographic image appeared before Bilik.

He was in a pale-yellow room with dark brown sinuously carved wood furnishings. It had a richness that showed his closeness to the center and all its attendant privileges.

With rudeness bordering on challenge-to-combat, he said, "There are voices near the center who speak your name. Voices to whom I must listen. So I must take you on the expedition to Kota. I've decided you will construct the drive system." Mata ChaLik directed the ship's construction.

"You'll also be the expedition's alien specialist since you discovered the aliens." Mata ChaLik heaved on his perch. A yellow-green bower of twisted vines and drooping ferns moved into view. Water dripped freely from a Podu tree with a scarred and torn trunk.

"Report to DalChik DuJuga on the ship," he said in a formal fashion. His head crest vibrated as though anger bubbled near the surface. "Now."

Bilik felt a surge of triumph. A stray thought intruded. That garden looks a little tattered, like it's been used recently for mating. *Is Mata ChaLik like most males? Or is he one of those who doesn't need female stimulation to become aroused?* It was rumored he sought out gravid females for trysts in his garden.

Ugh, Bilik thought. She barely hid her distaste.

Mata ChaLik briefly unsheathed his claws, indicating his growing impatience. He came from Ma, the smallest continent, whose inhabitants had a reputation for quick temper. "So, do you need more instruction?" He waved his limb in dismissal.

A bittersweet victory, Bilik thought. *I must leave my wriggler to my family, for they want me to succeed. Soon, I shall be male and be a Defender, like him.* The vision disturbed her.

~

When Bilik arrived at the partially constructed ship, the Egg-that-Flies at its orbit high above Qu'uda, he met with DalChik DuJuga.

"It's much larger than I imagined," Bilik said. Each end of the ship was made from a half of a hollowed-out asteroid, with a gigantic tubular fuel tank between the two ends.

"We intend to avoid the fate of the Star Seeker," DalChik said.

She referred to the exploratory craft that had died at the claws of the powerful alien lasers of the Hoo-Lii.

"Come, I want you to meet the navigator."

They descended from the outer rim of the living quarters toward the center of the ship at its forward end, which was also a giant centrifuge that provided gravity. It held a crew of five hundred and all the supplies needed for their thirty-year voyage. The forward part of the ship had an end-cap of one-half of the hollowed out asteroid. Its thick metal protected the crew from the hard radiation that would come from particle collisions at relativistic speeds.

"Meet Cha KinLaat DoMar, the navigator," said DalChik. "He's also an environmental analyst."

The room's solitary occupant turned and waggled his head crest. "Hello, DalChik." He glanced at Bilik.

Bilik noticed an odd smell, a distasteful smell.

"Cha KinLaat DoMar," DalChik said. "Meet Bilik Pudjata."

"Ah, you're the one who discovered the aliens in the Kota system. May you move ever closer to the center." Cha KinLaat flattened his head crest to indicate respect. "Welcome to the navigation station," he said. "It won't get much use now I have another biocomputer." Cha KinLaat indicated a lump on the inside of his upper limb, with fresh, green scar tissue. "I can navigate from anywhere on the ship." He pointed at a bundle of wire hanging from a console. "I had to replace the station's biocomputer with an electronic computer, because its life support system failed."

"Oh." Bilik recognized the odor of rotting flesh. *How does he control two biocomputers simultaneously?* "You're the one who gives commands to change the course of the ship?"

"Not really." Cha KinLaat's head wagged. "That's Mata ChaLik who speaks for the Defenders. I do as he bids. Only those orders which the Keepers approve." DalChik's head crest flared slightly.

The Keepers-of-the-Egg were the restraining claw on the Defenders. To get this ship built, Mata ChaLik and the Defenders had to accept quooning partners. Many still remembered the military sects' propensity to dominate.

"Well, yes." The topic seemed to make Cha KinLaat nervous. "A ship this size doesn't change course easily, nor stop quickly.

Most of the trip, I'll just confirm vectors and location. I'll also monitor the electromagnetic spectrum of Kota."

"What's it like on the ship?" Bilik wanted the real facts.

"It's been non-stop for almost two years. I feel like an overworked machine. I can hardly wait until we're underway."

"That won't be for several more years." DalChik's head crest rippled with amusement. "Don't rush things. Come, explain your system, and show Bilik its capabilities."

Without a word, Cha KinLaat activated the external monitoring system and focused on the planet below to show Qu'uda's five continents intertwined about the equator with oceans covering both Polar Regions. Mountains bisected the continents from sea to sea, with tongues of the ocean licking far inland. Even from orbit, the bright green of swamps and cultivated fields and the red-brown of mud flats were visible. The star's orange light gave the land mass an amber hue and the oceans a turquoise color. A swirl of white clouds covered a quarter of the vast northern ocean, with fluffy arms curving across the supine land.

"The first hot season storm." Cha KinLaat sent a thread of red to the heart of the white swirl. "It looks like a big one." The red thread danced across the image to the largest landmass following the equator. "That should fill the swamps and mudflats, even on the interior of Yata."

That triggered Bilik's memory of the initiation for gender change, crossing the ocean to Yata in an open wind-boat during a storm. On that passage, fear of dying had triggered hormonal changes causing the gender transformation. It was the only way to become female. It was horrible, seeing others drown and fearing that would be his fate, too. After he'd reached the safety of land, the gender change had come. Bilik sought out a mentor, MuLaak YataBu for an explanation.

Bilik initiated a sexual coupling with him, pushed on by a powerful drive. Afterwards, MuLaak explained a nubile female's powerful drive to couple came from the survival instinct of their species. Their world, subject to monster storms that roared out of its vast oceans, had periodic population collapses. All life on their world had a genetic mechanism to become female and breed furiously after such disasters.

She remembered dropping her egg in the birthing swamp that lay between high mountains. As her egg had ripened in the sun-warmed mud, her claws grew large and she developed a ferocity that surprised her. After her little wriggler clawed its way out, Bilik took him to the safety of a shallow pond. Through the cool, dry season, she guarded him. As the water level dropped, her wriggler's gills atrophied. Before the first rain of the hot season fell, she took her wriggler home.

A red line flickering out to a depression centered in the far end-cap of the ship brought Bilik back to the present. It was a short, stubby tube that was small in comparison to the massive ship. "That's the drive system," Cha KinLaat said. "The main propulsion tube still hasn't been made."

"Why not? I'm supposed to work on it," Bilik said.

"Well, it's behind schedule. We didn't get the zero-gravity metal-forming unit needed to cast the propulsion tubes." The droop in Cha KinLaat's head crest indicated that there was a story behind it. "You'll find out about it soon enough."

Cha KinLaat moved the red indicator to eight slender arms that radiated at right angles from the front of the Egg-that-Flies. The arms, connected together with a faint net of wires, extended like a giant frill several times the ship's length. Winking fusion torches outlined its structure.

"That's the magnetic sail. It'll gather deuterium from the atmosphere of Bata as well as provide deceleration at the trip's end." Cha KinLaat referred to the system's giant gas planet.

Bilik felt at ease with the young navigator. "I'd like to see more of your system, but I must go to another meeting."

"Do come again. Next time, you must tell me how you discovered the aliens in Kota, with all the technical details that PiRup left out." Cha KinLaat bobbed his head.

A TRIP TO THE PARK

"Take Shepherd Lane into the park." Skid jerked his chin to indicate the tree-lined road that curved and descended into the Metropark. "We'll cross the river there."

"Uh, sure." Knuckles slowed the van.

Skid whistled the opening bars of La Donna é Mobile right on key.

He'd been told he could have been the next Pavarotti if only he'd learned how to accept criticism. But the streets had never let go of him and his music career had come to an abrupt end when he'd beat up his music professor at Oberlin College for berating him about his work ethic. Scar tissue from a motorcycle fall covered the left side of his face. He found that and the Deacon's Death's Head emblem on the back of his black leather jacket shocked, even frightened people. He liked that.

I've got to find a way to make a buck, Skid thought. *This fuckin' war has changed everything. If only I could've worked out something with Blade Velasquez and his Diablos, but that asshole wants to run the whole show. Since he got that fuckin' armored troop carrier, he's had a hard-on as big as the Terminal Tower. We should've got to the Armory first an' got that armored troop carrier instead of him. Now he's got a shitload of firepower. It'd be suicide to take him on.*

Skid watched Knuckles, who drove slowly and deliberately. Skid knew Knuckles was dumb, had enormous strength, and would do as he was told, killing without any qualms. Skid liked that, too.

Knuckles slowed the van and steered it into the park, then stepped on the gas. The van balked and ran roughly until it built up speed, rattling and squeaking over the potholes.

This van sure is a piece of shit, Skid thought.

Knuckles stood on the brakes, abruptly stopping the van.

"What the fuck you doin'?"

"Uh, I think I saw a van back there. It looked new." Knuckles' smile revealed a mouthful of half-rotted teeth, the legacy of a lifetime of meth usage.

There was a shiny, metallic-green conversion van in a parking lot surrounded by tall pines. Behind it was a large, angular building made of brown-stained wood that overlooked a tree-lined river. It was the Metropark's Nature Center.

After Skid got out, he appraised the van with a practiced eye. It had no rust and sat low on its springs as though heavily laden. He glanced through the van's window and tried its door, but it was locked. He sighed and got out a lock-pick and went to work.

"Hey, hey, you." A burly man in blue work clothes lumbered forward, shotgun pointed at them. "What d'you think you're doing with my van?"

"Bingo, the keys." Skid said quietly. He put the lock-pick away and reached for the nine-millimeter handgun stuffed in the back of his jeans. He eased its safety off and stepped away from the van.

"This yours?" Skid asked in as pleasant a tone as he could muster.

"Yeah, what're you doing to my van?" The man moved between Skid and the van, shotgun at the ready.

"Well." Skid waved his left hand in the air. "You got a mighty nice van here. We're in the market for one. We'd like to check it out, and, er, take it for a test drive, okay?"

"It ain't for sale," the man said. "And we found this place first. So beat it."

"Stosh, Stosh," a woman called from the Nature Center. "Who's there? Is it Fred?"

"Naw, it's just a couple of drifters."

Skid grinned and waved his hand in a placating manner. "Hey, man, it's cool, no problemo. We're going."

"Sure, and keep moving."

Skid saw the man breathe a sigh of relief, glance back at the woman, and lower the shotgun. In one fluid motion, Skid lunged forward, knocked the shotgun aside, and jammed the handgun's barrel in the man's face.

"Drop it," Skid said. "Or I'll blow your fuckin' brains out."

The man blanched and dropped the shotgun.

Knuckles picked it up.

Skid smiled. "Let's go inside for a little chit-chat."

Inside the Nature Center, Skid saw a dark-haired woman wearing a plaid shirt and jeans stood with her arms around two teenage girls. One was tall and gangly with an angular face. The other was shorter, pretty in a young and plump sort of way.

Within the wood-paneled room, tall windows overlooked a slow-moving river. A wood stove crackled quietly, surrounded by several faded armchairs and a battered coffee table.

"A regular family scene." Skid spat on the floor. "Okay asshole, gimme the keys to the van. Unnerstand?" He pushed the gun's barrel into the man's nostril.

Anger stormed across the man's face as he pulled keys from his pocket. He dropped them into Skid's open hand.

The women's fear aroused Skid. The full, petulant lips of the smaller girl caught his eye and he felt his cock stir. "Hey, you, baby bitch." Skid waved his gun at the younger girl. "Show me your tits."

"W-what?" The girl's eyes opened wide.

"Now just a goddamn minute." The man stepped between Skid and the girl. "Nobody talks to my daughter that way.

Nobody. You get the hell out of here, like now." The man lunged for Skid's gun.

Skid fired. Blood and pink tissue exploded from the back of the man's head. He collapsed like an empty blanket.

The women screamed.

"Shaddup," Knuckles yelled.

They became quiet.

The smaller girl started to whimper.

"What's the matter? You deaf or something? I wanna see your tits. Come on, show 'em to me." As Skid pointed the gun at her, he saw her pupils dilate.

She's afraid, he thought. He felt his pecker grow harder. "Listen, bitch, when I say I wanna see your tits, I'm gonna see 'em, understand?"

"No, no, please, don't. No." The girl fell to her knees and leaned forward, putting her head to the ground.

Skid stuck the gun in the back of his jeans. He grabbed the girl's hair and dragged her upright. With both hands, he grasped her flowered blouse, ripped it open, and tore off her brassiere.

"You bastard." The older woman leaped at Skid, clawing for his eyes.

Knuckles grabbed the woman's shirt from behind and threw her to the floor, tearing her shirt open. "Shaddup, bitch." When she tried to rise, he punched her between the eyes.

"Nice tits." Skid twisted the girl's hair. He fondled the girl's breast as she tried to turn away. "Firm, too." He tightened his grip and pinched a nipple. Her closeness and the fear in her eyes made him want her even more. He unzipped his jeans and released his erect cock. "It's time to gimme some head. If you do it right, you won't get hurt. Understand?"

"No, don't, please, I can't." The girl tried to turn away.

"Don't say no to me." Skid backhanded her across the face. "Listen, bitch, that's just a taste of what you'll get if you don't do what I say." Blood dripped from her nose.

"Leave her alone, you bastard," the woman yelled as she staggered to her feet.

"Shaddup, bitch." Knuckles punched the woman on the side of her face. She fell, sprawling, face down on the floor.

Skid used his grip on the girl's hair to maneuver her head directly in front of his groin. "Okay, little girl, if you don't get your mouth in gear by the time I count to three, I'm gonna beat the piss out of you." He bashed her ear and yanked her hair.

"Please, don't," the girl said. "I can't."

"One." Skid twisted the girl's hair, tearing strands loose.

"Please, no more," she said.

"No more? Really?" Skid twisted her hair again. He grinned. He knew she'd give in. "Two."

"Don't, please don't hurt me anymore." Tears streamed down the girl's face. "I'll do it."

"Okay, little girl, do it nice and you won't get hurt." Skid yanked out his gun and stuck its barrel in the girl's ear. "If you get any ideas about doin' anything with your teeth, I'll blow your fuckin' brains out." He moved his hips toward her face.

The woman crawled toward Skid. "You filthy bastard, you no-good Goddamn son-of-a-bitching bastard—"

"Shaddup." Knuckles smashed his fist into the side of her head again. She collapsed. He dragged the woman's limp form to an over-stuffed armchair and draped her over one arm. He peeled off her jeans, turned her over—buttocks up—and spread her legs.

"Hey, you about done?" Skid zipped his fly. Behind him, the girl was on her knees and between sobs, retched and spat.

"Uh, sure," Knuckles said. "I got my rocks off."

"Say, wasn't there another bitch?"

"Uh, yeah. I guess so. I wonder where she went?"

"If that bitch is messin' with our new van, she's dead meat." Skid reached for his gun. "Come on, let's go."

"Uh, sure. We gonna take these ho's with us?"

"Fuck, no." *Man, my old lady would cut my cock off if she knew I was messing with another chick.* "We gotta take care of business, remember?" Skid winked. "I don't want no distractions, okay?"

"Oh, yeah." Knuckles scowled.

Skid knew that Knuckles was disappointed. He never seemed to keep a woman very long. With him, they always seemed to get old and wear out real fast, even the masochistic mammas that liked pain. He always had his eyes open for a new bitch to bang and bang around. "Let's go, we got a lotta things to do."

"Uh, yeah, sure. Like what?" Knuckles frowned.

"Put the gas from our old van into the new one. Gas is hard to find these days."

"Uh, yeah." Knuckles nodded several times.

Skid whistled a few bars of "Jesu, Joy of Man's Desire" as he searched through the van. It was full of food, clothing, and camping gear.

It's been a good day, he thought. *I got a buncha goodies—as well as some head—even if the young bitch didn't know how to suck a dick as good as my ol' lady. Now to business. Maybe I can work out something with those Deacons in Berea.*

A FAMILY GATHERING

Taylor woke to the sound of a distant gunshot. Early morning sunlight streamed in. Silence.

Outside the bedroom window, a robin began a tentative song. *Damn, I must've slept through the night. Just like a Sunday. It feels so peaceful*, he thought. *But Vivian isn't here.* A lump formed in his throat. *Dear Lord, give me strength to get through the day*.

He noticed the alarm clock next to the bed had stopped. He got up and checked the TV—it didn't work. A quick trip through the house confirmed his suspicions—no electricity or phone.

A volley of gunshots in the distance brought yesterday back. *Even though this house is made of brick*, he thought, *I'm a sitting duck. One firebomb—poof—it's all over. I've got to get away, to some place safe until sanity returns. The local Metropark, that'll do*. It was a place where he and Vivian had spent many happy days hiking through its densely wooded areas.

By the end of the day, Taylor had packed his Jeep and a small trailer with necessities. Valued items he couldn't take, he wrapped in a plastic tarp and buried in the sandy soil on the top of the embankment of the Rocky River behind his home.

It was after midnight when Taylor left. He drove his Jeep through deserted streets lit by a partial moon, dodging wrecked and abandoned cars. He turned down the road to the Metropark, where branches hung low, hiding the moon.

I can't see a damn thing, he thought.

With only the daylight running lamps on, the overhanging tree branches loomed like menacing giants. *Anyone can see me*, he thought, *and I can't see them*. He took a deep breath and drove on, nerves on edge.

Taylor saw two bright spots ahead and slammed on the brakes.

A deer, its eyes glowing from the Jeep's lights, turned and fled.

I've got to find the West Branch of the Rocky River. That's where there's a trail through the thickest part of the woods.

A stonewall appeared.

Ah, the bridge. Now I know where I am. Overgrown briars and dogwood hung over the metal gate closing off the trail's entrance. *Good*, he thought.

He pulled onto the graveled edge of the road. He got out of the Jeep, taking a shotgun and bolt cutters. He tiptoed through the grass to the gate. Dew slicked off his boots with a barely audible hiss. His breath caught the moonlight and glowed like steam. Every shadow took a shape and became a menace in his mind. He stood still and listened. *If anyone's here*, he thought. *I'm sure they can see me*.

The wind whispered through the trees. Branches groaned and clicked. A lone owl hooted mournfully.

As Taylor's night vision sharpened, the menacing shapes faded into trees and shrubs. He cut off the gate's padlock and returned to the Jeep. He drove through the gate and stopped to put a new padlock on the gate. He drove on, gravel crunching under the Jeep's tires. The trail narrowed and became dirt. He stopped, unable to see where the trail went as it entered the shadows of a dark stand of pines.

This is nuts, he thought. *I'd better wait for daylight.*

~

As Taylor sat up and looked around, pain stabbed his ribs. Sunlight glinted off the tips of dew-laden pine needles. The reddish-brown clay of the trail held no fresh tracks.

Good, he thought. *No one has come this way*. He started the Jeep and inched between the tall, pink trunks of Scotch pines. After negotiating between two large trees, he saw the trail veer left, out of the pines. Ahead, the trail rose steeply, winding through an area of tall, silver-limbed maples.

Finally, Taylor thought. *Indian Hill*. He unhitched the trailer and parked it in a thicket of dogwood. He drove the Jeep up the rutted trail until a fallen branch barred his way. He reached for an ax and hesitated. *This sucker will make a sound that'll carry. I'd better use the bow saw*. He got the saw.

"'Scuse me, d'you have any food?" a high-pitched voice asked from nearby.

Taylor grabbed his shotgun and whirled around to point it at a tall, gangly teenager with a dirt-streaked face who stood barely a dozen paces away, shivering. The youth had a pale angular face, an aquiline nose, and a small mouth, raggedly cropped hair, and wore a loose-fitting blue cotton plaid shirt stuffed into faded jeans.

Taylor guessed the teenager was a male, sixteen or eighteen years old. That clothing couldn't conceal anything, except, maybe a knife. "Hold it right there." He raised the shotgun and glanced around. He felt a tremor run through his hand.

"Don't shoot me, please, mister. I only want something to eat." The teenager started to back away, hands raised.

"Don't move."

Tears appeared in the young person's eyes.

"Who're you?" Taylor demanded. "What d'you want?"

"I'm Chris Kucinski," the teenager said, "I haven't had anything to eat for two days. I'm starving. Gimme something to eat, please."

I'm halfway up the hill and half my stuff is in the trailer below, he thought. *What a pickle. Maybe I can get a measure of this "Chris" and get the Jeep up the hill at the same time.*

"Okay, Chris Kucinski." Taylor pronounced the teenager's name exactly as he had heard it. "I'll give you food, after you help me clear the trail so I can get to the top." Taylor pointed up the hill. Something about Chris struck him as odd. *Then again*, he thought. *I don't have kids—they all seem weird to me.*

"Yes, sir, I'll help," Chris said.

"My name is Taylor MacPherson. Call me Taylor, okay?"

"Yes, sir, I mean Taylor, sir."

Taylor gave Chris the bow saw. He picked up the shovel and slung the shotgun over his back.

A shovel, he thought, *makes a damn fine weapon at close quarters*. As he filled the gullies in the trail, he noted Chris worked diligently. He became less apprehensive after they dragged several logs off the trail. He saw the teenager didn't have anywhere near his strength.

"I'm going to try it," Taylor said. "Wait at the top."

Head hanging down, Chris walked up the trail without a word.

The Jeep crept slowly up the hill, wheels spinning from time to time. It crested the hill, engine roaring.

"Yes." Chris dragged out the "s," and made a downward punch to indicate victory. "All right."

"Let's unload the supplies over there." Taylor pointed to a small clearing on the south side of the hill's plateau.

"Do I get to eat?" Chris asked after they'd emptied the Jeep.

"I've got more stuff at the bottom of the Hill."

Chris pouted but said nothing.

~

It took Taylor several tries to get the trailer up the hill.

"First things first." Taylor handed Chris an empty plastic container. "Get some water from the river. Clear water, no mud or debris in it. I'll get the food started. Make sure no one sees you."

"I hear you." Chris's voice quavered.

After Chris returned, Taylor boiled water on a camp stove and made a bowl of instant oatmeal.

Chris wolfed down the oatmeal. "I'm still hungry," Chris said, eyes glued on the remnants of food in Taylor's bowl. "Sir, can I have more food?"

"Nope. And my name isn't sir. It's Taylor, remember? We've got more work to do before we eat again." He'd read that starving people got sick if they ate too fast. "Coffee?"

"Yes, Taylor, thank you, Taylor." Chris looked away.

Taylor studied the hill. Its flat top had a dense plantation of mature pines with a perimeter of red oaks, beeches, and scrubby dogwood. Its north side sloped steeply down into a grove of maples. On the south and west sides were vertical cliffs formed by erosion of the Rocky River, which lay almost a hundred feet below. To the east, the former course of the river had formed a swamp. In the distance, the park road crossed over the river, just past the merger of the river's east and west branches.

It'll do, he thought. *It'll have to do.*

~

By late afternoon, they'd stored the supplies off the ground under plastic and bent boughs. They erected Taylor's pop-up tent. During this time, they shared few words other than those to work together.

"Chris, get me some pine branches."

"What kind? Ones with needles on them?"

"No, dry, dead ones for a campfire. It's time to eat."

"It's about time; I'm freaking famished." Chris got the wood.

Taylor built a fire that burned hot with little smoke. He sautéed a package of meat in a large pot and when the meat was browned, he added several cans of vegetables and seasoning.

"Okay," he said, stirring the pot. "How come you're in the woods by yourself?"

"I got separated from my family." Chris's voice became quieter, subdued. "I was afraid to go back to Cleveland."

"How did you get separated from your family?"

"My father ..." Chris started to cry.

"Why don't you start at the beginning and tell me the whole story." Taylor could see Chris was on the verge of losing control. "Look." He softened his voice. "Look, if you're going to eat with me, you're going to have to level with me. Okay?" He paused. "So, why don't you tell me about it?"

Chris took a deep breath. "My father was killed. Murdered."

Taylor's heart lurched. A lump formed in his throat and his mouth felt dry. "How did that happen?" he asked.

Poor kid, he thought, *I do know what you're going through. Oh, God, I do know it, only too well.*

"They killed him when he tried to stop them from doing things to Mom and Sis."

"And?" *Dear Jesus. It's worse than I feared.*

"They shot him, and then ..." Chris gulped. "They beat my Mom and Sis. I'm not sure, but I think the big guy killed my mom, too. He hit her so hard she didn't get up. Then he took her clothes off...." Chris's voice faded.

"Where did this happen?" Taylor stared at the pot of food. Bubbles started to rise. He stirred it.

"When things got crazy in the city, we went to the Nature

Center in the Park. Dad had packed our van full of food and clothes and stuff." Chris looked up, face owlish with eyes surrounded by grime. "We came here 'cause Dad thought it'd be safe. That was two days ago." Chris sniffled. "Two men ambushed us. They looked like bikers, y'know, wearing black leather jackets, long hair, and tattoos. One was huge, a real gorilla. The one with scars on his face did most of the talking. He's the one who killed my dad."

"How did you get away?"

"The scar-faced man wanted Cathy, my little sister, to, uh, do things with him. When she wouldn't, he beat her."

"I've got the picture." Taylor shook his head.

"It was awful. Mom tried to stop him from hitting her, but the big guy hit her so hard she didn't move any more. I couldn't watch. While they were doing things to Mom and Sis, I ran away. I should've done something to stop them. But I didn't do anything." Chris sniffled some more. "I really should've tried, but I was too scared."

"You probably couldn't have done anything, anyway. If you'd tried, they would have killed you, too." Taylor spooned steaming stew into a bowl. "Here, eat. You'll feel better."

Afterwards, they cleaned up with few words. As the light faded, Taylor saw Chris shivering. He got an insulated hunting jacket from the Jeep. "Here," he said. "Put this on."

"Thanks."

Taylor felt bone weary and saw Chris yawn. It had been a long day. "I think it's sack time."

Taylor woke with wet feet. He opened his eyes and saw water dripping from the peak of the tent's opening. A northeast wind had loosened the tent's door. Outside, under swiftly moving gray clouds, branches glistened dark, wet and waving.

He got up and started a fire. Upwind, he still could smell

smoke, acrid smoke. He sniffed several times. Smoke from locust wood burning. *Hmm*, he thought, *we're burning pine*.

"Well, where there's smoke, there's fire." He got guns out of the Jeep, including a Colt AR15. "Chris, do you know how to use a shotgun?"

"Er, yes," Chris said. "I used to go hunting with my Dad."

Taylor handed the shotgun to Chris. "Let's go," he said.

"Like where? Where're we going?"

"We're going to check out the Nature Center. To find out if those men are still around."

"Do we have to?" Chris stared at the ground, feet stirring pine needles and mouth pouting.

"Yes," Taylor said. "Let's go."

"If you say so." Worry pinched Chris's face.

"In front." Even though Taylor's instincts told him Chris was okay, he wasn't going to be stupid. On the way down the hill, he saw Chris held the shotgun like a hunter.

The rain eased. Water continued to drip from gaunt trees. Squatting below the skirts of stunted hemlocks near the Nature Center, Taylor could see shadowy shapes behind its windows.

"Look." Chris pointed. "That's Mom and Sis."

"Y'think so?" Taylor said. "How come you didn't see them before?"

"I was freaking scared those men might be here. Their van's still here." A shiver ran through Chris's thin body.

"I understand. Let's wait and see if they're alone," Taylor said. "It doesn't pay to be too hasty."

Inside, every now and then, someone moved. Misty rain began to drift through the quiet woods. Water trickled down Taylor's neck. "Chris, go to the Nature Center. If there are men there, drop your gun, act frightened. Got it?"

"Do I have to?" Chris's pupils dilated.

"Look, we've been here for almost an hour. Have you seen anyone else inside other than your mother and sister?"

"Well, no, but—"

"You're scared, right? That's nothing to be ashamed of. I'm scared, too. We've got to find out if it's just them."

"If you say so." Color drained from Chris's face.

"I'll back you up."

Chris slid out from the cover of the hemlocks and walked slowly toward the Nature Center, gripping the shotgun, knuckles gleaming white.

Taylor raised his Colt rifle. He peered through its telescopic sight, aiming it at the front door of the Nature Center, chest-high. He released its safety.

If anyone tries to hurt that kid, came an unbidden thought, *I'll blow them away*.

The door opened a crack. A pale face appeared for a moment.

Chris lowered the shotgun and stepped inside. A moment later, the door reopened. Chris leaned out and yelled, "It's okay, it's just Mom and Sis."

Taylor moved forward, rifle at the ready.

"Mom, this is Taylor MacPherson. Taylor, this is my Mom, er, Mrs. Franny Kucinski." Chris gestured toward a stocky, dark-haired woman. Two blackened eyes peered out from fine-boned features. "This is my sister, Cathy." Chris pointed to a teenage girl with torn clothing. Her face was bruised, too.

Taylor saw the older woman's eyes were unfocused; her stance slack as though exhausted.

Mercy, he thought, *she's had the crap beaten out of her. What do I say to her?* "Er, Mrs. Kucinski, how're you?" Taylor felt awkward as he offered his hand.

The woman stepped back. The front of her shirt was torn, partially open. "Go away," she said. "Leave me alone."

"Mom, listen. He's not like those other guys, really." Chris's voice broke the awkward silence. "Look, he gave me a shotgun. I can protect you now."

The woman's eyes watered as she grasped Chris's hand.

Taylor felt his skin crawl. *I've never seen anyone beaten like this*, he thought. *What should I do?*

Something he'd read came to him: All that is necessary for evil to triumph is for good men to do nothing. *I just can't run away from everything. If I do, I might as well kill myself.* Taylor made up his mind. *This family needs help. Now.*

"Let's go up to my camp," he said. "It'll be safer there until things get back to normal." *If they ever do.*

"I can't." Tears started to pool in Franny's eyes. "I can't leave Stosh, not in his condition."

"What d'you mean?" Chris said. "Mom, Dad's dead."

"No." Franny motioned toward the back door. "I just can't leave him here. Not like that."

"Where is he, ma'am?" Taylor said.

Franny moved stiffly to the back door and pointed outside. "There. There's my Stosh."

The man on the ground had a gray face, a bloated stomach, and was missing the back of his head.

Revulsion welled up in Taylor. "We'll give him a decent burial." He swallowed hard. "I'll get the shovel. I'll be right back." *Dear merciful God, and this, too.*

Chris and Taylor dug a grave that overlooked the Rocky River. As the hole grew deeper, Taylor silently cursed the tree roots they encountered. Three hours later, tired, sweaty, and rain-soaked, they placed Stosh Kucinski's body in a four-foot deep grave.

Raindrops mixed with the tears that ran down Cathy's cheeks. "They hurt me, too, Daddy," she said in a small voice as she placed a bouquet of wildflowers and hemlock boughs on her father's body.

Taylor offered up prayers vaguely remembered from his parents' funeral. In his mind, he said them for Vivian, too.

Chris filled the grave, shoulders heaving between each shovel of dirt.

Franny wept and said not a word.

As Chris finished smoothing the top of the grave, a distant voice called, "Stosh, are you there, Stosh? It's me, Fred."

Taylor grabbed his rifle.

"Uncle Fred, over here." Chris waved at a group of people barely visible through the conifers.

A heavily built man with black curly hair and a woman with long, dark hair approached. Two teenagers ran ahead to greet Chris and Cathy.

"So, where's Stosh?" The man gestured with his thumb at Taylor. "Who's this guy?"

"Um." Chris gulped and looked at the ground. "Dad's dead."

"Huh? What did you say?"

"Dad's dead." Chris's voice cracked.

"Jesus Christ. What the hell happened?"

No one spoke. Franny continued weeping.

Chris pointed silently at the grave, eyes watering.

"I'm Taylor MacPherson. I don't know the details, but these folks have been through a terrible experience."

"I'm Fred Del Corso and this is my wife, Maria." His mouth tightened. "What did you say your name was?"

"Taylor MacPherson. I'd like to help."

"Oh, yeah?" His frown deepened. "Like how?"

"First, we've got to get away from here."

"What's wrong with using this here Nature Center?"

"It isn't safe—it's too close to the road. And ..." Taylor took a deep breath. "It's got too many bad memories. Stosh was killed here. Franny saw it happen." He pointed toward the grave. "We just finished burying him."

"My God." Fred's weather-beaten face went pale. "Stosh, poor Stosh. He was a good man, he was good to Franny." His voice choked. "She's my sister," he said.

“Let’s go to my camp.” Taylor pointed up the hill. “We can talk there.” He hesitated. “I need to eat something.”

“What about all the stuff Stosh said he’d bring?”

“The van’s gone,” Chris said. “With everything in it.”

“Aw, no,” Fred said. “I got robbed, too.”

Taylor felt weak and almost irritable. He knew he needed food. “Let’s go. I’m sure you’re hungry and I haven’t eaten today,” he said. “I’ve got meat thawing and I’ve got to cook it before it spoils.”

“All right,” Fred said. “Let’s go.” He gestured to his family. “C’mon, Fran,” he said softly. “Let’s go.” He slipped his hand into hers. “Freddy will take care of you.”

FIRST STEPS

At the camp on top of the Hill, Taylor sent the teenagers to get plastic trashcans from the Park below. "Stay out of sight," he said.

In a large stew pot, he browned venison and onions for the meal. Once finished he looked up, eyes still watering from the onions, and he saw Franny shivering. Her jeans and red cotton shirt were ripped and pinned together. He went to his Jeep and got jeans, a wool shirt, and a sweater. "Here." Taylor handed them to her. "Put these on."

Franny stared blankly at the clothing.

Maria whispered in her ear and led her into the pine grove.

The rain returned.

Taylor got out a roll of clear plastic, and with Fred's help, erected an awning. While they worked, Taylor learned the Del Corso family had been robbed on Mastick Road while coming to join the Kucinskis at the Nature Center.

As Taylor decided he'd cooked the meat enough to eat, the youngsters returned with two empty trashcans, which they scrubbed with water that ran off the plastic awning. They put the trashcans under the awning to catch water.

Taylor ladled the venison stew into bowls. After the first bite, he realized the meat hadn't been cooked long enough, for it was still chewy and had a gamy taste. Nevertheless, after he'd eaten, all came back for more and emptied the pot.

"Where're we gonna stay?" Fred waved his hand in the direction of the pine grove. "There ain't no place up here."

"You put this together in less than an hour." Taylor pointed at the awning. "It's keeping us dry."

Already condensation had formed on the inside of the plastic sheeting.

"Let's get this stuff cleared away," Taylor said. "Then we'll figure out how to get comfortable."

Fred nodded. "Say, where's the crapper? I gotta go."

"There aren't any toilets up here. Here's a shovel." Taylor realized that sanitation had become more important with additional people. "When you get back, let's get a latrine dug. We don't want this area getting smelly."

"Yeah, okay. Just gimme the damn shovel, I really gotta go." He grabbed the shovel and hurried into the trees.

Before light faded, Taylor erected his pop-up tent and insisted Franny and Cathy use it to get some privacy. Fred and the teenagers spent the night under the awning.

By morning, the rain ceased. Under a sky the color of worn asphalt, silvery mist floated among the mossy-barked trees by the river. Birds sang their springtime arias.

Taylor watched his breath steam. *Well*, he thought. *So much for the warm spell*. He made coffee on the camp stove.

"I want to get even with those punks on Mastick Road. They took my van and all our stuff." Fred waved his coffee cup, spilling a few drops. "If they didn't have guns, I'd have kicked the shit out of them."

“Let it go,” Taylor said. “Wait until law and order is restored.” He wasn’t sure when that would happen.

“Bullshit,” Fred said. “Just gimme a gun. I know you’ve got more than one. I want our stuff back.”

“Think about it,” Taylor said. “You want to go up against men armed with Uzis, or whatever?”

“Well, I don’t intend to let punks rob me and get away with it. If you don’t want to help me, I’ll do it on my own. No one messes with Fred Del Corso an’ gets away with it.” He spat on the ground. “No one.” He stared through thick black eyebrows as though challenging Taylor.

Taylor looked around the camp. The last of the venison was simmering in a large pot. It no longer seemed like he’d brought all that much food. *Eight mouths sure go through it fast*, he thought. All of his spare clothing and bedding had gone to the Kucinskis and the Del Corsos. “Yeah, well, I guess it would get under your skin. How d’you figure on getting your stuff back?”

Fred frowned. “Mebbe I’ll go at night and surprise them.”

“Well, if you really want it back,” Taylor said. “I’ve got an idea. Here’s what I think we should do....”

~

“Are you sure this’s the house?” Taylor asked. “I can’t make out any details.” Not a light showed on Mastick Road. “There’s no lights in this neighborhood.”

“Yeah, it’s like that in the city, too. Haven’t seen a thing that looks like a repair crew from the electric company, either.” Fred pointed, “See the chain across the road? And those funny-looking windows?” The pre-dawn light revealed the outline of a brick ranch-style house with an attached garage and shuttered windows. “I noticed them when they made me pull my van around back. Yeah, I’m sure.” There was almost a growl in his voice.

“Let’s use those trees.” Taylor pointed to a row of hemlock

with low-hanging boughs in an adjacent driveway. "We can see both the front and the rear of the house from there. Now, it's up to young Chris to do his part."

"She's a helluva kid," Fred said.

"She? I thought Chris was a boy."

"Yeah, well she's kind of a tomboy." Fred frowned. "You see, Stosh always wanted a son. He took Chris with him when he went hunting and stuff like that. Chris ain't ..." He hesitated. "Well, she's kinda tall and not real well developed in a feminine way."

They slid beneath the hemlock, each using a trunk for cover. "Does she have a medical problem?" Taylor felt like he was prying.

"Naw," Fred said. "It's just that she looks like a beanpole compared to her sister, Cathy. She tries to make up for it by being good in sports. She's a tough kid."

As the sky brightened, Fred chambered a shell in the shotgun and sighted in on the front door. "Just like hunting deer from a blind," he said. "Except this is personal."

Taylor checked his rifle. *Is there going to be more bloodshed? Maybe.* He found that the idea was not only acceptable, but also exciting. *What's happening to me?* He realized he had a reservoir of anger that was threatening to burst loose.

The Jeep appeared and stopped at the chain stretched across the road. Chris got out of the Jeep and slammed its door. She crouched down behind the vehicle and pulled on the chain. It rattled. She jerked the chain again.

Moments later, three men emerged from the house. "Hold it right there," one of the men called. He pointed a short, stubby, gun with a long ammunition clip at the Jeep. "Don't move."

"Freeze," Taylor yelled. "We've got you covered."

"What the...?" The man with the assault weapon fired on full automatic. Holes stitched into the Jeep's side. Glass shattered. Chris was nowhere in sight.

"You son-of-a-bitch." Fred pulled the trigger.

The shotgun boomed.

"Take that, you bastard."

The man with the assault weapon stumbled and fell. The two other men turned, firing their handguns. Bark and branches splintered, showering Fred with debris.

Taylor aimed at a man with a handgun and squeezed the trigger. The man dropped his gun, grabbed his leg, and collapsed. The shotgun boomed again. The third man staggered backward, holding his arm as he sagged to the ground screaming.

Taylor jumped up. "Fred, cover me. I'm going inside to see if there are any more." He remembered what had happened to the intruders in his own home. *If there's someone inside, it's still dangerous*. It took him ten minutes to go through every room in the house, entering each with the rifle ready. No one else was there. "It's all clear," Taylor called from the doorway.

"See what they had?" Fred pointed at the assault weapon.

"Sheez," Taylor said. "We were lucky." He put the MAC-10 assault rifle in the Jeep and beckoned Chris. "Keep an eye on these guys." He gave her a semi-automatic handgun. "If they give you any trouble, shoot them." He pointed at the three men. They looked up, each with the slack-faced look of shock, eyes wide with fear. They'd heard him.

"Not a problem." Chris raised the handgun and pointed it.

"Fred, let's see what else they've got."

Behind the house, they found Fred's van, which was still filled with his possessions. They discovered gasoline cans in the garage, from which they filled the tanks in both the Jeep and Fred's van.

"Someone's coming," Chris called. She pointed to a group of people gathering across the street, none of whom had guns.

After a few moments, a tall, gray-bearded man with a long-hooked nose stepped forward. He stopped a dozen paces from Fred.

"What's going on?" the gray-bearded man said.

"These guys robbed me yesterday. I came back and took what was mine," Fred called. "Who're you?"

"John Wylie, I live down the street. Can we talk?"

"Sure, come on over," Fred said. "We've got no quarrel with you. We're about done here." He kept his gun ready.

"Can we have them?" Wylie pointed to the prisoners.

"Sure," Taylor said. "We're done with them." He felt a sense of relief; the men needed medical attention, and soon.

"Thanks, you did us a favor getting them off our backs." Wylie turned to the group at the street. "Hey, Colagrossi, you got the tool of justice?"

"Sure." Colagrossi held a coil of rope with a noose.

Taylor shivered in apprehension. *Lord*, he thought. *Are they going to hang them*? "Wylie, it's none of my business, but what're you going to do to these men?"

Wylie crossed his arms. "What we're doing isn't much different from what you did." He scrunched up his face. "You got your stuff back without any of the legal niceties."

"Well, yes, that's true," Taylor said. "What you're doing seems ..." He struggled for the word. "Well, it's barbaric."

"Barbaric, eh?" Wylie's mouth tightened into a thin line. "These bastards killed two of my friends. They ran our neighborhood like it belonged to them. They took what they wanted, including our women." He wagged a finger at Taylor. "Believe me, hanging's too good for them."

"I see." At that moment, Taylor realized his earlier encounter with neighborhood toughs had not been unique.

The first time a man bounced and struggled at the end of the rope, he felt queasy, almost like he'd become soiled, dirty. It gave him a feeling it was a lynching. When the memory came back about what had happened to his neighbor and his encounter with those who'd broken into his home, a cold hardness seized his heart. *Screw 'em*, he thought. *They deserve it*.

Wylie approached Taylor. "Where're you from?" he asked.

"We're staying in the Metropark," Taylor said.

"You in the Nature Center?"

"We're camped on the top of Indian Hill."

"Really? Kinda exposed, isn't it?" Wylie cleared his throat. "Um, er, we need guns. To defend ourselves."

"You want these?" Taylor pointed to the guns and ammunition they'd found in the hoodlums' house. He'd only taken the MAC-10 assault weapon and its ammo; the rest were stacked against the front steps.

"Sure. Hey, one good turn deserves another. D'you want some building materials?" Wylie pointed to a burned out house down the street. "There's plywood out back. No one's been there in a couple of months."

"Thanks," Taylor said. "Hey, Fred," he called. "Wylie says there's some plywood over there. Can we use it?"

"Yeah, sure can."

"Thanks. Well, got to get moving," Taylor said.

"Thanks for the guns," Wylie said.

~

The next day, Taylor finished sorting through his supplies. He pointed to the stack of cans and bags. "Fred, this's all the food I've got. It'll last a week or so." He'd figured that he'd brought enough food for at least a couple of months.

"Well, JB's has loads of food." Fred referred to a warehouse-style store that sold food and general merchandise.

"Oh, sure. I wonder if they'll take my credit card?"

"Y'think I'm being funny?" Fred said. "JB's was full of stuff a week ago. Then a buncha hoodlums took it over."

"Are you serious?"

"Yeah." Fred nodded. "Thugs with guns chased me off last week when I tried to stop to get stuff. I didn't see them last time I drove by."

"Want to do a little midnight shopping?"

"What've you got in mind?" Fred's eyebrows rose with a

quick smile. "Something similar to our last excursion?"

Taylor nodded, "Why not?"

Lights off, Fred drove his van slowly through deserted streets. A full moon peeked through scattered clouds. Not a house was lit up. "I hope you're right about this," Fred said, now nervous. "We ain't exactly an army."

"If it's guarded, we leave, okay?" Taylor said.

"Yeah, you've got that right," Fred said as he pulled the van in behind the gas station at the far end of JB's parking lot.

"I don't see anyone," Chris said.

The giant, windowless concrete building was dark. Moon shadows drifted over the parking lot. A half-hour later, they drove into the shadow of the building and stopped at a rear door. Taylor shielded the light with his body as he examined the steel roll-up door. Tire tracks ran under the door. "It's got a padlock," he said. "Fred, get the cutters."

"Move your skinny ass outta my way," Fred said, wielding a set of bolt cutters. "This's man's work." He flexed the bolt cutter. The padlock's hasp gave way with a dull crack.

Taylor inched the door open. He lay down and peered under it. All was dark, silent. "Let's get the van in. Move it." As Fred drove the van into the warehouse, Taylor boosted Chris on top of an overflowing trash container.

Lord, he thought, *have we fallen from grace so fast? Or have we always been savages, never mind our technological brilliance and high fashion?* He looked up at Chris sitting on trash, probably scared stiff. There was no one else to serve as lookout. He handed her a Colt rifle. He knew if she had to use it, its loud noise would penetrate even the walls of the building. "Chris, keep watch and be careful." Taylor worried about her being out here alone. "We'll be back in about an hour. Okay?" *Dear Lord, keep her safe.*

"I hear you." Chris looked tensely over her shoulder.

~

Later, after Taylor and Fred had filled the van with food and supplies, Taylor slipped out the door adjacent to the overhead door. He saw a rifle pointing at him from the trash container. "It's me, Taylor," he said quietly.

"There're men coming." Chris's voice was up an octave. "They're due here any time now." She pointed down the eastside of the building. "It sounds like they just came on duty."

"We'll have to outwait them." Taylor clambered into the trash container to join Chris. "How many?" he whispered.

"Two," Chris said in a low voice, holding up two fingers. "They don't know I'm here," she said. "They're just around the corner." She pointed to a corner a hundred yards distant.

Voices, indistinct at first, became clear. "Why we have to go on patrol at midnight is beyond me. I busted my fuckin' ass all day long. Now I gotta walk around this fuckin' building half the fuckin' night while Thompson's porking his new piece. It ain't fair." The flashlight's bright circle danced across the ground, closer and closer, and landed on the door.

"Thompson's worried someone's gonna break in. He's crazy." The light flashed to the overhead door, briefly stopping at the bottom. "See, tight as a virgin's pussy."

Still complaining, the two men continued in the same direction and disappeared around the next corner.

A minute later Fred eased the van out of the building. Taylor installed another padlock on the door. They took the same route as the guards around the warehouse. They paused at each corner, checking the way ahead was clear. Once at the front of the building, they headed for the exit road.

A flash and bang came as the van's rear window shattered.

Fred stomped on the accelerator.

There were several flashes from the building and bullets thudded into the back of the van. Tires squealed as Fred drove fast around a corner. The van's chassis creaked and groaned. On

Sheldon Road, he increased speed and soon they were out of range.

"Hey, hey, Fred, slow down." Taylor was afraid the overloaded van would tip over. "We've still got to get home."

"Yeah, you're right." There was an almost hysterical edge to Fred's voice. "It's time to go home to momma."

OUTWARD BOUND

Bilik argued with Mata ChaLik about the assembly of the drive system during the Egg-that-Flies' final construction because he refused to skip tests to confirm the reliability of the drive system. Angered, Mata ChaLik didn't allow Bilik to go on the ship's shakedown cruise—he had to stay behind and make spare parts for the drive. The ship would gather fuel from Bata, the giant gas planet's atmosphere just beyond the asteroid belt where they would deploy mining spacecraft.

"I'll miss you," Cha KinLaat said.

"Mata ChaLik had to accept a reduction in the Egg-that-Flies' self-sufficiency," Bilik said. "That means more space inside the gravity centrifuge."

"Yes and no. All the extra space is allocated to food production instead of supplies. Did you hear one of the hangars for space craft in the rear section was eliminated?"

"That, too?"

"Yes, and no armored scouts, no Birds-of-War."

"That won't make Mata ChaLik happy." Bilik had heard rumors the leader of the Defenders wanted to turn the Egg-that-Flies into an impregnable fortress. "Will we get the Birds-that-

Soar?" He knew the mission would be severely handicapped without the three fusion-powered heavy lift shuttlecraft.

"Yes, but Mata ChaLik insists they be fitted with beam weapons to give them some claws."

"What a surprise." Bilik lowered his voice. "Did you hear Mata ChaLik must now have every command approved by the Keepers-of-the-Egg?"

"That should give me comfort. Somehow it doesn't," Cha KinLaat said. "I'll let you know how that works out."

Bilik watched the Egg-that-Flies depart for Bata. Its drive made a long, thin blue-white trace of fire in the dark night sky. The ship's motion was slow to see as it descended below the horizon in a slow dance with Qu'uda's moons. The next night, its flame rose like a distant glow-fly, shrinking over the passing hours as it headed toward the outer reaches of their system.

Bilik felt alone, for he was the only crewmember left behind. He struggled to produce the spare parts on schedule. As his patience wore thin, his circle of friends shrank.

It was, Bilik thought, *the price I had to pay to be a part of the expedition*. He had little time to call Cha KinLaat, and when he did, his friend was too busy to talk for long.

The Egg-that-Flies returned, appearing as a twinkling light among the stars. The huge ball of deuterium ice attached to its front made it brighter in orbit than on its departure. The ship would use the ice first and reserve the fuel in its tank for deceleration at their destination.

"Bilik," Cha KinLaat called. "The commissioning cruise went well except for the loss of two mining craft. One collided with an asteroid, and the other lost control and crashed into Bata. We brought back lots of metals from the asteroid belt."

"How did the propulsion system function?"

"Thrust was within design parameters. No problems. No one said anything about it. So it must have worked—"

"All crew members report to stations." A voice overrode their biocomputer's comm-net.

"That's Mata ChaLik BuMaru," said Cha KinLaat. "He no longer seeks consensus. He just orders us around. I must go."

"I need the Birds-that-Soar to take the spare parts to the Egg-that-Flies," Bilik said. "I've got a mountain of material and parts for the ship."

Bilik shuttled equipment non-stop to the Egg-that-Flies and brought down the metallic treasures harvested from Bata's asteroid belt. Finally, he took a last load of water up to top off the tanks, bathing pools, and the food growing systems. The ship was ready.

Few attended the departure ceremony in person. Most watched the holographic images on the universal communications link. The Egg-that-Flies' trip to another star system was a historic event. Some feared the consequences, while others anticipated it would add a new world for their expansion. A few wondered if the aliens of Kota had anything to offer. Most viewed the mammalian species as vermin that could be safely eradicated.

Once on board, Bilik felt like an outsider. Everyone else had bonded during the trip to Bata. Cha KinLaat seemed distant.

This will change, he told himself. *It's just temporary. Maybe it's me. I need to rest and recover from this past year*.

On the outward acceleration leg, Bilik found Cha KinLaat still preoccupied while crossing the planetary orbits. When he did call Bilik, all he talked about was how he'd modified and corrected the thrust vectors, refining their course, adjusting for stellar aberration and relative system drift.

The deuterium ice-ball at the nose of the ship shrank as they passed the asteroid belt. The ship cleared the outer limits of their system and accelerated at one gravity to reach almost one-third the speed of light.

Once up to speed, the drive system shut down and the ship coasted on through the dark of interstellar space. There could be no turning back now from their thirty-year-long voyage to the Kota system. They only had enough fuel remaining to bring the ship to a stop. They would have to find fuel at their destination, Kota, the home of the alien vermin.

THE WAREHOUSE

"Mark, Mark." A fist pounded on the bedroom door. "Someone broke into the warehouse." The knocks grew louder.

Mark Thompson's erection wilted. "Shit. Perfect timing." He climbed off the tiny, brown-haired woman who quickly dragged bedclothes over her nakedness. Tears stained her face. A crack in the boarded-up windows above a chest of drawers barely illuminated the room. Empty beer cans lay scattered across the floor, along with discarded clothing.

"I'm coming. Listen, bitch," Mark said as he pulled on his jeans. "You'd better check your attitude. When I get back, you're gonna hafta get with the program. If you don't, I'm gonna give you to the boys. They won't be gentle like me."

"No, dear God, no," the woman said through bruised lips.

"Look, I own you, remember? If you piss me off, you'll be sorry." Mark slammed the door hard. He knew it had an intimidating effect. He checked the door's lock. He liked young girls, and in dim light, he could fantasize this one was a teenager. He got hard again thinking about her.

Mark's control of the warehouse gang had started after he'd lost his construction job. His unemployment benefits had run out and the Union hall had no jobs. He'd needed work, something, anything to put food on the table. He'd answered an ad for a security guard at JB's Warehouse Store.

Mark had been an MP in the Marines and knew the jargon used by police and security officers. He was six feet two inches tall, two hundred and fifty pounds and he liked to fight. He cultivated an honest and open expression that was deceiving, which helped him get jobs and con people.

Manny Jerzy, the manager of JB's Wholesale Food Club (Always the Low Price), a fat little man with thin, greasy hair, needed guards to prevent looting and vandalism at his store. "I've got over four acres under one roof," he said often. Now he talked incessantly about rioters targeting supermarkets. He wanted more security.

"... and I can start immediately," Mark said.

"Military police?" Manny asked.

"Yes, sir, Mr. Jerzy." Mark nodded. "Hand-to-hand combat, crowd control, whatever you need, whatever it takes."

"Can you get uniforms and security equipment?"

"Yeah, I know some police officers who'll help."

"You're hired." Manny shook his hand. "Start tomorrow."

Mark bought six AR15 rifles and fitted them with thirty-round magazines. "Mr. Jerzy, it's getting tougher out there. I'm good but I can't handle a riot by myself. I need more guards. Y'know, so people think the military is here."

Manny nodded. "Sure, Mark, sure, that makes sense." Sweat beaded on his forehead. The damp patches at his armpits grew larger. "Where can I get reliable people?"

"Well, I know a couple of ex-Marines. They were MPs, too. I could have 'em stop by tomorrow." Mark's construction buddies needed jobs and he was sure that he could teach them enough military buzz words to fool Manny.

"Do that. I really need to protect my store."

"Sure," Mark said with a wink. "Be glad to."

That afternoon, Mark coached Dave Luken and Bubba Eaton in security jargon for the interview. "Be at JB's first thing in the morning," he ordered. "Spic and span, got it?"

"You were in the military police?" As Manny looked up, he mopped his brow. "Is that right?"

"Yeah, I was a tough cop," Dave Luken said. "I didn't take no crap from nobody. I, uh, protected property from, er, getting damaged." He struggled to get the words right. Even cleaned up, he still looked like a thug.

"How would you prevent situations from getting out of hand?"

"Well, er, Mr. Jerzy, you gotta apply enough force and, um, use it early before the troublemakers can instigate others in their unlawful activities." Luken's eyes wandered over the ceiling as though he might find the words there.

"Thank you, Mr. Luken. Will you wait outside, please?" After Luken closed the door, Manny turned to Mark. "I'm not sure he's the right man. He doesn't project a military spit and polish image."

Mark wanted his buddies on the inside with him. "Yeah," he said. "They have some rough edges, but under that tough exterior, they've got solid family values, great loyalty, and they'll do what they're told." He paused. "I'm not sure I could work with someone I didn't know, especially in these times, if y'know what I mean."

Manny's nod was barely perceptible.

"Trust me," Mark said. "Those guys'll beef up security, so shoplifters will think twice. I can't work with anyone else."

"Well, if you put it that way, I guess it's okay." Manny narrowed his eyes. "They're your responsibility, you understand?"

"Sure, Mr. Jerzy, I guarantee they'll do what I say," Mark said. "Okay for them to start tomorrow?"

"Yes, the sooner the better. Make sure they're briefed on company policy. Have them wear the uniforms with the gold badges." It was obvious that he liked that appearance.

"Yes, sir. JB's security guards mean business."

"That'll be all, Mark," Manny said. A trace of a frown creased his brow.

~

In unison, the TVs in the appliance department showed the National Guard in action in Cleveland, Columbus, and Cincinnati. Later, there were unconfirmed reports of police losing control in major cities and rioters routing several Guard Units.

As Manny watched TV, sweat began to trickle down his back. Police from the west side suburbs had gone to contain a riot in Cleveland and had lost. Live coverage now showed armed mobs overrunning both the Police and the National Guard in downtown Cleveland. Only one television station remained on the air.

"Mark. Close the store," Manny said. "Chain the entrance and patrol the parking lot. We've got to keep looters out."

"Sure, Mr. Jerzy." Mark knew anything wearing a uniform would be a target for drive-by shooters. It was time for him to make his move. There was one more detail. He wanted his friends inside. And, he wasn't going to patrol the parking lot.

~

Mark locked the exterior doors and went up to the roof with his men. "You two, stay up here. If anyone comes in the parking lot, shoot 'em," he said.

Manny arrived, wheezing and puffing. "Why aren't those guards patrolling the parking lot like I told you? Who're these other men?" He pointed at a dozen armed men. "Who gave them store uniforms?"

"I did."

"Why?"

"Well, Manny, times have changed." Mark felt a smile start. "I'm in charge now."

"The hell you are. This is my store. You're fired. Turn in your equipment and get out."

"Luken, Eaton." Mark gestured toward the parking lot twenty feet below. "Get rid of this piece of shit."

"No, you can't." Manny screamed.

Luken and Eaton grabbed Manny and threw him over the edge of the parapet. As his body landed on the concrete sidewalk below, it sounded like a ripe melon bursting. He didn't move.

"Target practice." Mark took a shot at Manny's body.

His men started to shoot.

"Okay, okay," he said a moment later. "That's enough. Don't waste your ammo on him. He's history."

When a mob marched into JB's parking lot demanding food, Mark's men opened fire. The mob fled. He remembered another group of people, in a van, that tried to buy stuff. A couple more shots and they too, disappeared. Soon, no one came near the warehouse and it became safe to move into the nearby houses.

Really, Mark thought. *It was quite simple.*

Mark drove along the side of the tall concrete block warehouse for about a hundred yards. "Which dickhead got me out of bed with this break-in crap?"

"There really was a break-in," Luken said. "There're fresh tire tracks inside, on the floor. A bunch of stuff is missing. This door has a different padlock now."

"You're shittin' me," Mark said.

"Eaton and Weeks almost got them. It was a van." Luken creased his face with a grim look. "They nailed 'em—there's blood, lots of it."

"Yeah? Show me."

In the morning light, a trail of dark drops made a wobbly line down the driveway and turned onto Sheldon Road.

"There, see." Luken nodded toward the road.

Mark touched the fluid and rubbed it between his fingers and sniffed. "Asshole, this ain't blood." He tasted it. "It's tomato sauce."

"Look." Luken pointed to a trail of drops that went north on Sheldon Road. "It goes that way."

Mark glared at the men around him. "Get Baker and his dog to track 'em. Nobody screws with me and gets away with it. Nobody."

A SMALL JUSTICE

As the van leaned through the curve, its suspension bottomed out with a bang. Fred checked the rearview mirror. "Almost home," he said.

Shadows hid the road; no lights anywhere. Through the bare trees, moonlight glinted off the Rocky River, its appearance was like a ribbon of gems. Fred slowed the van as he crossed over the bridge and turned onto the trail to the Hill. As the track got steeper, the van's parking lights barely penetrated the tall trees.

"We'd better wait until daylight," Fred said. "It's too risky to continue." He halted the van and got out. "I wanna see what those punks did." He flicked a flashlight onto the rear doors. "Jeez. Will ya look at that?"

The rear window was shattered; tomato juice and olive oil trickled down the bumper. Fred opened the rear door and cans fell out, leaking spaghetti sauce and olive oil. Red liquid oozed down the doorsill.

He frowned. "Shit, that'll screw-up its trade-in value."

"Maybe your insurance will cover it." Taylor tried to hold his face straight. "Tell them it was vandalism. Y'know, it was done by vandals."

"You think they'll believe that?" Fred looked up and caught

Taylor's smile. "Aw, man. I paid a lot for this van. I really wanted ..." He closed his mouth.

~

A delicate peach rimmed the indigo sky in the east. Distantly, water tinkled. In nearby pin oaks, wood thrushes sang flute-like notes. A soft, southern breeze caressed the treetops.

"Let's go," Fred said. "I wanna go home to my family."

The van creaked and groaned, all four wheels scrambling for traction up the gullied trail. Taylor and Chris followed on foot as the van struggled over the crest of the hill.

"Oh, *Sant'Andon', grazia, grazia.*" A pale-faced Maria Del Corso stepped forward, hands clasped before an ample bosom. "*Caro mio*, are you all right?" Lines creased her round face.

Fred jumped out of the van. "Yeah, I'm fine." He slipped his arm around Maria's waist and pulled her close. "You worry too much about me. I wouldn't have you any other way."

"Not here." She pushed his hand off her buttocks.

"Let's get this stuff unloaded." Taylor pulled out a pair of jeans and a long-sleeved shirt. "Franny, look at what I've got for you. I hope they're the right size."

Franny stared wide-eyed, waif-like in her over-size clothing. The bruises on her face had faded to a greenish-yellow. "Uh, thanks." Blankly, she looked at Taylor's offering.

Cathy took the clothes. "Mom." She tugged on Franny's sleeve. "Aw, Mom, come on, let's go change."

"Oh." Franny's eyes came into focus. "I can't put them on. These clothes are clean. I need to wash first."

Taylor hadn't bathed since arriving on the hill and his clothes were dirty, too. It wasn't just a good idea—it was an excellent idea. "Hey, Fred, did we get detergent?"

"Yeah, I think so. Why?"

"Laundry. Let's go to the river, clean up, and do laundry."

"Hey, hey, hang on," Fred said. "I gotta pick out my clothes. I wanna be dressed right. Gotta look good, y'know."

~

After bathing, the sun warmed the day and Taylor found he could not stop yawning. The night had caught up with him.

"Mr. MacPherson, if you want to take a nap, I'll stand guard," Albert said. "I'll wake you if anything happens."

"Great, thanks," Taylor said and crawled into the sleeping bag in the small A-frame tent.

~

Taylor woke in the afternoon to the smell of garlic and spices. He joined Maria by the campfire that burned hot and smoke-free. Two pots sat on a metal grate. "Smells wonderful, what's cookin?"

"Pasta." Maria offered a brief smile. "But no wine. Franny, go roust those men of mine. It's time to eat."

"Yes, Maria." Franny's motions were stiff, awkward.

"How's she doing?" Taylor asked.

"Not so good." Maria shrugged. "Better, but not good. It was terrible what happened. She's a good woman. Losing her husband before her very eyes. *Sant'Andon'*, save us." Maria rolled her eyes and slipped the spaghetti into the boiling water.

~

Taylor ate until his stomach hurt. The sauce had been thick and flavorful. "Maria, that was delicious."

"*Non che male*, Maria." Fred used a Neapolitan phrase that meant "not too bad." He patted her buttocks and kissed her on the neck. "You make the best food in the whole world."

"Fred." She pushed him away. "Behave."

Later, around the fire, Taylor and Fred discussed their situation. They now had supplies, but still needed shelter. It wasn't comforting that all stations on the car radios only produced static.

~

Albert came running from his lookout station. He'd been on duty at the southernmost point of the hill that overlooked the road where it crossed over the river. "Dad, Dad," he said. "There're men on the road. They have a dog."

"Where?" Taylor and Fred asked in unison.

"By the bridge." Albert pointed.

From the top of the hill, they saw two men with a beagle that had its nose to the ground, tail wagging. They were at the gate where their van had stopped. After two minutes, the men left.

~

In the morning, high flat clouds the color of old concrete paved the sky. A cold breeze blew in from the north. It seemed like overnight the maple trees had acquired a yellow-green tinge with red that came when they blossomed.

Several hours later, Albert returned. "Dad, Dad," he called. "There're men on Cedar Point Road, they're carrying guns." He was almost out of breath.

"How many men?" Taylor asked.

"I don't know." Albert squinted his eyes. "Maybe fifteen."

From the edge of the hill, Taylor could see three tri-axle trucks and a large sport utility vehicle parked along the road. A large, dark haired man with a mustache appeared to be in charge. A short, stocky man held the same beagle that sniffed at something on the road. The dog led them up the road, past the gate toward Mastick Road. After a few moments of hand waving and shouting, the men got back into the trucks and followed the SUV up the hill.

Ten minutes later, Taylor heard the distinctive popcorn-popping sound from the west. “Uh-oh.” He straightened up from his task. “That’s gunfire.” Memories of the thugs who’d attacked him in his home came back.

Please, Lord, he thought, *no more*.

“Look.” Albert pointed. A column of dense black smoke rose from the direction of Mastick Road.

It’s happening again, Taylor thought. *This time, we have to be ready*. He got the guns from the Jeep. “In case we have hostile visitors.” He gave Chris a shotgun and a box of deer slug ammo. “Use them carefully.”

Chris nodded as she loaded the shotgun.

“Here.” Taylor handed Fred the MAC-10 submachine gun. “We don’t have much ammo for this.” He saw Franny’s eyes on him. “You want a gun?” he asked. *God, this has to be awful for her*.

“I don’t know.” Franny sighed. “I just don’t want anything bad to happen again.” She clasped her hands. “I’d like to help.”

“You can,” Taylor said. “Will you?” He held his breath. *Maybe I can reach her. Maybe she still cares.*

“I’ll try.” She bit her lower lip.

“Good.” From under the front seat of the Jeep, Taylor retrieved a small rifle with a plastic stock. “This is an automatic version of a Ruger 10-22. Was kind of illegal.” He shrugged. “Still, it’s effective.”

Franny’s eyes widened, and she frowned.

“Sorry, it’s a lightweight submachine-gun that fires .22 caliber ammo. It doesn’t have much of a kick.” He showed her how to put in its magazine and how to use it. “Got it?”

“I think I’ve got it.” She handled the gun gingerly.

“Albert,” Taylor called. “Can you handle a shotgun?”

“I know how. Uncle Stosh showed me.” Albert jumped up and down with excitement. “He did, didn’t he, Chris?”

“Well, yes.” Chris sounded hesitant.

"But?" Taylor watched her carefully.

"Well, he shot some targets, but he never went hunting with us," Chris said. "Dad thought he talked too much."

"Aw, Chris." Albert pouted. "Did you have to say that?"

Taylor hesitated before he said, "Well, okay, take this shotgun. I want you as backup. Chris'll show you how to use it." He saw Chris nod approval.

"Way cool." Albert's eyes got big as he took the shotgun.

"We need cover." Fred's eyes settled on the trunks of fallen pine trees. "They'll work."

Using the Jeep, he dragged logs to the edge of the hill and stacked them into barricades overlooking the trail from Cedar Point Road. It would stop a column coming up the trail, and would offer some cover against a broad attack up the hillside.

~

Three hours later, Albert ran down from the lookout point. "Dad, Dad, Mr. MacPherson. The trucks are back. They came down Cedar Point Road. They're at the gate to our trail."

From the top of the hill, Taylor saw vehicles on the road. A slender man cowered on the ground alongside a truck. A large, mustachioed man kicked him then grabbed his hair, pulling him to his feet. The large man seized the slender man at the neck and shook him several times before releasing his hold. The slender man pointed to the gate that led to the trail and moments later he gestured toward the hill.

Taylor flinched. *Now what?* he thought.

Men with rifles, shotguns, and handguns spilled out of the trucks. The mustachioed man waved his hand, shooing the men into a line. Once formed up, they entered the trail.

Taylor's heart beat faster. "Listen," he said. "They're coming, and they're armed. Take your positions and stay out of sight. Hold your fire until you hear me yell 'NOW.'"

They nodded agreement, even Franny.

"Maria, you and the children watch the back path up the hill. If anyone tries to come in that way, warn us. Okay?"

Maria's lips moved silently as she fingered her rosary.

"Don't be heroes. That'll get you killed. Fire only in short bursts. Understand? God bless us and preserve us."

Taylor watched the men move along the trail in the bright sunlight before they disappeared into the dark shadows of the trees. Pale faces flashed from time to time when someone looked toward the hill. They approached without any sound.

They reappeared at the base of the hill. The beagle, tail wagging, had its nose buried among the leaves. The mustachioed man kneeled briefly to look at the ground. He rose and pointed up the hill. Taylor heard a clatter. It was guns being cocked. He saw the men line up with their slender prisoner at the front.

Taylor swore silently. He held up his hand so his small band would hold their fire. *There're more of them than I expected.* He cocked his gun and sighted it in on the man who gave the orders. His heart began to pound, and his mouth felt like sawdust.

Mark always felt better after he jumped someone and kicked ass. He laughed. *Those doofuses on Mastick Road never knew what hit them. So what if we had to waste a butt-head who didn't have enough sense to quit when out-gunned? Too bad.* When his boys took turns on a woman, it made him want a piece of ass—one that was young and tight, especially young. *It's time to get a replacement for that little bitch. She just ain't young enough.*

Mark learned from the prisoners there was a family with a young chick in the park.

"Hey, dork." He kicked the young man. "On your feet. Where's the babe?" He dragged him to his feet by his hair then grabbed his shirt at the neck and shook him.

The lanky teenager had raw, oozing blisters on his face. "I don't know." He began to tremble.

"Gimme a cigarette," Mark said. "His memory needs help."

"No, please don't. Maybe on the hill. They said they was staying on the hill in the park." He pointed to a gate almost hidden behind a thicket of dogwood. "It's up that way."

"You sure?" Mark played with the unlit cigarette.

"Yes, sir." The young man's lower lip trembled.

"Luken, you an' the men on the rear truck, stay here," he said. "The rest, line up and move out." He pointed to the hill.

At the place where the trail became steep, the dog stopped to sniff something in the leaves. "What is it?" Mark asked.

"I don't know for sure," the tracker said. "Something liquid. Kinda looks like spaghetti sauce."

"Shit," Mark said. "It's those buttheads who robbed me." He eyed the hill. All was quiet except for crows cawing in the treetops. "I'm gonna surprise this bunch, too," he said. "Put those horse farm dip-shits up front." He chambered a round into his gun and pointed toward the hill. "Move it," he said. "An' keep your mouths shut."

The trail's steepness slowed their pace.

Mark heard a voice shout, "Now!"

Why, he thought. *That's what I say when ...*

At that instant, a small caliber high-velocity bullet punched a tiny hole in Mark's forehead. When the deformed, tumbling bullet exited from the back of his skull, it carried a storm of blood and bone fragments that sprayed a crimson halo onto the silvery-gray bark of the maple tree behind him.

As the lead person reached the top of the hill, about twenty yards away, Taylor shouted, "Now."

His Colt rifle banged loudly. A shotgun boomed several times. The MAC-10 made a giant ripping sound. The .22 rifle pop-popped away, almost toy-like.

The man with the mustache staggered and collapsed. He slid

down the hill among a flurry of leaves until he slammed into the bole of a tree where he stopped, unmoving. The rest of the gang dropped to the ground. Gun barrels rose to return fire.

Taylor emptied his clip at the intruders and paused. Screams filled the air. *I hope that's none of my people.* He leaned back and as he inserted a fresh magazine into his gun, he glanced up. Above, a pale blue cloud of smoke drifted through branches backlit by a pale luminous green from the emerging leaves.

The shotgun on Taylor's left fell silent. As he stretched around a tree to see if anything had happened to Chris, bark splintered just above his head. He jerked back. More wood fragments exploded from the tree where his head had just been.

Taylor crawled along the ground to another opening behind the log barricade.

Down slope, a kneeling man pointed a rifle at him.

Taylor ducked. Splinters flew from the opening. "Damn." He returned to his original position and peeked out. As he did, a shotgun boomed on his left and the man with the carbine shook like a rag doll and slumped backwards.

Taylor fired. The man's body jerked and was still. Angry, he fired his gun at the barely visible bodies among the trees and fallen branches on the hillside until he emptied the magzine.

"Stop shooting," called a voice from below. "Cease-fire."

Moans and cries filled the woods.

Taylor sat up, back against the tree. "Shut up and listen," he yelled. "Take your dead and wounded, and get out. Leave your weapons behind, all of them."

"Hey, man," a voice called back. "We need our guns. You know what it's like out there."

"Do as I say if you want to live. That's my only offer."

"Aw, man, you—"

"Shut up," Taylor shouted. He snapped a fresh magzine into his rifle and chambered a round. He fired once. The gun's boom echoed through the now-silent woods. "Take it or die. No weapons. Now move it."

The gang members called back and forth. "All right," one yelled. "Hold your fire."

"Throw down your guns and stand up," Taylor called. "Hands on your heads and face downhill. You." He pointed at the man furthest down slope. "You, in the red shirt. Pick up the man next to you and get out of here. Now."

"Four of us are prisoners," called a man close to the top of the hill. "Don't make us go with them. Please."

"Everyone who's a prisoner, put both hands straight up." Taylor yelled.

Four individuals raised their arms.

"You, in the camo outfit, grab the man on the ground next to you and get out of here," Taylor called. "All of you, right now."

One by one, he ordered the gang to carry off its dead and wounded. Three men struggled off the hill with the last body.

Four remained.

"Albert," Taylor said. "Go get the guns. We'll cover you." He knew the men holding their arms in the air were getting tired. If they tried something, they would be at a disadvantage.

Albert made four trips down the hill to collect guns. When he could find no more, Taylor sent him to the lookout point to watch the road. He beckoned to Chris who had a trickle of blood on the left side of her face. "Cover me."

"Sure, no problem." Chris's hands were steady.

"All right," Taylor said. "You, in the blue coat, come here." He pointed to the slender man who'd been in front when the gang came up the hill. Taylor patted him down for weapons but found none. "What's your name and where're you from?" He realized the slender man was just a teenager.

"Frank Colagrossi. I live on Mastick Road." His face was battered and pocked with burns. "They captured me today." He choked out the words, "They killed my dad."

"Sit over there." Taylor pointed to a log in front of the grim-faced Chris. Her gun followed him. "Next."

An older man, tall and rangy, stepped forward.

"What's your name and where are you from?"

"John Phelps from Barrett Road." A deep frown marked the man's face. "Those sons of bitches raided my home two days ago looking for guns, drugs and women. They used us as shields when they raided other houses on Barrett. Their leader was a nasty piece of work, always on the lookout for young girls. Whoever nailed him did the world a favor."

Taylor turned to the two remaining men.

"Ted Callioux," said the short, freckled man. "I used to live in Berea until those barbarians burned me out. I taught physics at the college. They took my wife, Sandy, and me as prisoners about a week ago. Then that bastard, Thompson, took my Sandy away. Dear God, I hope nothing's happened to her."

"You?" Taylor pointed to a slender, bespectacled young man.

"Harv Cubich," he said. "I'm from Chicago,"

"Chicago?" Taylor frowned. "What're you doing here?"

"I'm visiting my uncle, Dr. Shel Weitzman. He lives on Barrett Road. I made the mistake of going for a ride the other day. I was just poking along on a trail and pow, someone shot my horse out from under me. Why he shot my horse is beyond me."

"Phelps," Taylor called to the man sitting on the log. "Is there a Weitzman on Barrett Road?"

"Yeah, Weitzman is a dentist who lives on this end of Barrett," Phelps said. "I've met Harv before."

"All right," Taylor said. "You're free to go."

"Free? Just like that?" Callioux eyes widened.

"We don't want prisoners," Taylor said.

"Who're you?" Phelps asked. "What're you doing here?"

Taylor introduced his group. As they talked, he got out a first-aid kit and dressed Colagrossi's face.

Cigarette burns, he thought. *Whoever did that was a real prick.* As they left, he said, "if you come back, be sure to show a white flag."

"As long as you've got the first aid kit out," Franny said in a subdued tone. "Can you fix my shoulder?"

Taylor concealed his surprise at hearing her voice. "Sure, no problem." He struggled to find the right words. "Gosh, Franny, you've ruined your new shirt," he said as he cleaned a shallow flesh wound. "How'd you do that?"

"I don't know," she said flatly. "It must have happened during the shooting. I don't remember."

"Well, it isn't serious." He placed a bandage on the open wound. "I've applied an antibiotic. Should be all right. Let me know if it gets painful or tender." He looked at her with his eyes wide, looking for a response.

"Thanks." Her eyes remained blank. "You're a good man," she said and turned away.

"You're welcome," Taylor said. "Chris, you're next."

"Me?" Chris frowned.

"Yup, you," Taylor said. "Your cheek's bleeding."

"It is?" Chris winced when she touched the cut on the left side of her face. "Gee, I never felt a thing."

"By the way," Taylor said as he swabbed the wound with an antibacterial solution. "That was some pretty good shooting." *Probably saved my life*, he thought. *She was like ice while under fire. I owe her*.

"Thanks." Chris's eyes kept flicking to Taylor's face as he treated her wound. "You know, we were lucky."

"You're right," Taylor said. "And you're as good as new." He looked around. "Albert," he called. "Show us what you found on the hill." There were one Mini-14 rifle, two AR15s, five shotguns and six .22 rifles. *No handguns? Fewer guns than gang members who came up the hill, so they still have some. We're still outnumbered.* And the element of surprise is gone.

RECRUITS

Stars twinkled above the pink-lined horizon. Trees carried a faint silhouette of their emerging leaves. Frost traced ghostly patterns in the low-lying meadow.

It's like a camping trip, Taylor thought. *But my Vivian isn't here this time*. He turned away and put a pot of water on the fire.

Later, as he sipped coffee and stared at the glowing coals, Fred appeared, his breath steaming as he spoke.

"Got any more coffee? I got cold. I couldn't sleep anymore."

"Sure." Taylor moved to make space on the log. "Me, too. We need shelter." He reached for the pot.

A cup appeared in Fred's hand. "Yeah. This living in the woods sucks. The damp aggravates my arthritis. Everything seems to get dirty twice as fast." He blew into the cup. Steam rose.

"Camping is a lot more fun with hot showers and clean beds."

"Or the House of Pancakes is just around the corner."

"Hah, you got that right." Taylor had to smile at the image.

"Y'know, I was thinking, there're park shelters in this valley. It wouldn't take much to move one up here."

"Y'think so?" Taylor cocked his head to look at Fred.

"Sure. Shelters are pole barns without sides." Fred waved his hands. His voice got louder. "Even if we hafta cut the poles off, there'll still be plenty of headroom."

"Shush, Fred," Maria called. "You'll wake the children."

"Momma, I'm already awake." Albert's voice came from under the plastic awning. "I can't sleep any more."

"Well, I guess that means it's breakfast time," she said. "Excuse me, I need the fire."

"Yeah, sure," Taylor said. "Come on, Fred. Let's go and check out one of those shelters you were talking about."

~

"Dad," Albert yelled. "There're men coming, on horseback."

"Where?" Taylor asked.

"On the road by the river."

Among the trees, riders in plaid shirts bobbed in and out of view. They stopped at the bottom of the hill and waved something that looked like someone's old underwear tacked to a garden stake. "Taylor MacPherson," a voice echoed.

"Yeah, I'm here," Taylor called.

"Can we talk?" a horseman asked.

"Come on up." Taylor stood and pointed to the trail.

The riders hunched forward on their horses as they jolted up the steep track. Two of the riders had rifles in scabbards.

"I'm Taylor MacPherson. Who're you?"

"I'm Shel Weitzman." The man in front was slight of build, with dark hair starting to recede and a touch of gray at the temples. His face, narrow and dominated by a long, straight nose, carried a full harvest of worry. He dismounted and held the reins with hands that never stopped moving.

"Harvey Cubich is my nephew. I want to thank you for freeing him from those horrible people." His eyes flicked back and forth to the guns held by Fred and Chris. "My wife and I feared something terrible had happened to him. He's like a son to us."

"You're welcome," Taylor said. "You didn't make this trip just to say thanks. What's on your mind?"

"Well." Weitzman frowned. "I was talking with John Phelps. He lives down the street from me." A hand fluttered toward the south. "He told us how you ambushed that gang and got their guns and ammunition. We want to buy ammunition." The lines between Weitzman's eyebrows deepened. "We'll pay a fair price."

"I'm sorry." Taylor held up his hands. "We have no use for money, and, we can't part with the ammo."

"Surely you got plenty from the gang."

"We got some guns, but no ammo." Taylor sighed. "We didn't search them. I just wanted to get rid of them."

"We've got to get more guns and ammo," Weitzman said. "The gang from Berea just torched two more farms. They'll be back."

"Yes, they will," Taylor said. "If you live alone on a farm, your days are numbered. The gangs will pick you off." He looked into the distance. "I left my home because I knew I wouldn't last long there."

And for other reasons, too, he thought. "You should pick a farm that's easy to defend and move into it with your neighbors. There's safety in numbers." The memory of the killing came back. He was afraid to count how many had died.

"We don't want to leave our homes. Besides," Weitzman said with a sigh. "The horse farms weren't designed with defense in mind. They're spread out, y'know, with out-buildings."

Taylor shook his head. "It's your choice. This hill is the most defensible location I know and I'm still worried."

"Can't you even spare even some twenty-two ammunition?" Everyone knew that twenty-two ammo was the most common variety.

"No," Taylor said. "Band together, build defenses. Then you might stand a chance."

"I'll talk to my neighbors." Weitzman's lips compressed into a thin line. "Can we visit again?"

"Sure. Just make sure you show a white flag."

Weitzman got on his horse. "We've got to do something." He backed up his horse and as he turned around, he saluted. "Bye."

"Good luck," Taylor called as the horsemen left. He turned to his group. "Time to get back to work. Albert."

"Yes?"

"Guard duty." Taylor winked. "Keep up the good work."

"Yes, sir." Albert beamed as he trotted off.

"You know," Fred said. "We ought to ask those horsey folk if they want to join us here, on the hill."

"Oh, sure. They can join you under the awning."

"Look, I'm serious. We could use the Park shelters for housing. That might solve the problem of working in an exposed area since there'd be more of us, right?" Fred's voice rose.

"I hear you. Do we really want others joining us? I came here to be alone, to hide in the woods. I don't need anyone. I can disappear into the woods anytime I want to. Now you want me to take even more people under my wing?"

"Taylor, I don't know what the hell is your problem." Fred put his hands on his hips. "There're a lot of good people who're suffering through no fault of their own. Now, I know you've been generous, but didn't you just get through lecturing those horsey folk about banding together in a defensible location?"

"You made your point," Taylor said. "Well, that may help if the gang comes back. Maybe we've got to grow to survive."

"If they come back, we'll talk to them about it—"

"Dad, Dad." Albert ran up. "There're more people coming."

"From which direction?" Taylor reached for his Colt rifle.

"Down Cedar Point Road, from Mastick." He pointed west.

Five men in faded work clothes were at the bottom of the hill. One shook out a white cloth, almost self-consciously.

"Taylor MacPherson," a voice called. "It's me, John Wylie."

"Wylie, come on up." Taylor hadn't recognized him. The five men who climbed the trail didn't have any weapons. That, he realized, could be either good news or bad news.

"Hello, Wylie, what brings you up here?"

"Hi, Taylor. I hate to admit this, but you were right."

"What d'you mean?"

"You got one bunch of bullies off our backs. We weren't ready for that group yesterday. They attacked without warning. They killed Marty Colagrossi and gang-raped Jenny Pokopac."

"Sweet Jesus." Taylor tightened his jaws.

"It was horrible." Wylie shook his head.

"We heard the shooting and saw smoke your way."

"Yeah, they burned Colagrossi's house." Wylie had pronounced bags under his intense green eyes. His gray hair looked stringy and greasy. "We heard the shooting on the hill. Until young Frank Colagrossi came back and told us what happened, we figured you were a goner, too."

"Yeah, well, I guess we surprised 'em."

"I'd have enjoyed doing the same thing to them, too," Wylie said with a trace of bitterness. "Let me get to the point. Earlier, you offered us a chance to join you on this hill. Does that offer still stand?"

"Er, as a matter of fact, we were just discussing something like that." Taylor beckoned to Fred.

"We were fools to turn down your offer. We had no idea how bad things were. We've got to move to a safer place, like this hill. We'd like to join you folks, if we can."

"Well." Taylor hesitated. "How many of you are there?"

"Thirty-four. Eight families."

"That's a lot of people. What's your condition?"

"Well, two men and a woman took a beating from that gang. And they stripped us clean. If we'd only had more guns." Wylie sighed. "We didn't stand a chance." His shoulders sagged as though deflated. "We'd like to join your group."

"Let me talk with Fred and Chris," Taylor said. "I didn't know you had so many in your group. Excuse me." He rejoined Fred and Chris. "Well, Fred? Is this what you want? Have the hill overrun by refugees?"

"Aw, shit, MacPherson, where's your spirit of charity?"

"Charity, my ass." Taylor grimaced. "Where do we put them?"

"We'll put up some buildings."

"Oh, sure. That's easier said than done."

"Aw, come on, it's not difficult." Fred spat on the ground. "I do it all the time, I'm a journeyman carpenter."

"Chris, what d'you think?" Taylor asked the thin teenager.

"Me?" Her eyes widened in surprise. "You want *my* opinion?"

"Yes. Take them in or tell them to take a hike?"

"We could defend the hill if there were more of us," Chris said slowly. "Shortages of ammo and food are problems."

"Chris," Taylor said quietly. "Don't worry about ammo, worry about taking in the Mastick Road folks. Well?"

"Well, overall, we'd be better off with them," Chris said after a pause. "We'd be safer. So I guess that's a yes."

"John Wylie," Taylor called. "Welcome to the Hill."

In that instant, something softened that raw, empty feeling he had each time he thought about his dead wife and abandoning his home.

"You're sure?" Wylie's frown eased.

"Yes. Let's get moving. I want everyone over here in one day. Otherwise, you'll be vulnerable to attack during the move."

"Can you let us have some gasoline?" Wylie asked hesitantly. "The gang took every drop of ours."

"Use Fred's van. It's a big all-wheel drive unit."

The van's first load brought three injured people. Taylor examined them on picnic tables under the awning area. None were conscious.

When will this end?

"Franny," Taylor called. "Come here, I need your help." *Christ, what do I do now?*

"Me?" Franny looked up, eyes wide.

"Yes. Help me with these people, please." His voice softened and he pointed to the injured. "Get me some boiled water, we need to wash their wounds."

"Yes." She put her hand to her mouth when she saw the woman. "I understand." She swallowed hard.

Taylor removed the dressings on the battered woman.

Franny gasped. She bit her lip, paled, and hurried off.

~

By late afternoon, all the people from Mastick Road arrived. They erected plastic sheet awnings and dug another set of latrines.

"Welcome to the Hill," Taylor said from atop a picnic bench. Clusters of families stared at him, faces pale and drawn, amidst the jumble of piled-up possessions. "As a condition for living with us, I ask all of you to work together as a group. We are, in effect ..." Taylor hesitated, seeking the right word. A memory of something that his father had told him about his Scottish ancestry came to him. "A clan, an extended family, banding together for mutual protection and survival."

Faces looked at one another, hands rose to mouths. "You mean like those fuckin' Ku-Klux—" a voice said.

"Don't impugn my ancestry by comparing me to those bigots," Taylor said. "An extended family, like a clan in Scotland."

"Yes," Wylie said loudly. "An extended family, a clan."

"Yeah, sure," a voice said without much enthusiasm.

"If you don't like it," Taylor said. "You're free to leave." He lowered his voice. "In the meantime, supper is ready." He pointed to tables set up in the clearing in the pine trees. Steam rose from hot food in the cold air. "Let's eat."

~

At dusk, a lone horseman with a white flag appeared at the base of the hill. "Hey, Taylor," the horseman called. "Can we talk?" It was Shel Weitzman.

"Sure." Taylor waved him to come up and led him to the fire. "Hi, Shel. What's on your mind?" He pointed to a seat.

Shel shook his head and remained standing. "This morning, the Wisnofskeys were burned out. I discussed your ideas with my neighbors. We can't stay on Barrett Road any longer."

"Yes?" Taylor waited for him to speak.

"Can we join your group, here on this hill?"

"Hmm." Taylor hesitated until he caught Fred's barely concealed grin. "How many are in your group?"

"Twelve families, thirty-six people. And fifty horses."

"Fifty horses?" Taylor hesitated. "We can't keep fifty horses on this hill. They'll need pasture, won't they?" An idea came to him. "Wait a minute, what if we set up a communal farm in the Oxbow section of the park? It's just upstream from here."

"That's not on this hill." Weitzman frowned. "How will that be safer than a farm?"

"It's surrounded by water and we're on your northern flank. There's pasture for your horses, too. If we work together and pool our resources, we should be too much for the gangs."

"It might work," Weitzman said, "I'll talk to my neighbors."

~

A line of figures, silent and gray, appeared like apparitions in the early morning fog. A damp white cloth hung limply from a stick propped on the lead horseman's saddle. They stopped with a clatter of tackle. The horses snorted and stamped their hooves, steam rising from their flanks.

"Taylor," Weitzman called. "We came to join you." His voice echoed off the steep walls of the valley. Silently, the snake-like procession resumed its slow movement up the hill. Their numbers almost equaled those of current Clan members.

A DAY IN THE LIFE

"You what?" Mata ChaLik BuMaru said.

"I discarded the propulsion tube. It was eroded from the acceleration phase. I replaced it with a spare."

Bilik stared at the room behind Mata ChaLik. It was like a swamp in Ma; Podu trees perched on spindly elevated roots and its symmetrical branches laden with dense yellow-green vines dripped water. It reminded him of a scene from an erotic story.

"There are two spare tubes left."

"You launched it into space. Why?" Mata ChaLik's head crest rose in anger. "Our resources are limited, irreplaceable."

"It had no further use. It was worn, its walls so thin it would not last through a sustained burn—"

"Even so, it could have been used in an emergency." Mata ChaLik's head crest engorged. "You wasted resources."

The cold claw of fear clutched Bilik. That was a serious charge. "I sought a use for it, but its wear made it too dangerous." *And you, builder of sumptuous bowers*, Bilik thought, *complain of wasting resources*. "I decided, as engineer in charge of the propulsion system, safety considerations outweighed the benefits of keeping it. So I got rid of it."

"Its velocity makes it dangerous to anything in its path."

Mata ChaLik paced left and a pool came into view. It was like he was flaunting his new quarters. "What if it strikes an inhabited planet? Have we not had enough problems with hostile aliens?"

"Its course will take it through Kota's outer cometary belt. The navigator told me it is unlikely to collide with debris in that orbit."

Well, Bilik thought eyeing the pool, *he really does have a place to get wet. Perhaps the rumors are true. Maybe Mata ChaLik does know other males who want to get wet and share erotic experiences.* Another rumor was he tortured young males into gender change. None of the crew appeared pregnant or abused so it was product of idle chatter. *With so much time on our claws, we grasp at any rumor.*

"Should it reach a planet, it would burn up before reaching the surface. I believe I acted responsibly," Bilik said. "Besides, discarding mass reduces the energy demands of deceleration."

"You always seem to have a clever answer," Mata ChaLik said. "Remember, our resources are limited. In the future, consult me before you make any decisions." His voice had become loud, his head crest swollen with anger. "I know our needs better than you."

Yes, I'm sure you do, Bilik thought. *You, who take our scarce resources and build a palace for yourself for doing who-knows-what. You know how to take care of your own needs far better than I do. Because of your activities, some varieties of foods are no longer available when you and your fellow Defenders created dwellings in the biozone by eliminating rare food plants. Now there are more Podu trees with vines—a classic mating setting. It's obvious that unbalanced the ecological flora.*

"Yes, Mata ChaLik BuMaru," Bilik said in a formal manner. "I'll consult you before I scrap another propulsion tube."

"You know well what I mean." Mata ChaLik's head crest grew larger, pulsating. "I shall remember your insolent attitude." His voice rumbled as though he was about to make a battle cry. "For a long time."

"Yes, Mata ChaLik BuMaru." Bilik flattened his head crest. *Oh, Egg, now I've done it. I'd better report this conversation to DalChik.*

Even as spokesperson for the Keepers-of-the-Egg, DalChik might not do anything. Since departure, Mata ChaLik had taken control of the Egg-that-Flies, rendering the Keepers impotent. There was no effective counterforce to the Defenders.

The holographic image of Mata ChaLik disappeared.

~

"Did you know that DuKlaat YataBu actually ate some of MikLak's decorative plants?" Cha KinLaat referred to an incident that had taken place at a social gathering. "It's almost as though his diet is unbalanced. Maybe that's causing his aberrant behavior."

Cha KinLaat brought up a holograph of surf breaking on a sandy beach. He changed it to that of a steamy swamp. He stared at it for a moment and then went back to the surf. The roar of breaking waves grew louder.

"You think so?" Bilik wondered if he would be sane when the voyage ended. Minor items often became major sources of social condemnation. If one fell out of favor, it could mean exile from the daily discourse so essential to sanity. Even these quiet meetings in Cha KinLaat's resting area had an element of strain.

Every detail, every plant in the pale green room was familiar to the point of tedium, including every strand of the sleeping nest upon which they sat. "Does the medical staff have data on this? It could be important."

"Well, it could be," Cha KinLaat said. "You'd think someone like DuKlaat would show some restraint."

"Do you know why certain foods are no longer available?"

"Don't ask that question," Cha KinLaat said. The holographic image with which he had been playing abruptly contorted into the test pattern that blocked surveillance. "You know the answer. I told you some time ago. Those responsible know more about fighting than you or I."

"Well," said Bilik. "We've only got to survive twenty more

years." Perhaps, the Defenders' reputation for toughness seemed overblown. He'd met the combat qualifications when he defeated the instructor sent to test him. In fact, he was sure he could have beaten the instructor if needed. That was one of the benefits of being female and raising a wriggler. "It'll be figured out by the time we arrive at Kota."

Defenders tough? I don't think so.

"This conversation is making me uneasy." Cha KinLaat's hologram collapsed into a pinprick of light and disappeared. "I'd better check the external monitoring system focused on Kota. They're wearing out faster than anticipated. It's difficult to replace them, and for what? Nothing ever happens out here."

OXBOW

Taylor placed a full ammo magazine on the flapping sheets of paper that lay on the weathered picnic table.

In spite of the sun, the April breeze coming up the cliff from the Rocky River below had a cool edge to it. A hawk screamed as it circled above the valley.

Shel Weitzman and John Wylie faced each other across the table representing different groups within the Clan.

"Yes, we've got people who know how to shoot." Weitzman ran fingers through his thinning hair. "When do we get ammo?"

Taylor pointed to the list. "These are their guns?"

"Yes. What about the ammo?" Weitzman frowned.

Taylor again ignored the question. "We need two squads, militia, to escort your people during their move into the valley."

"What about the ammo?" Weitzman said. "Do we get it?"

"You'll get ammo." Taylor hesitated. "For defense only. No one carries a gun inside the community. That's a Clan rule."

"Y'think you can make that stick?" Wylie asked.

"D'you want people carrying guns when they're tired and hungry, or when the pressure's on?" Taylor's eyes flicked back and forth. "If you can't agree to this, no ammo." He sighed. "Look, too many people have died already." He had a feeling of dread like he was on the edge of falling into a bloody abyss.

"Why should we give up our weapons?" Weitzman asked.

Taylor's lips tightened. "If you want ammo and if you want to be part of this Clan, you'll agree to it. Only the militia carries guns."

No one spoke. Wylie and Weitzman exchanged glances.

"I see," Wylie said. "Your ammo, your rules."

"Yes." Taylor's voice left no room for compromise.

"Some won't like it." Weitzman shook his head. "I'll explain it to my people. Maybe it'll work out."

Taylor looked up at Weitzman. "I'd like to talk to the guy with the backhoe. Can you send him over?"

"Klaus Stolz?" Weitzman said. "Why?"

"To build defenses around the Oxbow."

"Ah, I see." Weitzman's frown lifted partially.

Taylor turned to John Wylie. "Next. Find out who has gardening tools, seeds and whatever." He pointed at Weitzman. "If anyone has horse-drawn farm implements, bring them. We're going to need them."

"Okay," Weitzman said. "I'll check, too."

"We've got to get seed in the ground and soon. Our food will only last for a month or so."

The afternoon meal was carp from the river, fixed Cajun-style by Marie and Frannie. Afterwards, a frowning Weitzman collared Taylor. "The south entrance to the Oxbow is wide open. There's nothing to stop anyone from coming in."

"Put militia at both entrances until we get a proper gate built," Taylor said.

"A truck could roll right through our foot militia," Weitzman waved his hands. "We need a barrier of some kind."

"You're right. Talk to the backhoe guy," Taylor said. "Have

him drag something over there that'll stop a truck." He cleared his throat. "Next, food inventory. Do you have it?"

"Not yet." Weitzman scratched an emerging beard. "We're okay on grain for the horses. I guess everyone stocked up because they expected prices to go up."

"What kind of grain?" Taylor hadn't thought about food for the horses; it seemed to him that they'd eat grass or hay.

"Oh, oats and cracked corn," Weitzman said. "There's feed for our other farm animals."

"What kind of animals?" Taylor asked. "How many?"

"Let me see." Weitzman paused. "I think there's six cows, four goats, three pigs and two flocks of chickens."

"I see." *Maybe*, Taylor thought, *things aren't so bad after all. The weather's warming up. We could substitute grass for grain. Maybe we don't have a food shortage after all.*

Toward evening, Taylor visited the Oxbow. Its shelter was an open structure with a metal roof that had sandstone walls on two sides. It had a fireplace with a built-in grill and warming oven. Beside the shelter was a large yellow Ford tractor, equipped with a bucket and a backhoe. It sat next to two hay wagons loaded with boxes and bundles. On top of one wagon was a four-post mahogany bed.

"Whose bed is that?" Taylor pointed.

"That belongs to Shirley O'Connor," Weitzman said. "She insisted on bringing it. It's a family heirloom."

"Jeez. Why?" Taylor asked.

"I just found out about it. It's causing bad feelings. Others left valuables behind. She's got her husband, Jack, wrapped around her little finger. He can't say no to her."

"Point her out to me."

"The woman near the fireplace." Weitzman nodded his head.

"Mrs. O'Connor," Taylor called in a voice honed at noisy construction sites.

Conversation faded into silence.

"Yes?" Shirley O'Connor was statuesque blond, with athletic shoulders and a long graceful neck.

"Why did you bring such a fine piece of furniture?" Taylor pointed to the bed. "It'll just get ruined outside."

"It won't get ruined." Shirley looked down her long nose at him. "It'll be in here, under cover and protected."

"Well, that's a problem. It's too big for the shelter with this many people." Taylor smiled innocently. "If you want to give up your share of the shelter and use the bed outside ..."

Several people chuckled.

"What? Why should my bed go outside?"

"There's not enough room for you and the bed."

"What right do you have to tell me what I can or cannot do? Does this shelter have your name on it? That bed has been in my family for three generations. I'm not leaving it to a gang of thugs." She had the nasal pitch of a New Yorker. "It's staying in this shelter with me. And that's final." As her voice rose, she put her hands on her hips and stamped her foot.

"Fine." Taylor's jaw tightened. "Who d'you propose shall sleep outside so you can have more room than anyone else?"

She opened her mouth to reply. The man at her side nudged her with his elbow. She gasped and shut her mouth.

"Mrs. O'Connor, take a good look around. Everyone is going to sleep in this shelter, everyone will have shelter from rain, and we can each store a few possessions."

"But—" Shirley began.

"If you don't like the arrangements, Mrs. O'Connor," Taylor said loudly. "You're free to leave."

"Honey, I'll cover the bed with plastic. We can store it under the trees," the man said quietly.

Shirley's eyes snapped toward her husband, hard and flashing. "Jack, shut up. I'm not sleeping on the ground." Her voice rose.

"Why do we have such primitive accommodations when he gets to sleep in comfort in the Nature Center?" She pointed a brightly painted fingernail at Taylor. "Well?"

"For your information, no one sleeps in the Nature Center. It's too close to the road and can't be protected." Taylor lowered his voice. "You're welcome to stay on the Hill and enjoy our palatial accommodations. We've got room under our star-view canopies filled with fresh air and convivial company." He referred to the clear plastic sheet awnings.

Several people laughed. They had seen the living quarters on the Hill. This shelter was better.

Jack put his arm around Shirley and whispered in her ear. She started to sniffle. He guided her away from the now-silent crowd and walked her to the nearby trees.

"Thanks, Taylor, for taking the heat," Weitzman said. "I should've done that."

"If that's the most difficult thing I've got to do, then it's going to be a walk in the park." Taylor shrugged. The memory of the dead bodies in his home flashed into his mind. He turned to Weitzman. "Give me a rundown on your gardeners. What did they bring?"

Weitzman pulled out a list. "Here it is. We found a small plow, so we'll have to jury-rig a horse collar to use our horses." He looked up. "Here's the seed list."

"Good," Taylor said. "I'll send John Wylie's people down tomorrow morning to join them. Who's in charge?"

"Er, I think it'll be Phelps."

"Fine." Taylor looked at his list. "Is Stolz around? I still haven't caught up with him and need to talk to him about using his backhoe."

"He's over there." Weitzman pointed to a tall, blond man.

~

"No problem." Klaus Stolz nodded. "I can dig a ditch ten, twelve feet deep, as long as I don't hit rock. D'you really want to cut the road? That'll make it more difficult to move stuff into the Oxbow."

"Right. Start with a ditch from the edge of the road to the water." Taylor knew Weitzman was uncomfortable about the open road into the Oxbow. "We need deep ditches from the end of the lake up to the edge of the road." He pointed to where the Rocky River had carved a U-shaped lake in the valley, with cliffs sixty feet high on its outside bank. At each end of the oxbow lake, narrow gaps provided access to the land inside, which consisted of fifteen acres of flat land with two baseball diamonds surrounded by Scotch pines.

"Sort of like a medieval moat?" Stolz pointed to the thin ribbon of cracked blacktop passing through the one hundred yard wide gap at each end of the oxbow lake and the river.

"Exactly." Taylor stroked his chin.

"What about the road itself?"

"Block it with a row of logs as a starter. Later, we'll put a drawbridge over the ditch."

"The same thing on the river side of the road?"

"Yes," Taylor said. "Can you dig a ditch on each side?"

"Sure."

"How long will it take?"

"How wide do you want each ditch?" Stolz asked.

Taylor got down to the details. It was comforting in a way, because it was something he was used to doing.

FOCUS

Dave Luken glared over the cherry wood desk in the office that had belonged to the former manager of JB's. "What d'you mean, they're moving outta their farms?"

Dust shadows and carpet indentations were ghostly evidence of previous filing cabinets and other office paraphernalia. As he leaned forward, his high-backed chair squeaked. "Well?" Luken now led the warehouse gang.

Bubba Eaton shuffled his feet. "They've been loading stuff onto wagons and taking it down to the Metropark."

"Where exactly? In the park?"

"I dunno. Mebbe the hill." Bubba avoided Luken's gaze.

"Tomorrow we're going back. And Bubba, you're gonna scout 'em out." Luken banged his fist on the desk. "Got it?"

Bubba examined the floor. "I got it, Dave."

The next morning, dawn brought a low sky the color of hammered pewter. A cold wind out of the northeast blustered around the edge of the warehouse.

Luken chivied his men into two rusty red dump trucks. "C'mon." He scowled. "Move it."

"This sucks," came a voice from the back of a truck. "Do we hafta go out today?"

Luken stared hard. "What was that?"

No one said anything.

"If you don't like it here," Luken said. "Piss off."

No one spoke.

"Let's go."

The trucks bumped and lurched through side streets of Berea. The few people about had vanished. On Barrett Road, the trucks stopped on the section without houses. Trees and undergrowth hid the nearby Rocky River Valley.

Luken called, "Bubba, it's scouting time."

"Yeah, sure, Dave." Bubba jumped down from the truck.

"I want to know where they are and how many. Be back here in an hour. And stay outa sight. Got it?"

"Sure thing, Dave, I got it." Bubba took a breath and trotted off. It was less than a quarter mile to the park.

Bubba reached the Metropark's entrance and was halfway down its road to the Rocky River Valley when he heard a chain saw bray into life and then drop to a quiet rumble. A saw revved and groaned into work.

Someone's working in the Oxbow section, he thought. *Even closer than the hill.* He listened for a while and heard a diesel engine running. *Sounds like a regular construction job*, he thought. *Had to be a lot of people; it had to be them. That meant loot, and mebbe even women. This has to be the info that Luken wants.* He headed back at a run.

Bubba ran out of breath going uphill, so he walked the rest of the way back to the trucks parked on Barrett Road.

"Dave," Bubba said. "They're just down the road, in the Oxbow section, lots of them, working. They won't expect us."

"How come it took you so long?" Luken's hand dropped to his gun. "What were you doin'? Pullin' your pud?"

"Aw, Dave, you know how it is when you're scouting—"

"Time these dudes learned who runs things around here," Luken said. "To the park. Nice and easy-like."

At the Metropark entrance, Luken ordered his men out of the trucks. "We're going in on foot," he called. "Column one, on the right side of the road. Column two, on the left. Move out." He'd seen enough war movies to know how it was done. "As soon as you see them, open fire. Got it?"

His men mumbled assent.

"Let's go." The men marched down the narrow, curving road overhung with branches. They hit a stride that had an almost rhythmic cadence, thudding and jangling along.

High-pitched voices, children, began to shout. The chain saws stopped. Deeper, male voices called distantly.

"Shit," Luken said. "We've been spotted. Move it, double time."

As they rounded a corner, Luken saw a rubber-tired front-end loader—bucket raised—backing away, engine racing. A solitary rifleman stood with his back to the retreating machine, rifle raised. Freshly fallen logs lined the roadway.

"Get him," Luken yelled and fired.

Simultaneously, from behind the logs, guns boomed.

"It's a fuckin' ambush." Luken dove for the ground and rolled off the road into the ditch.

Shortly after the shooting ended, Taylor arrived on the run, along with Chris Kucinski and other militia. "Well, well," he said, breathing heavily. "What've you got here?"

"These scumbags attacked us," Stolz said. Out of eleven prisoners, nine were wounded. A dozen lay dead.

"Doesn't look like you need our help," Taylor said.

Grim-faced men surrounded the silent prisoners, guns at the ready. Weitzman leaned over the militiaman stretched out on a battered picnic bench and cut open his shirt. The left side of his chest was shattered, and as he gasped, frothy blood and air bubbled in and out.

Weitzman's long face sagged and he mopped the wound for a moment. He sighed. There were tears in his eyes as he glanced at the two workers who sat on a log waiting for medical attention. Blood saturated their clothing.

"The kids warned us," Jack O'Connor said. "So, we were ready for them. They didn't expect we'd be waiting."

"Who's he?" Taylor pointed to Weitzman's patient. "What happened?"

"That's Hauer." O'Connor shook his head. "He was protecting Stolz. He's hurt bad."

Weitzman sighed. "He's got a major chest injury. It'd be touch and go even in a hospital. I'm just a dentist. I've got some morphine with my gear. All I can do is ease his pain." His voice cracked. "He's not going to make it."

Taylor turned to the captives. "Who's in charge?"

No one spoke. Eyes flickered.

Taylor followed their glances to an uninjured captive, a big muscular man who stared steadfastly at the ground. "You," Taylor said. "In the camo jacket, what's your name?"

The man said nothing, not raising his head.

Taylor strode over to him, followed by Chris. He pointed at the man and nodded to Chris who poked him on the shoulder with the barrel of her Colt rifle.

The man waved off the rifle, glanced up. "Cut it out."

"What's your name?" Taylor almost snarled. "Where d'you come from? On your feet."

"I'm Dave Luken." The man rose slowly to his feet. "I live in Berea." He glanced around as though looking to leave.

"Why did you attack us?" Taylor took a deep breath.

The man called Luken said nothing and looked away.

"He asked you a question." Chris's mouth got thin. "Answer him."

"Fuck you, bitch."

Chris whipped the rifle's barrel up between the Luken's legs. He screamed and slumped, holding his crotch.

"When he asks, you answer." Chris's mouth was razor thin.

"You fucking cunt," Luken said. He spat at Chris.

Chris swung the rifle butt up into Luken's face. He staggered backward and collapsed to the ground, both hands to his mouth.

Chris stood over him, gun ready. "Want more?"

"Chris—" Weitzman said in a reproachful tone.

Taylor stepped forward. "Leave her alone. He got what he deserved. For what they've done, they've forfeited all rights." He pointed to Luken. "Like the lady said, I asked you a question."

Chris raised her gun.

"You ambushed us two days ago in the woods." Luken spat blood. "We were returning the favor."

A ghost of a cold smile flickered across Taylor's lips. "Looks like your return favor didn't work."

~

Over the next hour, Taylor learned from the other prisoners, the gang used JB's Warehouse, which was now lightly guarded. Satisfied he had no more questions, he turned toward Chris. "I guess we'll take their weapons and turn them loose—"

"No way." John Phelps stepped forward. "These hoodlums are the ones who attacked our farms, killed people, and burned us out. Ted and Sandy Callioux are still missing—"

"They're the bastards who killed Marty Colagrossi and raped Jenny Pokopac," Wylie's face became flushed. "They're not walking away. Not a chance."

Taylor took a deep breath. *So, this was the gang that'd victimized the people on both Mastick Road and the horse farms.* He knew what was coming. *Dear God, stop me before I become like them. They're thugs who've raped and killed, and burned people out of their homes. They'll only get what they deserve.*

"Okay," Taylor said. "They're yours."

"Stolz," Phelps called. "Dig a hole big enough to hold all of these slime-balls."

The prisoners heard him. Their faces blanched.

Taylor took Weitzman aside. "Look, Shel, this is our chance to get supplies and finish off this warehouse gang."

"What've you got in mind?"

"We go and clean out the warehouse."

"You really want to do that?" Weitzman's long face grew longer. "I mean, what if they resist and we fail?"

"We won't. There're more of us than them. The warehouse is almost deserted. Someone else will do it if we don't."

"I don't want anyone else getting hurt," Weitzman called as Taylor walked away. "I don't want us to become like them."

But I am becoming like them, Taylor thought. *And it doesn't seem to bother me. Lord help me.*

The Clan's midnight raid caught the warehouse's inhabitants by surprise. The guard surrendered after a gun was stuck in his ribs. No shots were fired.

They found Ted Callioux, battered and bleeding. His first question was about his wife, Sandy. No one knew what had happened to her, except that Mark Thompson had taken her away. They put Callioux on the first truck back to the Oxbow.

"Y'know," Taylor said, looking around. "There's a lot of material here. More than we can haul in one load."

"Yeah." Phelps nodded. "Still, we'd better get the stuff moved, and quick. Did you know that there's a tank of diesel fuel behind the automotive section?"

"Really?" Taylor's eyes widened. "How much?"

"At least five hundred gallons." Phelps smiled wryly. "I guess I'd better let Stolz know about that right away."

"Did you see all those canned goods?" Taylor waved his hand toward the aisles of racks. "Fruit, vegetables, salmon and meat. Man, I'm getting hungry thinking about it. Even fruit juice. And rice, sacks and sacks of it. Did you see all that pasta? Cases of it. I can almost taste one of Maria's great Italian meals."

"If you keep that up, I'm gonna need something to eat."

Taylor gestured at the food section. "I'm really surprised at how much is here. Y'know, there's an awful lot of space taken up by totally useless things, like TVs, computers and electronic junk where there could be food."

"Yeah," Phelps said. "Funny how your values change."

Taylor worked until dawn and through much of the next day to get the warehouse stripped of its food.

Wow, he thought, *between grain from the horse farms and this, we've got enough food to last through next winter*. They even found a half-dozen rifles and several cases of ammunition. He began to feel more secure.

LAGER

Bright sunlight woke Taylor, streaming through the peak of his A-frame shelter. As he dressed, he remembered the dream, no, the nightmare about those who'd died. Mark Hauer was dead and his wife, Kristy, was now a widow with two babies. *When will it end?* He'd tried to protect them and failed. He shivered and felt the urge to run away. He prayed and hoped for guidance that never came. After breakfast, he sent for the team leaders.

"We've got to improve our defenses." Taylor leaned forward over the picnic bench that served as his open-air conference center. The day was warming rapidly.

"Oh?" Stolz said. "I thought I built our defenses the way you wanted them. Something wrong with what I did?"

"No, what you did was fine. They've got to be stronger."

"Yeah?" Stolz's chin moved forward. "Like how?"

"Fred," Taylor said. "Tell us your idea."

"Well, we can build walls real easy-like." Fred described how to build a wall from two parallel chain link fences filled with rocks and rubble to make gabions. When he was through, the room was silent.

"Any objections?" Taylor looked around the room. "No? Well, Mr. Stolz, that's how you'll do it. Okay with you?"

"Well, okay, I guess." He frowned and pursed his lips.

"Good." Taylor looked at his notes. "Next. We need shelter, fast. Any ideas?"

"Yeah." John Wylie jutted his chin forward. "How about moving a metal building here? Like one of the barns at the horse farms."

"Now just a minute." Jack O'Connor glowered at Wylie. "First you take all our animal feed, now you want our buildings? Are we bank-rolling this entire operation?"

"You came here to be safe." Taylor frowned. "When things get better, you can have your buildings back."

The corners of O'Connor's mouth turned down.

"Anyone know how to move these buildings?" Taylor asked.

"I do," Phelps said. "I've put 'em up. I think I have an assembly manual back at my house. Plus, I've got tools."

"Can you start first thing tomorrow?"

"Sure, but I'll need help moving the frames and stuff."

"How about moving a park shelter to the Hill?" Fred said. "Can we do that?"

"I've moved whole buildings," Stolz said. "We just don't have the right equipment here to move them."

"What about taking them apart to move them?" Fred asked.

"That'd damage the roof," Stolz said.

"No, those roofs are built in sections," Fred said. "Just split them along the roof seams."

"But—" Stolz started to say.

"Enough." Taylor raised his voice. "Discuss it together after the meeting. Let me know if you can do it. Mr. Stolz, don't leave yet." He furrowed his brow. "On the way back from the warehouse, I saw Medina Supply on Front Street in Berea had concrete block. Would they also have cement?"

"Yeah." Stolz nodded. "I'm sure they do."

"Hey, Stolz," Phelps said. "What's your charge number?" A grin grew on his face.

"Well, Fred." Taylor winked. "It looks like we've got masonry supplies, now show us your bricky tricks."

"Hey, I'm a carpenter, remember? I'm not a bricky."

~

The next day, Phelps' crew moved a thirty by eighty-foot metal building to the Oxbow. Chris Kucinski's squad shuttled trucks back and forth from the building supply yard, bringing cement and building block. With scavenged chain link fencing, Wylie's crew closed off both ends of the Oxbow. Every so often, they reported glimpses of faces in the woods, watching.

Stolz widened the ditch on the south side of the Oxbow and used the excavated materials to build an eight-foot-high earthen embankment. Within the barrier, he made alcoves for guards and formed a funnel-shape entrance to the gate.

~

A guard called from the lookout point that offered a view of the trail up the Hill. "Four people with a white flag."

"We heard noise in the park. What's going on?" asked a gray-haired man with rimless glasses.

"I'm Taylor MacPherson. Who're you? Where're you from?"

"Patterson Rice from Edgepark. We're just east of here, next to the NASA Glenn Research Center. There's about three hundred of us. We heard shooting, and when the tractor and chain saws started up again, we knew you'd survived."

"That was the warehouse gang. They won't bother anyone anymore," Taylor said with a shrug.

"Good, but watch out for the Diablos gang," Rice said. "They shot up a section of Fairview, across the freeway, last week. They've got some kind of armored vehicle with a machine gun."

"Jeez," Taylor said. "Y'think you can hold them off?"

"I don't know. We've blocked the roads. We're low on guns and ammunition. Have you got any you could spare?"

"No." Taylor paused. *Who're these people, anyway?* He decided to find out. "Maybe there's other ways we could help. Can I visit and get an idea of your needs?"

"Um." Rice looked at his companions. They nodded. "Tomorrow, about nine, come to the Metropark's east entrance."

~

Taylor visited Edgepark but refused to give any commitment about supplying them with equipment. Instead, he redoubled efforts to reinforce the Clan's settlements in the valley. Within a week, the Oxbow had metal gates guarding its entrances. Two rows of chain-link fence with barbed wire crowned the dirt embankments.

Taylor began to feel safer.

The large metal building erected on the concrete pad in front of the Park shelter went up more quickly than Taylor believed possible. He'd intended to store extra food in it, but as more refugees arrived, it became an overflow dormitory.

Now the Clan population exceeded two hundred, Taylor learned from Franny their food would last barely two months. Food. That reminded him of the afternoon when Albert Del Corso complained he never got to use the bow anymore after he'd started to catch fish with it.

The words came back clearly to Taylor.

"If I had a bow," Albert had said. "I'd go hunting."

Sam Wylie, a retired machinist had spoken up, "Tomorrow, I'll show you how to make slingshots and bows."

"Hey," Albert called to his young friends. "Ol' Mr. Wylie is going to make me a slingshot and a bow."

"No, show you how," Sam Wylie said. "Not make them."

Taylor smiled, for Albert's hunting efforts with the newly

acquired bows, slingshots, and snares had brought in a steady supply of fish and small game. Every little bit helped.

As he walked back to the Hill, he caught sight of water flowing slowly through a newly excavated channel. He'd had a twinge of conscience when Wylie raided an abandoned construction yard to bring back a small bulldozer and a tracked excavator.

Now he felt better since Stolz had put the construction equipment to work on improving the Hill's defenses. They used the dozer and track-hoe to widen and deepen the swamp-like former river. With the excavated mud, they built a low, sinuous embankment, effectively surrounding the Hill.

The only way into the Hill was through the swamp on the south over the causeway or by the old township road on the north. There was also a narrow set of wooden stairs by the Nature Center that snaked up the steep eastern flank of the Hill.

They were now more secure.

~

A small, rusty, green John Deere tractor jerked to a halt in the garden at the Oxbow. "Hey, Taylor." Weitzman grinned. "Look what I found." He rubbed his hand on the farm tractor's hood as though polishing it. "It may be old and not very powerful but it sure runs well. It's made farming much easier."

"Good." Taylor noted that its appearance belied his claim. "How much land is ready for planting?"

"There's four acres in the Oxbow. We're going to plant it tomorrow." Weitzman made a wry face. "We had to sacrifice a baseball diamond for root crops. It was the only place with sandy soil. There was some bitching about that."

"Yeah, I'll bet. What else?"

"We've got a couple acres of peas, beans, and corn planted just north of the Hill."

"Where exactly?" Taylor realized he'd lost track of some of the projects.

"Just inside the old river bend, behind the pine trees."

"Ah, yes." Taylor nodded. "What about livestock?"

"We're using the cows and goats to keep the approaches to the Oxbow clear. We're grazing the horses in any odd spot that we can find, away from the meadows," Weitzman said. "We want to grow hay in the meadows, so we can put it up for next winter."

"Sounds good." Taylor frowned. "Shel, will there be enough food to last through next winter?"

"If the harvest is as good as I hope it is." Weitzman beamed. "We might even have a surplus."

"So, you're Los Diablos, is that right?" Chris asked, looking at the three young men who sat with tied hands on a fallen tree trunk alongside the road leading to the Oxbow.

Guards had caught Eddy and his two companions trying to sneak into the Oxbow early in that morning and subdued them after a brief struggle.

"*Sí*," Eddy said. "Blade sent us."

"Blade, eh?" Chris pulled out a hunting knife and began to play with it. "Tell me about him."

"He heard the warehouse boys tangled with your gang."

"If you refer to the Clan as a gang," Chris's voice took on a hard edge. "I swear I'll lose control." She held the knife close to his face. Sunlight glinted off its honed edge. "Do I make myself clear?"

"Yes." Eddy tried to back away from the knife.

"That's better." Chris drew the knife back. "Why did you come here? Who sent you?"

"Blade. Y'know, *el Jefe* hisself," Eddy said. "He wants to know everything about this place. How many people, the lay of the land, guns, ammo an' stuff like that."

"Really? D'you know what we've got?"

"No, but he got people watching you all the time."

Chris smiled. "I hear Blade's gang has twenty members."

"Naw, it's more than fifty, mebbe eighty."

"D'you reckon he could beat us in a fight?"

"Sure. We got that tank." Eddy looked up with a trace of a proud smile. "It's got a big gun an' a bad-ass machine gun, an' carries six dudes with full auto AR15s. No one gives Blade shit now he's got the tank."

"Where do the Diablos hang out?"

"*No se*," Eddy said with a sneer. "Here an' there."

"Where are the Diablos?" Chris poked him with the knife.

"Hey, bitch, that hurt."

"Eddy, watch your language." She raised the knife.

"I don' know. We Diablos jus' keep movin'."

"Why?"

"Food. It's getting hard to find." Eddy narrowed his eyes and cocked his head to one side as he stared at her. "Blade planned on movin' onto Berea, but he heard you got some food. He's comin', and he's gonna getcha, bitch."

Chris made jerking motion with her thumb. "Toss 'em out."

"The Diablos have machine guns and artillery?" Taylor asked. Through the open door of the metal building, he saw a light mist of rain drift over the Oxbow's newly planted fields.

"That's what it sounds like," Chris said. "I've sent out scouts. They've seen gangs but no armored vehicles."

"This changes everything," Taylor said. "I thought we had enough people and guns to be safe from the gangs."

"Well," Fred said. "What d'you think we should do?"

Taylor looked around the table at the team leaders. Even

after only a short time, Taylor knew them well from the daily contact.

"The only way to be safe from a force like the Diablos, is to keep them away from here," Clayton Nicholas said. He was an African-American engineer with a military background who'd been made a refugee by the West Side gang several weeks ago.

"Easy to say, difficult to do." Taylor frowned.

"Maybe we can get the Edgepark people to join us and establish a common defense," Fred said. "We help them with their defenses and they help us."

"They're settled and won't want to move," Weitzman said. "They're certain to fight hard for their homes."

"True," Taylor said. "I'm sure Stolz could improve their defenses. I didn't suggest it because I want to get ours finished first. Does anyone have connections in the Edgepark area?"

"Yes," Ted Callioux spoke in a small voice. "I know people there from when I was at Baldwin-Wallace University."

"Ted," Taylor asked. "You want to talk with them?"

"Yes, I suppose I can."

"Good. Now, Clayton, what d'you think we should do?"

"We should have a defense-in-depth strategy," Clayton said. "If we keep our lines of internal communication short, we can flex quickly for a more effective defense. We might even sucker them into a trap. That'll take preparation."

"Get your ideas together," Taylor said. "Anything else?"

"Yes," Callioux said. "There's a bunch of folk in Berea that would like to join us."

"How many? How well d'you know them?"

"About a hundred. They're from the section of town where I used to live. When I went back looking for Sandy, they asked me about joining up." His voice trailed off, his eyes downcast.

"Another hundred people. Oh, man, we've only just got everybody under a roof. Where'll we put them?"

"To work." Callioux's voice held a hint of defiance. "I told them we have a shelter problem. They're ready to help."

"Like how?" Taylor asked, his eyebrows rising.

"They'll bring plywood from the local lumber yard. They reckon there's about four truckloads of plywood, plus several truckloads of other lumber and building supplies. They've got construction skills." Callioux's voice strengthened. His face reddened. "What they don't have is ammo for their guns. They're defenseless."

"All right, tell them they can come. We'll split them between the Hill and the Oxbow," Taylor said with a sigh.

"If you don't mind, they'd like to stay together for a while," Callioux said. "I think they'd prefer the Hill, even if there's less shelter. They are willing to work."

"Ted, they're your problem now. Keep me posted." Taylor wondered why they preferred the Hill. "Next item. Warning of impending attacks. Chris, we need more scouts. Ted, since you're from Berea, how about getting scouts in there? Wylie, take Mastick Road and points north and west." Taylor looked up from the list. "Shel, can we get horses for the scouts?"

"Er, yes. I'll get with Chris and Wylie, too."

"Okay, that's it. Let your people know what we're facing."

Three squads, Taylor thought. *Each with twelve people armed with high-powered rifles, and ten groups with eight adults each, with less powerful guns than our militia, against a gang with an armored vehicle. It isn't a fair match.*

NEIGHBORS

"If you lie to me again, you'll eat your own *cojones*." Armando "Blade" Velasquez waved a bloody knife.

Antonio Morales now knew how the *Jefe* of Los Diablos got his nickname. "I swear on my mother's grave I saw a tanker."

"Gillipolas." Asshole. "You think I'm stupid? There ain't no gas deliveries." His knife flicked. Blood flowed.

"I swear it went up Sheldon Road with a jeep following."

"Find that tanker or else." Blade wiped his knife on Morales's jacket. "Skid, Knuckles," he said. "*Señor* Morales will find us a tanker full of gas. If he can't, waste him."

Skid Vukovitch silently appeared from the corner of the manager's office at JB's Warehouse. The Deacons had joined up with the Diablos because the firepower of the Diablos' armored troop carrier exceeded anything the Deacons could muster.

"Sure, Blade." Skid's laugh was forced. "A road trip will be fun." He glanced at Morales like a cat sizing up a mouse.

"Take the Maquinez brothers with you." Blade gestured toward two hulking men slouching behind him. "Jus' so you've got some company." He leaned back in the chair and smiled.

Skid swallowed. His smile faded. "Sure, Blade. The brothers

gonna do as we say? Y'know how they're always trying to find something to fuck, drink, or kill when no one's watching."

Blade frowned. "Enrique, Jose, obey him. *Ya se va?*"

"Si, Jefe." The Maquinez brothers' faces went dark.

Morales shivered. *I'm in for a bad time*, he thought. *Will I survive this trip? Why did I ever join up with Los Diablos?*

~

"Move it, asshole." Skid kicked Morales in the buttocks, who'd paused to look up and down Sheldon Road.

"Ow, it's this way." Morales pointed north on the road. "The tanker went on an' the Jeep, she stop here." In the distance, he could see a ten-foot-tall dirt embankment on which there were armed guards and workers.

"Okay," Skid said. "We're goin' through these trees quiet-like to take a look-see. I don't want to hear one peep, understand?" He stared at the Maquinez brothers until they nodded. "Knuckles, keep an eye on these turkeys, understand?"

"Uh, sure, Skid." Knuckles unholstered his Browning handgun and snapped its magazine in and out several times.

They stopped under a clump of spruce trees, water dripping from the drooping foliage. Ahead, a narrow bridge crossed a flooded ditch leading to a stone-lined opening in an embankment.

"Looks like a regular fuckin' emplacement," Knuckles said. "I don't see no gas tanker, Morales. You fuckin' with us?"

The knot in Morales's stomach grew bigger.

"There's only three guards." Enrique Maquinez raised his laser-sighted .44 magnum Ruger pistol and aimed it at the guards. He reached for the lasers' switch. "I can off them."

"Don't mess with those guards, asshole." Skid showed his teeth. "They've got rifles and cover." He spat on the ground. "Stupid shit." He turned to Morales and grabbed him by the hair. "Where's that big green gasoline tanker?"

Morales could smell Skid's hot breath. It stank.

~

Morales woke with a start, a sharp pain in his ribs. "Ow." For a second—just a second—he didn't know where he was. He remembered they'd stopped for a break and he'd fallen asleep leaning against a big maple tree.

"Okay, asshole, we ain't seen no green an' white gasoline tanker." It was Skid. Reality returned. "Now where?"

Knuckles balled a fist. "Got any other bright ideas where to look?" He grinned and raised a hand as though to strike Morales.

"Please." Morales hurt all over. He'd found it hard to remember the park's layout. "Mebbe if we take the horse path to the road in the park. I found it when I was on a picnic with the Asemblas de Dios. I was porking this *muchacha*—"

"Yeah, yeah. Fuck tellin' me all the dirty details," Skid said. "Just show me your secret fuckin' path, asshole."

"It's, it's—I gotta think." Morales scratched his head.

"Think faster." Skid cuffed him, hard.

"Ow. You don' have to do that, I'll tell you." Morales tried to scramble away on all fours.

Enrique Maquinez blocked his way, smiling.

"Get up asshole, an' move it," Skid said. "If you steer me wrong, I'll stomp the shit outa you." He wagged his finger at Enrique. "An' if you touch Morales, I'll give your head to Blade."

Enrique licked his lips nervously.

~

An hour later, Morales' couldn't see out of his left eye as blood oozed from a split eyebrow. In the distance, diesel engines rumbled under a load. He had gotten lost twice. Each time, Skid had pistol-whipped him to improve his memory. Ahead, a road crossed the tree-enshrouded trail, which made it look like an opening.

"Morales, macho man, check out that road," Skid said. "Let me know if it's safe on the other side, understand?"

"*Sí.* When you want to cross?" Morales asked. "After dark?" No one crossed open areas in enemy territory during daylight.

"Now," Skid said, his voice hissing harshly. "Get going." He banged Morales' swollen ear with his pistol.

Morales stumbled across the road, almost wishing for a bullet to end his misery, heading for the path where leafy branches made it look like a sanctuary. As he entered the path, a sound on his left made him turn. From behind a tree protruded an M-16 rifle.

"Shut up," a camouflaged uniform said in an exaggerated whisper. "Don't move."

Morales raised his hands. "Don't hurt me. Kill me, but don't hurt me no more." *The fates have it in for me. I have gone from one set of devils to another*.

"Who's across the road?" the camouflaged uniform asked.

"They Diablos, man."

"Why're you here?"

"We lookin' for a gas tanker that came here yesterday. They sent me ahead to see if it's safe." Weariness consumed Morales; he was hurt, he was hungry and very, very afraid.

"Tell them to come over," the person in camouflage said. "Tell them it's safe."

"Please, you don' understan'." Morales fell to his knees and clasped his hands together in front of his face. "They kill me for doin' that. Knuckles an' Skid, they Deacons." He started to shake. "Jus' kill me, please. I can't take no more." He put his forehead to the ground and began to cry.

"Jeez," the person in the camouflage uniform said. "This little shit is somewhat the worse for wear."

"Chris." Morales heard a whispered voice say. "They're coming. Two are wearing colors. Looks like a gang to me."

Morales saw a dozen people in camouflage—each with a rifle —appear out of the woods.

Oh, Dios, he thought, *I've led them into a trap. Blade will slice me into pieces, soak me in salsa, and piss on me. I'm a dead man.*

"Wait 'til they get to this side of the road," the person called Chris said. "See if they'll surrender."

The Deacons and Diablos started across in single file.

"Freeze," a voice called. "Move and we shoot."

Knuckles, in the lead, raised his gun and rattled off a volley of shots. Guns replied from the woods.

Jose Maquinez staggered, holding his thigh. The rest fled into the woods.

Six men in camouflage advanced to the edge of the road, firing constantly. "Don, Pete, follow them," Chris said. "Find out where they came from, but be careful." The one called Chris turned and said, "Get that vermin off the road." She pointed at the downed man.

Morales saw it was Jose Maquinez.

"Okay," a man in camouflage said. "On your feet, scumbag."

Maquinez screamed as the two men pulled him to his feet. There was a pool of blood on the road.

"Charlie, Jack," Chris said. "Warn the guards at the entrances there's a gang nearby. We've got to tighten security right away."

After being assured he would not be sent back to the Diablos, Morales talked freely. He told the person named Chris that the Diablos had raided the National Guard Armory in Brookpark, where they had gotten an armored troop carrier and fifty full-auto M-16 rifles.

Jose Maquinez passed out and never regained consciousness.

PREPARATIONS

That evening, after Chris's encounter with the Diablos, Taylor met with the team leaders in the Hall on the Hill.

"Perimeter defense." Taylor's eyes lit on Stolz. "Stolz and Clayton, that's your responsibility. Give us an overview."

"Well ..." Stolz detailed their defenses. "It's still a large area to protect."

"It won't stop a serious attack. We don't have any heavy weapons," Clayton Nickolas added. The room grew quiet.

"How about the road entrances?" Taylor said.

"All the roads into the park have been choked down to a single lane." Stolz shrugged. "We used big concrete cubes."

"Well, Clayton," Taylor said. "What about the troop carrier?"

"If it gets inside or has a clear shot at us, it'll be a disaster," Clayton said. "We've got to ambush it."

Taylor pointed to one of Stolz's workers. "Higgins, how's the perimeter defense around the Hill?"

"We're completely surrounded by water that's at least three feet deep." Jim Higgins was a thin, tired-looking man who spoke rapidly. "The embankment is from four to ten feet in height. That swamp mud was a bitch to pile up. I couldn't build a barricade on it. I even got the track-hoe stuck." Higgins' face reddened. "As well as the dozer."

Taylor caught Clayton's faint smile. An embankment of soft mud would stop the troop carrier. "How wide is the old river?"

"Thirty to sixty feet. Much of it still has water," Higgins said. "I didn't dig there 'cept to get material."

"Thanks," Taylor said. "Let's see, we've got to move the food stores onto the Hill." He looked up from his notes. "And get the cisterns filled. Shel, can you take care of that?"

"Yes, I'll do that."

"Thanks. Any comments?"

"Why don't we try a sneak attack on this gang?" Shirley O'Connor asked. "Like we did on the Warehouse gang?"

"Ted, what do you think?" Taylor said. "You've seen more of this gang than anyone else here."

"Unfortunately." Callioux cleared his throat. "This gang's different than the Warehouse gang. First, there's about two hundred—all well-armed. Second, they're sending out patrols, so I don't think we could surprise them." He furrowed his brow. "Also, they've covered a half-dozen or so trucks with planking and sheet metal, which I'm sure, is in preparation to attack us."

"I didn't know that." Shirley sounded resigned.

"Maybe we should all move to the Hill," Taylor said. "Fred, does the Hill have enough shelter for everyone?"

"No. Lately I've been working on the defenses, not housing." Fred shrugged. "Which means we sure don't have enough for the Edgepark people on the Hill."

"Fred, you're relieved from all work except to build shelter on the Hill," Taylor said.

"If you say so." Fred's eyebrows rose.

"Stolz, have one of your crews help Fred. Got it?"

"Yes," Stolz said, "but what if—"

"If you run into any bottle-necks, solve them. See me only if you have a major conflict. Is that clear?"

"Yeah." Stolz did not look happy.

"From what Ted said, I'd guess we've got very little time left. Wylie, help Shel with the food and water."

"Sure, Taylor." Wylie nodded. "No problem."

"Chris, put your squads on higher alert. Coordinate your efforts with the Edgepark people. Set up a horse courier system." The furrow between Taylor's eyes deepened.

"Taylor." Chris Kucinski hesitated. "The Edgepark folks have walkie-talkies. I talked them into giving us two."

"Good." Taylor's eyebrows rose. "Very good, Chris." It confirmed his hunch promoting her was a good decision. He'd seen she was cool under fire and was mature beyond her years and had a toughness unusual for one so young.

"They've also prepared some surprises for the Diablos," Chris said. "Y'know when we got the stuff from the construction yard? Well, we gave them a couple of generators and some fuel. They've been busy ever since. They made eight big crossbows out of pickup truck leaf springs," Chris said. "They gave us four. They really make the explosive bolts fly."

"Explosive bolts?" Taylor looked up. "What kind?"

"They got two kinds," Chris said. "One explodes on contact. The other has an armor penetrating head."

"Armor penetrating?" Clayton's normally sleepy eyes opened wide as he sat up. "Through how much armor?"

"In tests, it punched a hole in half-inch mild steel," Chris said. "The problem is, no one knows if they'll penetrate the troop carrier's armor."

"Chris, get together with Clayton." Taylor felt a sliver of hope. "Figure out how to get the most mileage from them."

Clayton nodded.

"Tactics. Clayton will brief each squad individually." Taylor pointed to the slender black man with close-cropped grizzled hair.

"We now have three squads armed with high-powered rifles; there're two more from Edgepark. We've brought the Clan militia up to about one hundred, with forty more from

Edgepark. Unfortunately, they've only got small bore weapons," Clayton said.

Taylor looked up from his notes. The room became silent. "Evacuate the horses at the first sign of trouble. We don't have fodder or water on the Hill. Nor do we need to deal with panicked horses in the middle of a battle. Jack, you're taking care of that, right?"

"Yeah." Jack nodded. "We've got contingency plans."

"That about covers it." Taylor folded his checklist. "A determined and well-prepared force can hold off three times its own number. Remember that." He saw most of the leaders nod. "I expect all of you will do your duty to protect your family and the Clan. Is that clear?"

TEMPERED BY FIRE

Blade leaned over the table and stabbed his finger toward Skid. "You will attack the south entrance before dawn."

"Sure." Skid picked his teeth. "We gonna get any support?"

"Take the truck with the machine gun," Blade said. "When we hear your attack, we'll start at the north entrance."

"That road is blocked with a ditch, here." Skid pointed to the map spread out on the table. "How you gonna get past that?"

"Don' worry, I got it all figured out." Blade explained his plan. "An' you move out at 3:00 AM. Unnerstan?" He pointed his knife at Skid.

Skid sniffed and nodded, just barely. "Yeah, I unnerstan." He imitated Blade's pronunciation.

"Everyone else moves out at 4:30 AM. Unnerstan'?"

~

Leaves rustled in woods around the Oxbow. Water gurgled over the spillway. A hint of pink in the east brightened the dark sky.

A dark shape overtook the Clan guard on the Oxbow's south embankment. A guard dog tore into the fray with savage growls. Two Molotov cocktails arced through the air and whoofed into flames, lighting the embankment with smoky yellow light.

More explosions on the road revealed a line of shadowy figures. Guns flashed and boomed from the guardhouse at the Oxbow's entrance.

~

Phelps awoke. It was dark. Through the door of the shelter, he saw flames flickering by the distant guardhouse.

"Up, dammit, get up," he yelled.

In the distance the gunfire intensified. Around him, militia struggled with their gear. "Move it," Phelps yelled. They trotted toward the guardhouse outlined by flames.

"Heads up," Phelps said. "Someone's over there."

A gun fired, flashing brightly among the trees.

Phelps fired twice. A figure dropped. When he got to the fallen figure he examined it. "Gang member," he said. "He has a full auto M-16."

Phelps led the squad toward the gatehouse. As the shooting slowed, he positioned the squad between the bank of the oxbow lake and the pine trees. Gunfire picked up.

"They've never attacked at night," Shirley O'Connor said. "That's what MacPherson told us. He should've warned us." She wore her resentment openly. She hadn't gone with Jack, her husband, when he took the horses to safety. Before their move to the Oxbow, rumor had it their marriage was on the rocks. In these close quarters, there was no concealing their stormy relationship.

"It isn't his doing," Phelps said. "He's not the one shooting at us." He pointed. "Go to the shelter. Get the families moving to the Hill, now. Take Jones and Diaz and have them keep the north gate open—it's our way out."

"Anything else?" she said.

"Find out if we're going to get reinforcements. Send a report to the Hill that there's no sign of the troop carrier here. Also, the bridge into the Oxbow is still holding." He gave her a gentle shove on the shoulder. "Okay, O'Connor, scoot."

Shirley disappeared into the trees.

The squad resumed its advance.

As the day brightened, they saw gang members in leather jackets among the trees approaching the south entrance to Oxbow. They slowed in the face of crackling gunfire.

"Jeez, they've all got automatic rifles," Phelps said.

On the road from the south, a boxy-looking dump truck moved toward the entrance to the Oxbow. A booming chatter came simultaneously as chunks of wood splintered off the gatehouse.

Phelps lowered the binoculars. "Shit, that dump truck's got a heavy machine gun. Uh-oh," he said. "They've seen us." As branches shattered above, he embraced the ground. "Fall back toward the shelter house," he called. "We can't do anything against that."

Shirley crawled up to him. "Phelps." She was panting. "They haven't finished evacuating the children and old people."

"Damn. Did our trucks arrive?"

"Yes. Two came from the Hill. They said they put militia at the north gate and have come to pick up the noncombatants."

"Any word from MacPherson?" Phelps aimed his gun at a figure silhouetted against the brightening sky and fired. "Gotcha, you bastard."

"Yes, he said to abandon Oxbow. The north perimeter of the Hill is also under attack." She was still panting. "Our trucks will come back after they drop off the civilians."

The bang-bang-bang of rapid-fire guns erupted in the vicinity of the Park shelter house. Automatic weapons started to chatter.

Nearby, somebody screamed, "Help me, I'm hurt."

A half dozen leather-clad men emerged, firing as they moved toward the shelter house.

“They’re behind us, too.” Phelps swore. “Stop them from reaching the shelter.” He raised his gun and began firing.

Ten long minutes later, from the north, two trucks with boxy appearances from the wood planking used to armor them, rumbled toward the Park shelter. The trucks turned around and approached the shelter in reverse.

“Shirley, get a load of this.” Phelps handed her his binoculars. His frown eased. It was the Clan militia.

“About time,” she said. Her voice had a scolding tone.

The militia in the back of the trucks opened fire on the attackers. Four men wearing colors broke cover and ran from the truck toward Phelp’s squad in the pine trees.

“Phelps,” Coughlin said. “Look.” He pointed to another group of men in leather jackets moving from tree to tree, approaching from the opposite direction angling toward the shelter.

“More of them. Damn,” Phelps said. “Hold your fire until I say so. We’ve got to take care of the ones in front first.”

The original four came closer.

“Fire,” Phelps yelled.

The volley caught the men before they reached the pine trees.

“Hey, want a lift?” a voice called from the trucks.

“Stolz? Damn right we do.”

“Anyone injured?”

“Got a couple who can’t walk,” Phelps called.

As the truck moved closer, he saw the heavy machine gun on the dump truck had begun to fire again. Bullets that missed the guardhouse stitched through the trees, shredding bark and branches. Shots continued to ring out from within the guardhouse. Phelps’ squad loaded the wounded into the truck. As the truck headed toward the shelter, the squad used the shelter’s stonewalls as a screen while boarding the truck. Once loaded, the trucks drove to the north gate where they stopped.

“Ferris has to set up his things,” Stolz said.

"Can we stop them here?" Phelps asked.

"No, because the troop carrier's gonna break through the outer perimeter. If we stay, we'll be trapped outside of the Hill."

Bryan Ferris, a former NASA electrician, knelt in the center of the road by the north gate, working. He stood and with his foot, spread gravel. To the south, at the shelter and guardhouse, it had become quiet. Guns crackled in the north.

"Bryan, are you finished?" Stolz asked.

"Yes, I'm making sure it won't be seen."

"Hurry." Stolz turned to the squad. "Barricade the gate. We've got to slow them down."

The militia piled debris against the gate, wedging it tight before they scrambled into the truck and left.

~

At the south entrance to the Oxbow, Terry Whiteside saw the Clan militia trucks leaving, heading north. "Ah, shit." He was also almost out of ammo. His partner, Jimmy Corbach, lay on the floor with a bullet in his throat.

"It's over," Terry said. "Hey." He waved a white rag. "I give up," he shouted. "I surrender." The shooting ceased. He threw out his rifle. "I surrender," he called again.

"Come out," a voice answered.

Terry stepped out with hands raised.

"Lower the bridge," the same voice called.

Terry released the wire cable holding the drawbridge and cranked it down. As the bridge bumped to the ground, the dump truck's engine roared and it rolled across the bridge.

A dozen Deacons followed, weapons at the ready.

Skid strode over to Terry who stood with his hands on his head. "So, you're the dumb-shit who wouldn't give up, eh?"

"Just doing my job." Terry stood still, hands up.

"A wise ass, too." Skid raised his handgun to Terry's forehead.

"A bad mistake." He licked his lips. "You shot some of my boys. That was a bad mistake too."

"But," Terry said. "You attacked—"

Skid pulled the trigger.

~

Behind the plastic sheeting that served as temporary walls for the shelter house, Skid found only remnants of clothing, bedding, and a few children's toys. "We're going next door." He pointed to the metal building.

Skid peered through the open doors. Inside were tables, chairs, and beds. One table had a teddy bear propped up next to a half-eaten bowl of cereal. "Fuck, they've cleaned it out." He kicked a chair out of his way.

"Uh, Skid, what d'you want us to do with this stuff?" Knuckles pointed at the furniture.

"I don't care," Skid said. "It don't mean shit to me."

"Uh, sure." Knuckles nodded to several nearby Deacons. "It's cool." They piled up the furniture and set it on fire.

A Deacon laughed and threw the teddy bear into the flames.

From the north the rattle of gunfire started.

"Let's go." Skid climbed into a truck and pointed in the direction the Clan truck had gone. They followed the curving road through the pine trees to a gate piled with logs blocking their exit from the Oxbow.

"Do these assholes think a fuckin' gate is gonna stop me?" he said to no one in particular. "Hey, Wheelman." He beckoned the truck's driver. "Knock this damn gate down."

"Sure thing, Skid." Wheelman backed the truck into the gate. It took three runs before the gate tilted over and crashed down to become a bridge over the ditch.

Skid picked out a half-dozen Deacons. "You, check it out." He gestured at the road on the other side. "Make sure no one's waiting for us." The men trotted over the bridge.

Alongside the road, the Deacons poked their guns into the thick underbrush. Nothing. After ten minutes, Skid waved to Wheelman. "Okay, move it forward."

The truck crunched into gear and rumbled into the narrow confines of the gate entrance. Something clicked loudly.

A ball of flame erupted skyward with a monstrous roar. The truck lofted into the air, its cab shattered. It rained down pieces in all directions. The heavy machine gun and its crew in the truck's box split off and crashed to the ground thirty yards away. A mushroom-shaped cloud of smoke rose.

The truck's box slammed down near Skid. "Mother-fuckers! They tried to kill me. I could've been in that truck. They're gonna pay for this."

Clayton Nickolas watched the attack develop on the Park road north of the Hill. The Clan had built a ten-foot-high dirt embankment as its outer defense perimeter to block the road. A ditch carrying water from a small stream to the Rocky River ran alongside the long dirt mound.

Clayton glanced at the large crossbow. *Ford pickup truck springs*, he thought, *must have at least a four-hundred-pound draw*.

The string—a length of emergency brake cable—was held by a latch made from a claw hammer. A three-foot length of two-inch diameter iron pipe—the bolt—sat in a slotted channel made from white oak. Beneath the crossbow's stock was a long lever that operated a mechanism similar to the old-style car jacks—it was the only way to pull back the crossbow's string.

He'd found the design of the armor-penetrating bolt ingenious. *Damn good engineers at the Glenn research center*, he thought. The pipe held an explosive charge that would propel a hardened steel rod upon impact. *What was it? At four thousand feet per second? Whatever, it sure punched a hole in steel plate. I just hope it works on that troop carrier*.

Clayton raised his hand. A bolt streaked from the crossbow to the troop carrier and hit the machine gun. It exploded in a shower of sparks and scattered in all directions. Ammunition exploded like a string of firecrackers.

The crossbow team stood and cheered.

Damn fools, thought Clayton. *They should've aimed at the driver.*

The Bradley slewed its cannon, hunting for a target. It boomed loudly several times in rapid succession. Its cannon shells shredded the crossbow's emplacement. The second crew dragged its crossbow below the crest of the embankment.

A minute later, three trucks covered with planking backed-up to the ditch and dumped rubble and dirt into it. Two more trucks arrived and filled the ditch. The troop carrier's turret continued to move back and forth, seeking a target.

Clayton watched from behind a large tree. He knew it was just a matter of time until they broke through the perimeter. "Try again," he said.

The second crossbow rose and fired at the Bradley with an armor-penetrating bolt. Flame and sparks erupted from the impact, leaving a splash mark in the Bradley's metal skin. It hadn't penetrated the armor.

The Bradley swiveled its cannon toward the crossbow. The crossbow dropped below the embankment. The cannon fired, raising a plume of dirt.

"Pass the word," Clayton said. "Start the retreat. You," he said to a small group of Clan defenders. "Get the Molotov cocktails ready. Wait for the troop carrier to get between the walls of the embankment." Clayton joined them as the rest of the Clan force dispersed into the woods.

After the trucks filled the ditch above its banks, Blade waved his men on from the troop carrier. His men surged forward and scrambled across the ditch. Three Molotov cocktails exploded among them. They halted and began shooting. More Molotov cocktails flew over the embankment. After five minutes, they stopped. The rate of fire from the Diablo's guns slowed.

Blade pointed at the embankment. "Forward."

Three trucks lurched across the rubble, each compacting the fill in the ditch.

Blade followed in the Bradley. Water began to accumulate behind the ditch crossing.

~

A line of Clan militia climbed the Hill, silent except for the moans of the wounded and the jingle-clack of their equipment. They were the last defenders from the embankment on the park road. They moved into prepared positions on the Hill and noncombatants brought them food, water, and ammunition. A breeze from the south brought warm, moist air. The day began to heat up.

Franny silently handed Taylor the casualty report.

Taylor shook his head; five men and one woman dead, fourteen wounded and out of action, and four missing. And, Clayton Nickolas was badly wounded.

Damn, he thought, *he's our best tactician*. He clamped down on his feelings. *Later. I've got a battle to fight. Right now, we're outnumbered and out-gunned*. He began to feel as if he were trapped on the Hill.

~

Blade scowled. The troop carrier's cannon had only thirty rounds left. Each one had to count. "Advance."

At the bridge over the Rocky River, a ball of flame exploded low on the lead truck's cab. Liquid fire flowed out of the truck's fuel tank and spread across the road. Flames roared into the air, crowned with black smoke.

"*Dios*." The word slipped involuntarily from Blade's lips as he backed away from the intense heat. "They have some kind of artillery." He backed up the troop carrier behind a clump of large maple trees. He stared at the hill, looking for a telltale puff of smoke. Nothing. "Put more planks on the trucks."

An hour later, three trucks with crate-like appearances again drove onto the bridge. A ball of fire exploded on the side of the lead truck, showering wood fragments in all directions. The truck continued to advance.

Blade saw a flicker of movement on the hill five hundred yards away. He opened fire with the troop carrier's cannon.

The second and third trucks started over the Rocky River bridge. Blade's men used the bridge's stone parapet for cover. The troop carrier followed at the end of the column.

At the mid-point of the bridge, an explosion rocked the lead truck of the convoy. Shredded metal raked the men. Several fell screaming, their blood staining the asphalt paving.

"Pigs." Blade had seen movement on the point overlooking the river, which jutted out like a prizefighter's chin. He rotated the turret of the troop carrier toward the point and fired, again and again until he'd reduced the trees on the point to straggly, splintered wood. Over half of the cannon's ammunition was gone. "Follow me," he said. "Behind the troop carrier."

The column rolled over the bridge to the tall maple trees lining Cedar Point Road. Ahead was the road leading up the Hill.

Blade's men ran behind the vehicles until they turned down the gravel trail. The lead truck slowed as it approached the old riverbed at the base of the hill.

Something whistled through the air and a huge explosion lifted the lead truck a foot off the ground. Smoke and dust enveloped it as it burst into flames. Something else streaked in and an explosion smashed into the side of the troop carrier.

"*Dios*." Blade crossed himself. "Back to the trees."

"Where the fuck are those Deacons when they're needed?" Blade said. "They should lead this attack." He'd forgotten his promise to join them. "Enrique, go get the Deacons." He had only a hundred able fighters left—he needed more.

"Sí, Jefe." Enrique saluted and hurried out.

"Careque." Blade called to a Capitan. "Move your men closer. If anyone on that hill raises a head, blow it off. *Ya se va?*"

"Sí, Jefe."

Blade studied the hill and reviewed the map. The only way up the hill with the troop carrier was on the west side where the grade was not so steep. That meant crossing the old riverbed. It was time to have the trucks fill the riverbed.

"Where the fuck were ya?" Skid had arrived with twenty-five Deacons. "You said you was goin' to join us at the south entrance. We took our lumps waiting for you." He glanced at the Troop carrier. It looked battered; its machine gun was gone, and along one side metal was bent with blackened marks.

Blade ignored Skid's question. "There's been a change in plans," he said. "You will attack the east end of the hill. Enrique is your *capitan*. Unnerstan'?" He pointed to Enrique Maquinez.

"Sure thing, Blade." Skid's smile was forced. He turned and gave his fellow Deacons a wink. "Right, boys?"

The Deacons nodded silently.

"*Señor* Maquinez," Skid said. "Lead the way."

"Pico," Blade called to a young *capitan*. "Get the trucks loaded with stone." He pointed to a gravel bar in the river.

Upon reaching the east side of the hill, Enrique raised his hand and called, "Halt."

Skid nodded to Knuckles who grabbed Enrique from behind. Skid slipped on a pair of brass knuckles. "You an' me, *Señor* Maquinez," Skid said, "are gonna have a little chit-chat."

"Let go," Enrique said. "You make a big mistake."

"Yeah, right." Skid punched Enrique squarely on his nose. Blood splattered. "First, you've gotta learn no one orders me around unless they've got real muscle. An' you don't, see?"

"Ugh." Enrique gagged, blood streaming from his nose.

"What happened to the troop carrier, chump?"

"I don' know what you mean." Enrique struggled. "Let go."

"Asshole." Skid kneed Enrique in the groin. "Answer my fuckin' question." He punched Enrique on the ear.

"They, the worms on the hill, used a big bomba on her. It was terrible, they destroy the gun."

"How much ammo does the Troop carrier have?"

"I don' know."

"Wrong answer." Skid hit Enrique again.

Bone fragments protruded from Enrique's left cheekbone. Blood streamed down his face. "Aaagh, I don' know."

"Don't be a stupid chump. Just tell me how many shells are left in the fuckin' troop carrier," Skid's voice rose an octave. Spittle frothed at the corner of his mouth. He hit Enrique with a roundhouse blow on the side of his head.

Bones cracked in Enrique's skull. His mouth sagged open and his right eye opened wide, empty. His muscles contracted and then went limp. His bowels and sphincter released.

"Fuck." Knuckles pushed him away. "He shit his pants."

"Yeah, that's the last time that turd will shit you." Skid removed the brass knuckles. "Okay, what do we do about this?" He pointed at the stairs that led to a barely visible structure at the top of the hill made of logs and sandbags.

"It'd be fuckin' crazy to attack," Knuckles said. "A couple of guns up there would eat us alive."

"Yeah, that's what I thought, too." Skid spat on the ground. "Let's just lay off an' watch for a while. If that greaser's got a lotta ammo for the troop carrier, we'll pretend to attack the hill. If he don't, then we'll find a way to waste him."

~

Taylor reviewed the battle reports. "That troop carrier has hurt us," he said. "We've only got one large crossbow left and only three armor-penetrating bolts."

"What's the casualty count?" Weitzman asked.

"Twenty killed and many more wounded." Taylor's voice rose. "Most by that damn troop carrier."

"How many left?" Fred asked.

"Less than one hundred in both the squads and the militia." Taylor paused. "Okay, Clayton what d'you think?"

"Counter-attack after their next move." Clayton's words came out faint and wheezing. His chest wound made it difficult for him to speak.

"Oh, sure. All ninety of us will charge down the hill and chase them away." The instant Taylor spoke he regretted his words. Clayton didn't have time for jokes.

"Edgepark still has bolts for their crossbows." Clayton coughed. Froth tinged with blood bubbled onto his lips. "Coordinate your attack with them. Have Edgepark attack their rear. The gang will break and run. They don't like what the crossbows do." He closed his eyes and sighed.

Weitzman gently pushed Taylor away. "He needs rest."

What Clayton really needs, Taylor thought, *is an intensive-care trauma unit. Many of our wounded will die from wounds that would've been routine care in a hospital*. Each time he thought about it, his throat constricted and his heart ached.

As Taylor surveyed the valley, the wind changed direction and picked up, blowing dust and leaves around. The sky had become slate gray, low clouds scudding in from the south. Heavy drops of rain plopped down, raising puffs of dust. Trees swayed and rattled in a gust of wind. A veil of rain swept across the valley obscuring its far side. A blue-white lace of lightning flickered. Thunder pealed.

"Pat, come in, Pat," Taylor spoke into the walkie-talkie. It was a NASA security encrypted walkie-talkie.

"Patterson Rice here, I can barely hear you." His voice sounded faint through the static.

"Yeah, there's a lot of interference," Taylor said. He laid out Clayton's plan, explaining Edgepark's role.

"I don't know, that sounds mighty risky."

"Look," Taylor raised his voice. "We've been the ones on the receiving-end all day. It's time for you to do your share."

"If this fails," Rice said. "They'll walk all over us."

"Yeah, well, we're in the same spot." Taylor let his annoyance show. "Look, there's only about eighty Diablos by the bridge. We actually outnumber them. The only problem is the troop carrier." Taylor wondered if he'd made the right decision to share ammo with the Edgepark community.

"Well, okay, I guess. Let us know when to move."

"I'm turning the walkie-talkie over to Chris," Taylor said. "She'll keep you informed. Okay?"

"Okay." Rice's voice lacked enthusiasm.

The day darkened into an almost-twilight. Rain poured down. In the lightning, Taylor saw sheets of water running down the glistening clay on the flanks of the Hill. *Now we're safe. The Hill's slopes will be too slippery, even for a troop carrier.*

The rain stopped and the air was sharply colder with a crystalline clarity. The Diablos fired from time to time from the riverbank near the base of the Hill's cliff.

"Have some sharp-shooters give those Diablos a taste of their own medicine." Taylor pointed to the men by river. "Phelps, bring up those drums of gasoline." He indicated the path leading down the steep slope to the main entrance. "If the troop carrier tries to cross the ditch, it's gonna get a warm welcome." He forced a smile. He didn't feel like smiling.

Franny came running. “Taylor,” she called. “They’re moving on the main entrance.”

“What’re they doing?” Taylor strode to the lookout point.

“They’re bringing up trucks loaded with rock.” She trotted alongside him.

One by one, the team leaders joined him as he viewed the situation. “Wait for them, make them come to us.”

The walkie-talkie squawked. “It’s Patterson Rice,” Chris said. “He says that he can see some Devil’s Deacons in the vicinity of the Nature Center. But they’re not moving.”

“Tell him to wait for the signal,” Taylor said. “I want the Diablos to commit themselves before we do anything.”

“Sure.” Chris reached for the walkie-talkie.

“Where’s O’Connor and the horsemen?” Taylor had no real need to know but he was nervous. “Tell him to get ready.”

“Sure thing.”

A cloud of blue exhaust smoke rose as the Diablos’ trucks lined up with the troop carrier at the rear.

“Chris, have Rice take a shot at the troop carrier.”

“He wants to know why so soon.”

“Just tell him to damn-well do it.”

The bolt from the crossbow seemed to float in a lazy arc across the width of the valley. It struck the Troop carrier with a bright flash, followed by a puff of white smoke. A clump of Diablos went down like wet wheat before the wind. A boom echoed through the valley.

“Good shot.” Taylor said.

“Look out,” a voice screamed.

Before the bang-bang of the Troop carrier’s gun reached them, branches shredded around them. As one, the group on the point dropped, some moaning. Blood flowed. The troop carrier turned its cannon again, but its gun did not fire.

Taylor grabbed the walkie-talkie from Chris’s hand, “Rice. Hit them now,” he yelled into the mouthpiece. “They don’t know where your shot came from. They’re about to shoot at us again.”

Another explosive bolt hit the back of the troop carrier; its cannon remained silent. The Diablos' trucks backed up to the old riverbed and dumped fill into the water across from the main entrance. Even after the last truck dumped its load, the waterway was only partially filled. The troop carrier advanced to the edge of the water and from behind the trucks, Diablos emerged in a ragged line and started to wade across the waterway.

Taylor rubbed his head. "I don't believe it, a human wave attack. Chris," he yelled. "Let 'em roll."

One after another, three drums filled with gasoline bounced down the hill. The drums came to a halt at the base of the dirt embankment near the front entrance. The leading edge of the Diablos emerged from water and climbed the embankment by the entrance, firing continuously.

"Now," Taylor yelled.

A crossbow bolt streaked down the hill and struck a drum filled with gasoline.

A ball of fire erupted with tongues of flame shooting out in all directions. A huge cloud of black smoke rose. Another dull boom accompanied a fireball that climbed high into the air. Even from the top of the hill, Taylor could feel its heat. Another explosion blew a sheet of flame across the moat's water. As the flames subsided, blackened figures crawled out of the water. A few struggled on board the truck that had backed up to the water's edge. The troop carrier's engine roared and it backed away.

"Rice," Taylor yelled into the walkie-talkie.

"Yes?" Rice answered. His voice was tentative.

"Start the counter-attack, now. We got 'em. We fried 'em. They're running. Push them west, push them up Cedar Point Road." Taylor began to hope for victory. "Do it now."

"Wilco," Rice answered.

~

An explosion rocked the troop carrier. "*Madre de Dios*," Blade said. A wave of flame engulfed his machine and it hesitated briefly. He checked its instruments for malfunction, then crammed it into reverse. He headed back to the entrance from which he had come, followed by a truck laden with his men.

"This whole thing has gone wrong, very wrong," Blade said to himself as he drove. "These Clan people have artillery, they ambush me. This is not supposed to happen to me. I am Armando Diaz Velasquez, the Blade, the one who deals out death, not these worms." He drove north on the Park road.

Blade slammed on the brakes and screeched to a halt. The fill in the ditch over which he'd made his initial assault was gone. It was now a stream, full to its banks with brown, raging water. *What happened?*

He turned the Troop carrier around and headed back. Several Deacons waved to him but he kept going. *Let those smelly pigs rot in hell*, he thought.

As he entered Cedar Point Road, the troop carrier's metal structure rang like a bell as something crashed into the armored car's side and exploded. He remembered there was another way out of the Park, up the hillside out of the valley. He turned west on Cedar Point Road and accelerated through the opening in the concrete blocks of the barricade.

Buried beneath the center of the road, within a thick, reinforced concrete casing was five pounds of smokeless powder carefully sealed in a section of a thick-walled four-inch diameter steel pipe. Its only opening was at the top. Above it was a thirty-gallon drum filled with polystyrene-jellied gasoline.

The weight of the troop carrier compressed a truck spring used as an electrical switch. Current flowed to a solenoid that snapped a steel pin briskly into a shotgun shell at the bottom of the steel tube. The shell coughed a small tongue of fire into the smokeless powder. It exploded.

Constrained by its steel and concrete corset, the explosion front went upward, the shock wave atomizing the jellied gasoline and accelerating it.

A gigantic blowtorch of flame engulfed Blade's vehicle and threw it high into the air. The troop carrier landed on its side, rupturing its fuel tank. The fuel burst into flames and sent a large cloud of black smoke into the cool, clean air.

~

Bryan Ferris heard the explosion and smiled. He knew what had happened. He'd never imagined his electrician's training would come to this.

~

Taylor stared at the rows of laid out bodies. Corbach, Whiteside, and Coughlin—*I barely know their names—and now they're dead.* Around him lay the bodies of men and women whose faces he knew but whose names he couldn't recall. *Butchery*, he thought.

Why? Why? And Clayton—quiet competent Clayton. In just the short time I knew him, I thought that I'd found someone to help me lead. They came here to be safe and now they're dead. For what? Food and a place to stay? Some of those that I sent out to fight didn't know how. Is this what I've come to? A bringer of death and destruction?

Fifty-five dead, out of the one hundred and forty men and women who had fought for the Hill. It was a Pyrrhic victory, Taylor thought. *We can't afford this, ever again. If I'd walked away, they might still be alive.*

A SEASON TO GROW

"Dearly Beloved, we are gathered here today to mourn the passing of the brave men and women who gave their lives in defense of our community...."

Franny listened to Father Scaravelli, who had his arms raised, eyes closed, standing on top of a weather-beaten park bench before the Clan in the grassy meadow below the Hill.

A clump of tall maples behind him provided shade. He'd organized a group funeral service because too many had died for private services. As yet, there was no church or chapel. However, they now had a large, new cemetery.

Franny knew how those around her, sweltering in the afternoon sun, had suffered. For two days after the battle, she had tended the wounded with no time to think about her own problems. As she prayed for the dead, she felt thankful, that in spite of her suffering, she and her children were still alive.

I know there's nothing I can do to change what happened, but if I try, perhaps the future will be better. I've been so wrapped up in myself, she thought, *I've driven people away from me*. As the opening notes to "God is our Fortress and our Rock" sounded, she opened her heart and raised her voice to God.

~

At the funeral service, Taylor sang almost without feeling. It brought back memories of Vivian and the life they'd once shared. His heart ached to hold her again. As he scanned the faces of those present, he recognized the Clan needed a sense of continuity and he knew for many, religion was a source of comfort and mysterious strength. He supported the establishment of formal religions even though he no longer felt any need. Something inside him had died.

Taylor's sense of self-reliance forced him to look within to find solutions. He found what kept him going was a sense of responsibility to others. The loss of Vivian and the devastation of the battle lay on him like a black fog.

I have done evil. My only chance of salvation lies in helping others.

~

After the funeral service, Taylor assembled the team leaders. "We took too many casualties and sustained too much damage."

Heads nodded.

"We can't let this happen again. So, what should we do about it?"

"Well." Weitzman cleared his throat. "The Oxbow residents would like to move onto the Hill, where it's safer."

"All right." Taylor paused. "What about your animals?"

"Maybe we can use the Oxbow area as farmland." Weitzman had a distant look. "However, I'm still concerned about its security. We'll have to strengthen its defenses."

"Let's schedule a separate meeting on that," Taylor said. "Any objections to the Oxbow people moving to the Hill?"

"No, but I'd like to say something." Pat Rice cleared his throat. "Edgepark has some natural defenses, but they're not as good as the Oxbow and nothing like the Hill. Even though we took only minor casualties, we're vulnerable, too. We'd like to move to the Hill, as well."

Taylor stroked his chin. "In reality, there's a lot of space on top of the Hill if we're not concerned about hiding our presence. By now, the gangs know we're here."

"How're we gonna get enough shelter built in time for winter?" Fred's frustration showed. "There'll be more problems with people living so close together," he added.

"Any other objections to the Edgepark and Oxbow people moving to the Hill?" Taylor saw heads nod agreement. "You're right, Fred, but security comes first. It's agreed then. They can move in."

Taylor found the different factions seemed to turn to him for guidance. Perhaps they recognized he represented all of them and was committed to being fair. His leadership skills, honed in project management and the fact he was the first to settle on the Hill after the Collapse, had, de facto, put him in command.

As summer progressed, Taylor pushed to get more shelter and improve their living conditions. He organized the construction of two dams on the Rocky River to raise its level and provide better protection and more water. They used the large sandstone blocks that came from an old railroad overpass in nearby Berea for the dam.

While building the dam, Stolz dug two channels to connect the existing river to the old riverbed. The first channel, upstream from the first dam, diverted water into the old riverbed. At the east end of the Hill, a second channel returned the water via a weir into the Rocky River. The channels maintained the water level in the old river course, which formed a "moat" that completely surrounded the Hill.

By the end of the summer, Stolz had finished both dams, complete with fish ladders. The new reservoirs quickly found use as swimming holes. The downstream lake, directly below the Hill, became the accepted bathing area and the taboo of being naked in public faded fast. Bathing alone in a remote section of the river was just too risky.

"Sir, please sir, let us in, please." It was a small Asian man in a torn shirt. "We afraid, sir, they took everything." His face was a mass of bruises and cuts.

Shel Weitzman glanced up from his notepad. "D'you know anyone here?"

The woman behind the man had a blank look on her bruised face. She clutched a tiny child who sucked a grimy fist. They were gaunt and emaciated. "The gangs, they rob us, they beat us, they take everything. My wife, they ..." The man fell to his knees and placed his head on the ground in front of Weitzman.

"Shel, let him in." Taylor helped the Asian man to his feet. "What's your name?"

"Nguyen Van Minh. Thank you, sir, thank you," the man said. His wife's expression was unchanged. It had the same blank look seen on the faces of many refugees.

"What d'you do?" Taylor realized they were like many who'd been caught up in events that had stripped them of possessions, pride, and dignity. Yet he knew all had to work together so they might survive.

"I had restaurant in Cleveland. They burn it."

"Mr. Van Minh, we'll find you a place. I'm Taylor MacPherson. This is Dr. Shel Weitzman. He'll help you." Taylor led him through the gate. "Shel, send him up to see me after they've had a chance to settle in." He shook Nguyen's hand.

"Thank you, sir, thank you. Thank you very much."

~

More refugees came to the Clan. Some wanted food, others sought protection.

Weitzman examined them, turning away those with tattoos and missing teeth that suggested a gang affiliation or the scars on their arms indicating heavy drug usage. The newcomers had to swear an oath of allegiance to the Clan. All had to work. Those without skills worked as laborers on the fortifications or in the fields.

Among the refugees who joined the Clan was Dr. Meltem Encirlik. She had been a surgical intern at the Cleveland Clinic and Weitzman knew her socially. He welcomed her gladly.

~

"Look, if you feed a man a meal, you satisfy his hunger for one day." Sam Wylie's voice got loud. "If you teach him to fish, you show him how to feed himself forever. Don't you see? We need the equipment and materials to make tools. Then we can make machinery for farming and manufacturing. We don't need the scraps and leftovers of society to survive." He referred to the Clan's practice of sending out regular scavenging parties.

"Yeah, well, sure Sam, I get your point," Ted Callioux said. "We need food to get through the winter. None of us know what kind of tools to get."

"We can grow food." Sam Wylie's voice cut through the conversation.

"Sam, you're right, we'll grow our food," Taylor said, joining them. "Soon, we'll start looking for tools. And Sam, you'll be involved, I promise."

"Is that a real promise?" Sam Wylie's eyes narrowed. "Or are you just saying that to shut me up?"

"It's a real promise." Taylor's mouth tightened.

~

"Ted, I hear you're going north today," Taylor said. "Mind if I come along? I could use a break."

"Why, sure." Ted Callioux's eyebrows rose. He led the scavenging team because he still hoped to find his wife. "We're going out further each time. It'll take most of the day."

"I used to live north of here. I left some things behind," Taylor said. "Can we stop to take a look?"

"Sure."

Taylor's home had been stripped and trashed. Behind the house, he found three skulls, white and grinning, along with a scattering of bones. The cache of buried items was still intact, from which he retrieved a generator and books. He wasn't sure if his personal computer would be of any use, but brought it anyway along with reference data on memory storage devices.

Blackened shells of houses lined the streets, and those not burned, had broken windows and doors hanging ajar. Tall grass grew throughout the formerly tidy neighborhoods. Lines of weeds delineated the cracks in the roads and sidewalks. Crows circled above. "How come we haven't seen anybody?" Taylor asked.

"The survivors hide when they hear a vehicle," Callioux said. "Only the powerful have gasoline."

~

By late summer, the Clan's population grew to more than a thousand. Even with the labor surplus, Fred could not keep up with the ever-increasing demands for shelter.

"All right, how many damn buildings do you want?" Fred had had enough. "Every time I get started on a building, you tell me to make it bigger. I can build anything you want. It'd be a whole lot easier if I knew what you wanted ahead of time."

"Point taken." Taylor held up his hand. "We need a plan to develop the Hill, something to follow."

"What about services?" Fred put his hands on his hips. "There're too many people on the Hill already. It's getting unsanitary. We've gotta deal with that, too."

"Yes, you're right," Taylor said, thinking hard.

"So, what're you going to do about it?" Fred's voice took on a belligerent tone.

"Let's work on the problem. Have Stolz join us tomorrow. Let your people know that I'll need you for the whole day."

~

The next morning, Taylor unfolded a drawing and spread it out before Fred and Stolz. "Here's some of my thoughts on what we should do. I'd like your input before we get started."

"That'll be a change." Fred examined the drawing.

"Look," Stolz said. "This is going to be a problem area." They went through item by item, developing the plan's concepts.

The next day, Taylor presented them with a revised plan. "It will incorporate existing buildings as well as those under construction," he said. "Under this plan, the Hill will become a high-density living area within a wall. We'll need warehouses to store food and supplies in case of a siege...." Taylor warmed to the subject.

~

Within a week, the plan expanded to include sewers and water lines. There would be a main entry road that crossed the Hill to a meeting square in the center, with a perimeter road around the top. There would be no buildings along the edge of the Hill so as to preserve the trees and aid defense. It also reserved four sections of the Hill for Clan buildings and service facilities.

"This is better," Fred said. "Now I know what I'm doing."

"No more of that dig a hole, fill a hole shit," Stolz said.

"You really want to develop the 'Lower Hill,' don't you?" Fred pointed to the land adjacent to the Hill.

Stolz pointed to the drawing. "This is where we'll put a sewage treatment plant." It was the land next to the marsh. "We need this if we want to keep eating fish from the river."

"Yeah," Fred said. "We gotta get something done, and soon. The place is starting to smell."

The mud that Jim Higgins had excavated with so much difficulty from the old riverbed dried out. It was now a gently sloping four-foot high mound that followed the inner bank of the old river course. On top sat an eight-foot high wall made from rock-filled gabions to completely enclose the Lower Hill district. A similar wall encircled the top of the Hill. Taylor was sure they were now safe.

AUTUMN'S HARVEST

Chilled, Taylor got up from his chair and put on a jacket. *Late summer and early autumn had been busy*, he thought. *Good thing Stolz's crews had installed sewers on the Hill*. He hoped those septic tanks that cleaned up the sewerage, which was now discharged into the marsh. Ted Callioux said he's positive the cattails and water lilies will purify the water before it drains into the Rocky River. So far, the swamp is thriving and the river seems cleaner.

As the light faded, Taylor lit several candles. The gray, weathered plywood walls of his office reflected light poorly. *Days are getting short and I really miss electricity*, he thought.

He picked up another report, squinted his eyes, and began to read. John Wylie and a group from Edgepark have built more large crossbows. *Good*, he thought. *That adds to the four catapults they made from heavy lumber and automotive coil springs*.

He picked up another report. *Harvest is over*, he thought, *but Franny's calculations show hungry times could still lie ahead. Even though our people worked long hours drying and canning vegetables, and smoking and salting fish from the river, we'll have to find more sources of food.*

~

"Taylor, look at this." Franny pointed to five partially chewed rats in a bucket. "Ol' Puddinhead brought them to me."

"Who?" Taylor put his pencil down.

"I'm sorry," she said. "Y'know, he's the big, old tabby who hangs around the food storage warehouse."

Taylor glanced at the ceiling of his office. *Now what?*

"The point is," Franny said. "There're too many rats around here for one cat. We're losing food."

"So, get more cats."

"I asked Albert to catch cats for me." Franny paused. "He believes hunting for game is more important."

Taylor waited for her to continue.

"Would you talk to Albert?" Franny reached out with her hand as though to touch him. "Please, Taylor, as a favor for ..." She hesitated. "For the Clan."

"Why would a feral cat stick around?" Taylor frowned. "Especially after being trapped. Wouldn't it run away as soon as it was released?"

"Oh, no." Franny's face brightened. "You bring them to me. They'll stick around, trust me."

"Maybe I can get Sam Wylie to build a trap." *There was something familiar about Franny. No, she doesn't look like her.*

Chris barged into Taylor's office. "It was a gang attack," she said. "They killed the men guarding the group gathering berries south of the Oxbow. They kidnapped six workers. They left one behind with a demand for a truckload of food for their release." A fierce frown knitted her forehead.

"Damn," Taylor said. "They kill our people and hold others for ransom. We can't afford the food, or let them start blackmailing us. Stall them. We're going after them."

Weitzman, Phelps, and Chris gathered around the table in the plywood shack that served as Taylor's office.

Chris was pale. "We found five bodies at the south gate."

Taylor swore. "Who were they?"

"It was the men in the foraging party," Chris said. "They had their, their ..." She gulped. "... cut-off. They were mutilated."

"Oh, God, what else?"

"There was a message carved on one of the militia's body. They now want two truckloads of food for Kristy Becker," she said. "Our scouts tracked them to the old National Guard Armory in Berea. That's where one of them got killed. It's a gang called the Deacons, a bunch of ex-motorcycle thugs. They're holding Kristy there."

"Look, either we pay tribute, and keep paying, or we fight." Taylor's voice rose. "I say we fight."

"Isn't there's another way?" Weitzman wrung his hands. "We lost so many fine young people last time."

"Well," Taylor said. "What's the alternative? Give them our food?"

Weitzman said nothing.

"All in favor of rescuing Kristy Becker, say 'aye.'"

Only Weitzman abstained.

~

On the edge of the ravine, Chris peered through binoculars. The National Guard armory lay on the north side of the former business district of Berea. It was perched above the West Branch of the Rocky River, which flowed through a heavily wooded ravine. The three-story brick building had a large central hall that had originally been a garage. All the openings on the ground floor, except for the front and rear entrances, were boarded up.

A six foot-tall chain link fence surrounded the armory complex with a gate directly in front of the main door. Four guards hung around the main door, talking. A lookout on the roof smoked a brown-paper cigarette. Empty beer containers and a scattering of wind-blown paper littered the weed-filled drive running along the side of the building.

The aroma of food and the absence of people convinced Chris the Deacons had started their evening meal. She waved to her platoon. All of the camouflaged fighters crawled out of the ravine one by one. They assembled, crouched in the long grass at the edge of the road opposite the armory's entrance.

Chris raised her hand and pointed first at the doorway, then at the roof of the armory. A dozen crossbows rose, cocked and ready.

She dropped her hand.

Feathered bolts streaked through the air, thin, silent, and fast. Four bolts struck the man on the roof. He staggered, coughed out his cigarette, slumped, and fell thirty feet to the driveway. He landed with a sound like a watermelon smashing. His body jerked and then lay still.

At the door to the Armory, two Deacons slumped, feathered bolts quivering in their chests. They started screaming.

"Go," Chris yelled.

The platoon rose as a unit. Another cloud of bolts whistled into the Armory's entrance as the two remaining guards raised their rifles and fired wildly.

Two of the Clan militia collapsed. The rest of the platoon reached the building's entrance. They paused to hook the crossbows to their belts and then unslung their M-16 rifles. Together, they burst through the Armory door, firing.

~

At the sound of gunfire, Phelps leaned out of the lead truck, raised his hand and pointed.

Two big tri-axle trucks rumbled into life and rolled down the tree-lined street. In the back, militiamen readied their rifles. Above the cab of the leading truck, two men crouched over a catapult designed to throw Molotov cocktails. The catapult was an Edgepark invention made from automobile coil springs and a lever arm that could lob a gallon jug of gasoline almost four hundred yards. They'd practiced with it and were confident of their aim.

~

As gunfire echoed through the armory, Skid jumped up from the table. "What the fuck?" He ran for the front door, Knuckles close behind. As he reached the main corridor, more shots rang out and the edge of the door erupted into a shower of splinters.

"Shit." Skid slid to a halt and reversed direction. "We gotta get outa here." At the rear entrance, he dove through the door and rolled on the ground.

The Clan's trucks, armored with heavy planking, entered the driveway at the side of the armory. A volley of gunfire erupted from the back of the trucks.

Mud splattered around Skid. "Aw, crap." He scrambled behind the corner of the building just as the militiamen in the lead truck fired their catapult. A gallon jug Molotov cocktail streaked a trail of black, greasy smoke.

As it struck the ground, a huge ball of fire erupted behind Skid. He felt its sudden heat. He ran to the next building. Once around the corner, he took a quick look.

The trucks had stopped, but the Clan militia continued firing at the armory.

"Bastards." Skid retreated around the corner.

Two Deacons crowded past him and rattled off quick shots at the truck. Empty cartridges clattered off the wall, bouncing onto his arm.

Within the shelter of the door, several Deacons hung back.

"Stubby," Skid said. "Bring the boys. Tell them to bring ammo, too. Get them here, pronto. Understand?"

"Here?" Stubby scratched his crotch. "To this building?"

"Yeah, and move it, move it, move it." Skid felt his face begin to twitch. He licked his lips and bit the corner of his mouth.

"Okay, Skid, I got it." Stubby scrambled away from the building, ducking and weaving out of the line of fire.

Inside the Armory, Chris fired at the two shadowy men in black leather who ran toward the rear of the building. She followed with a platoon of militia close behind. As the men leaped out the rear door of the building, Chris saw the Deacons' colors on their backs. The smaller of the two was the scar-faced man.

My God, she thought, *that's who murdered my father*.

Chris sprinted after him. Shirley O'Connor and half the platoon followed. At the back door, Chris peered out. A bullet whined off the door's metal edge. She pressed against the wall behind her. "Damn, damn," she said, "he's getting away."

"What's up?" Shirley arrived, breathing hard.

"Nothing." Chris shook her head. "Search the building for Kristy. If anyone offers resistance, kill them." She replaced the M-16's thirty-round magazine and cocked the gun. A truck rumbled past the back door. It was a Clan truck.

"Hey, Phelps."

"Yeah?" A face appeared at a vision slot.

"Get a truck at the front." Chris pointed in the direction from which the truck had come. "We may need to leave in a hurry."

"Gotcha." The truck growled, transmission whining as it reversed. From a nearby building came the rattle of automatic weapons. As the truck backed up, its catapult heaved a smoking Molotov at the next building. It struck the building and flame washed down its side. The gunfire paused.

Upstairs, on a bare, stained mattress, Shirley found Kristy Becker chained to a radiator. She was naked and semiconscious, face swollen and eyes blackened.

"Bastards." After Shirley undid the chain, she carried Kristy through dim, dirty hallways acrid with gunfire fumes and down the stairs. Shots echoed in the building. Broken glass crunched underfoot. Several militiamen appeared out of the gloom.

"C'mon, help me get her out of here." Between pants, Shirley lowered Kristy to the floor.

Two militiamen carried the moaning woman to the front door. "Now what?" The militiamen looked up after placing Kristy on the ground inside the doorway. A militiaman returned with a blanket, which he wrapped around Kristy.

Chris waved to a truck.

Moments later, it rumbled around the corner and stopped in front of the building. "Get her on board and let's go."

"Wait, Chris, there's ammo and medical supplies," said a militiaman who staggered out of the building with a box of ammo.

"Go get it," Chris said. "You, cover this side." She pointed to the rear of the building.

Within a minute, the militiamen returned with eleven M-16 rifles, four cases of ammunition and a box of medical supplies. "Okay, we've cleaned it out. Nothing left worth taking."

"What do we do about this place?" someone asked.

"Burn it," Chris said.

A Molotov cocktail flew into the building through an upstairs window. A dull thud preceded a ball of flame erupting from the upstairs.

"We're loaded, time to leave," Chris spoke into her walkie-talkie. It was eight minutes since the first shot had been fired. The second truck rumbled up. "Let's go," she yelled.

"It's those assholes from the park," Skid said. "They pulled a sneak attack." He pointed at the trucks. "Don't let them get away." He couldn't stop his face from twitching.

A fireball exploded at the corner, blazing fuel splashed

toward them. “C’mon,” Skid yelled and ran.

Flames blossomed out of the armory’s upstairs’ windows. As the Deacons advanced, they fired continuously. As they rounded the corner of the armory, trucks were pulling out of the gate.

“You yellow-bellied pricks.” Skid shook his fist at the trucks. “I’m gonna kill you. Every damn one of you.” He felt spittle run down his chin.

Flames licked out of every window of the armory. The repetitive bang-bang-bang of ammunition cooking off began.

“Which dumb-ass let those Clan bastards in?”

No one looked up. No one said anything.

“Who was on guard duty tonight?” Skid clacked home a fresh magazine into his rifle and cocked it. “Knuckles. Bring those shitheads to me. This chapter’s gonna learn a lesson. No one lets me down an’ gets away with it. No one.”

“Uh, Skid,” Knuckles said. “They already dead.”

As the Clan trucks pulled out of the gate, slugs slammed into their tailgates. Through the drifting smoke, Chris counted a dozen Deacons on the ground. Eleven more had been left for dead inside the building. Still, her heart was heavy.

Oh, Daddy, why you? Why did it have to happen to you? I need you, Daddy, but you’re not here. She wiped away a tear. *I couldn’t save you. I swear I’ll get him, Daddy. I promise.*

Something within Chris began to grow, something hard and cold.

“Taylor, we need to get more land under plow.” John Phelps looked at his companions. “We’ve got to get the winter wheat in right away so we’ll have food next summer.” It was obvious he’d rehearsed his argument.

"If we don't," Franny said. "We'll be out of food."

"Okay," Taylor said. "What do you want?"

"Well, even with rationing, we'll need ..." Phelps described their requirements and the land he wanted to use.

"D'you need all twenty acres?" Taylor asked.

"Well, yes, we'll need to get at least that much in over the winter." Phelps's face held a frown.

"Okay, you'll get fuel," Taylor said with a sigh. "I'll notify Chris about your need for guards. Is that all?"

"Yes, I guess so."

Taylor guided them out of his office but Franny lingered.

Taylor's eyebrows rose. "Something else?"

"Umm, yes." Franny took a deep breath. "Albert brought me a litter of kittens. He said you talked to him. Thanks."

"You're welcome."

She touched his arm briefly. "You'll have to come over and see them. They're so cute and Puddin-head plays with them."

Her touch reminded Taylor of another ... *No*, he thought. *It's not the same*. "I'll drop in after supper to see them."

Franny's face lit up. "I'll expect you."

Work continued on the House of Worship. With limited resources, Taylor knew they could build only one place to pray. Already its bare unfinished interior had seen weddings, funerals, far too many funerals.

As it grew colder, the pace of activities slowed and Taylor realized there were more women than men on the Hill, many of them young and with children. Most were widows from the battles with the gangs. Some of the older couples adopted young widows, providing care for their children while they worked. Men died, women grieved, and children wept.

Taylor felt a terrible sense of failure.

DOMESTIC TRANQUILITY

The weather turned colder and the trees became gaunt and gray. As the leaves fell, Taylor felt his mood slowly spiral downward.

Seeking company, he joined Clan workers harvesting the late fall run of shad. While they salted and smoked the fish, he heard someone tell a joke. It was the first time in what seemed like forever he found a reason to smile. It almost hurt to laugh.

Winter arrived with a lake-effect storm dumping a foot of heavy snow overnight. Some believed the snow was due to the smoke in the air from the war; others claimed it was an act of God. Bitter cold soon followed with more snow. As winter deepened, the Hill became a more closed-in community. People huddled around stoves and fires to soak up precious heat.

"It's amazing. I now know more people than I ever did. It's like there's no barrier to meeting people," Franny said.

"Yeah, I guess so." Taylor bent over a tablet of paper in front of the window. "TV and cars were really barriers to meeting people; they were agents of isolation. TV and movies didn't require any mental effort." He kept his face serious. "All you had to do was just lay back and get a mental massage."

"Maybe you're right," Franny said. "I can see how it could

limit interaction, erode social skills, and produce a breakdown in civilized behavior, which contributed to the Collapse."

"You sound just like a sociologist."

Now that Franny had come out of her shell, Taylor found he enjoyed her visits. *I may have underestimated her*.

Even when the paths were shoveled clean, few went out into the bitter cold. On still days, the blue-gray smoke from the wood stoves hung over bare trees in the valley like a wraith of despair.

Franny cut the food rations again. Soon, everyone had the foul smell of fasting on their breath. Tempers grew short and occasionally, fights erupted. The rule of no weapons on the Hill prevailed and Chris Kucinski's tight discipline preserved order.

Young Albert, not so young anymore, won the respect of many with his steady supply of game and fish. He also patrolled the river, making it safe for ice fishing. He'd had no luck hunting deer, so he went to Taylor for advice.

Taylor welcomed the diversion from the never-ending tasks of administration and decision-making. He had hunted regularly in his previous life and took a day off to go out with Albert.

"Look," Taylor told him. "See how these tracks converge? They're going in that direction. If we circle around, sooner or later, we'll find where the deer went." He pointed to the spoor outlined in the snow. The naked gray-barked trees creaked tiredly in the wind. Light was fading.

"In the winter," Taylor said. "Deer gather into groups after the rut in areas that provide food and cover, such as swamps or thick scrub. The only time deer are vulnerable to, say, wild dogs and coyotes, is when the snow gets too deep. That's when they get trapped because they can't outrun them."

"Like the section down there?" Albert blew into his hands and pointed to a tangle of briars surrounding clumps of stunted willow and dogwood bushes near the river.

"Maybe." Taylor pointed to a trail in the snow where hoof prints disappeared through a prickly hedge. "See this? It has fresh tracks going in both directions. It may go from a yarding area out to a feeding area. Let's come here tomorrow, before dawn. Maybe we'll see something."

Albert's eyes lit up. "Let's do it."

Over the winter, Albert tracked three herds of deer to their yards and culled them to get much-needed meat for the community. He also broke ice on the river to provide swimming areas for waterfowl, which he harvested using snares and crossbows. Nothing was wasted; the feathers and down from the Canada geese went to the sewing circles that gathered around the stoves during the cold, empty days of winter.

Taylor didn't bathe often since there was no running hot water and the only warm place was next to a stove. The sour smell of unwashed bodies had become an accepted norm.

One morning, Dr. Encirlik came to Taylor's office.

"Our sanitation worries me. People aren't washing themselves or their clothes enough. I'm concerned about public health." She paused. "Something has to be done before it becomes a real problem."

"Problem? What kind of problem?"

Dr. Encirlik looked over her glasses in the manner of a lecturer looking at a student. "The sanitary conditions on the Hill are atrocious. We're ripe for infestations of body parasites, such as fleas, bedbugs, or other vectors to spread disease. If there were an outbreak of a bacterial infection, our community wouldn't stand a chance."

Taylor became acutely conscious of his own body odor. "Doesn't the cold suppress these vectors?"

"Yes, but there are no antibiotics left. An outbreak in our over-crowded living conditions would be like the Black Death."

Dr. Encirlik removed her glasses and polished them while watching Taylor. “I hope I haven’t alarmed you.”

~

It took Taylor a week to organize the construction of a public bathhouse. It was next to the river just below the dam. They ran a water line from the river to a large wood stove to heat the water. The stove produced a steady stream of hot water and warmed the interior to a comfortable temperature.

Women and small children used the facilities in the early afternoon, followed by the men and boys. During the mornings, the bathhouse was the community laundry. Laundry flapped like flags from clothes’ lines and gave the Hill a festive appearance. The bathhouse brought a major uplift in the Clan’s morale—it was a touch of civilization.

~

“You bitch. If you go near my husband again, I’ll kill you.” Shirley O’Connor yanked the slender woman’s hair and hit her face with the back of her hand. The ring on Shirley’s finger drew blood.

The woman was clad in a partially open gown. Shirley struck the woman’s upraised arm. The woman stumbled and landed hard on the muddy ground.

Shirley kicked her. “Take that, you slut.”

“No, no, don’t.”

As the woman scrambled away, Shirley kicked her again. The woman gained her feet and ran down the narrow alley, gown flapping.

The woman ran into Fred Del Corso’s arms.

“Now just a damn minute.” Fred grabbed the bloodied woman and pushed her to one side.

The woman closed her gown, crossing her arms over her breasts.

"Hold everything, both of you, right now." Fred barred Shirley from advancing. "What the hell's going on?" he asked.

"This bitch—"

"She's crazy." The woman's voice cracked into falsetto.

"Shut up. Both of you, shut up," Fred yelled. "All right, who're you?" He pointed to the injured woman.

"I'm Noelle Smith and I—"

"You're a slut." Shirley's voice echoed down the alley. "A whore." A door cracked open and a face peered out.

"Enough," Fred said. "Shirley, what happened?"

"This slut is screwing my husband."

"She's insane," Noelle said. "She tried to kill me."

Fred glanced up.

More people emerged from houses, staring, eyes wide.

"All right, let's go." Fred pointed down the alley. "Move it. You're both under arrest for disturbing the peace."

He led them into Taylor's cluttered office. "These two were disturbing the peace. That means you're involved."

"Hmm." Taylor was taken aback by how different each looked from the other.

Shirley's long blond hair went in all directions, starkly outlining her pale, tight-lipped face. She wore a tan over-sized winter jacket that almost reached her jeans-clad knees. Shirley towered over the bare-footed woman whose torn house-gown was splattered with mud and blood.

Noelle was in her twenties and thin to the point of emaciation. Her heart-shaped face and dark hair, cut short in a style many women now favored, made her look almost elfin. She shivered and dabbed a grimy rag to the cut on her bruised face.

"You, sit here." Taylor pointed to Noelle. "And you, sit over there." He indicated that Shirley should sit on the opposite side of the rough-sawn plank table. "What's going on?"

Both women started speaking.

"Shut-up," Fred said loudly. "You." He pointed at Shirley. "State your name and what you were doing."

"Shirley O'Connor. This whore is screwing my husband and—"

"That's enough." Fred's voice drowned out Shirley's words. "You." He pointed to Noelle. "State your name and what happened."

"I'm Noelle Smith. This woman tried to kill me—"

"You deserve a fate worse than death, you whoring bitch."

"Hey, hey, that's enough." Taylor raised his voice to a level that usually got obedience. "If this involves Jack O'Connor, we need him, too. Fred, get O'Connor."

"This slimy, disease-infested slut—"

"Shut up," Fred said. "I'm not gonna tell you again." He stood over Shirley and wagged his finger at her. "We're gonna wait 'til Jack arrives. Got it?"

When Jack entered, Noelle rose, one hand holding her gown closed and the other extended to him. "Jack, tell them—"

"You slut." Shirley jumped up. "If you look at my husband again, I'm going to claw your eyes out—"

"You're mad."

"Fred, get this under control," Taylor said.

"Everyone shaddup." Fred slammed his ham-like fist down.

The table bounced. The room became quiet.

"These are the rules: You speak when I tell you. You." Fred pointed to Shirley. "Tell us your side of the story. No name-calling, yelling, or finger pointing. Understand?"

"This tramp—"

"No name-calling." Fred's voice rose. "Remember?" His hand extended until his index finger almost touched Shirley's nose.

She swallowed and nodded. "This, thing," she said, acid dripping from every word.

Fred raised an eyebrow and cleared his throat.

"Jack started coming home late. He'd go to the bathhouse in the afternoon and not return for hours. He never told me where he'd been. Well, I finally realized what was going down when I saw him sweet-talking to that ..." She pointed at Noelle. "Her. Right away I knew something was happening. He was grinning like an idiot, oblivious he was making a fool of himself. So, I decided to have a discussion with ... her."

"Shirley," Fred said.

"I went over to her grubby hovel this afternoon. It's really disgraceful." She sniffed. "It matches her appearance."

"Please," Fred said. "Spare us."

"Well, after this slut serviced this weak-minded husband of mine, I went to see her."

"Shirley," Fred raised his eyebrows and cleared his throat.

"I'm sorry. When this lady opened her legs for the whole world, he had to take a turn, too—"

"All right," Fred said. He frowned. "You've had your say."

"It's just not true," Noelle said. "It's not the way she says it is. She makes it sound so cheap." Her voice quavered and sank in volume. "I got to know Jack after he made a snowman for my little Martha. He's the only man, other than her father, who ever took an interest in her." She paused and smiled at Jack.

"He likes children, he likes mine. As we talked, we found we like a lot of the same things. He wouldn't spend time with me if she gave him the affection he needs and the children he wants—"

"How dare you say that, you bitch. Just keep your filthy claws out of my Jack, or I'll—"

"Or what, Mrs. O'Connor?" Fred asked.

"Nothing." Shirley's nostrils flared.

"This afternoon," Noelle said. "After Jack and I were—"

"In bed," Shirley's voice rang out. "Screwing his brains out."

"Shirley, please," Fred said. "You've had your say."

"Well, after Jack left, after we'd, you know, been together. The first thing I knew, this madwoman burst in and grabbed my hair and hit me. I couldn't stop her—she's bigger and stronger than I am. So I ran and she chased me." Noelle sighed.

"I don't want to hurt anyone. I just wanted to be with Jack." She dabbed her eyes. The bloodstained rag left red traces on her cheek.

"Jack," Fred said. "Are you seeing her?" He nodded toward Noelle.

"Well, yeah, I guess I am." Jack looked up, voice hesitant. "It's kind of hard to explain. Because in a way, I still love Shirley; she's my wife. I also love Noelle." His voice became stronger. "Y'see, Shirley takes me for granted. Noelle is more exciting. And she has a child."

"How dare you?" Shirley jumped to her feet. "Why, you selfish, sex-crazed, self-centered son of a bitch—"

"Oh, shut-up," Jack said. "I'm tired of your temper-tantrums and excuses in bed."

Shirley flinched as though she had been struck. Her face went ash white. She sat down slowly like something was broken, as though every movement caused pain.

"Shirley, you'd better get used to it," Jack said. "You can still have me, but not exclusively, not anymore. The world's changed. I've changed. I won't put up with you running my life any longer. Life's too short and too uncertain for me not to do what I want to do—not when I could die anytime."

"But, Jack, our marriage vows—"

"Noelle and I have a relationship. Period. We can stay married, but there're things I want that you can't or won't give me, I'll get elsewhere." Jack wagged his finger at Shirley.

"How can you do this to me?" Shirley's voice quavered. "We're husband and wife. You have a duty, you took vows, you can't ..." She sagged into a chair as though wounded. Tears filled her eyes. Her lower lip quivered.

"Shirley, you've been my best friend and partner. I've trusted you with my life." Jack grasped her hand. "But there's aspects of our relationship that don't work. You're too hard, too competitive and sometimes, too mean. At times, I need a relationship that's not so demanding. Noelle gives that to me. That's the way it is, that's the way it's going to be. The choice is yours. You can have a part of me, or none of me."

Shirley withdrew her hand.

"Noelle," said Fred. "What've you got to say?"

"I like Jack. I need company ... his company." She lowered her eyes. "I've been alone since I lost my boyfriend. Now, since Jack came into my life, I look forward to getting up each morning instead of dreading the day. He pays attention to me, he fills up my empty life, and he likes my little girl."

"Did you know that Jack was married?" asked Taylor.

"Yes, but I don't care. I don't want to be alone."

"Did you know that Shirley is his wife?"

"Yes, and she threatened to kill me. I'm not trying to steal him from her. I'm not even jealous when he goes home to her. I'm just grateful for what little time we have together."

Noelle shivered and drew her ragged gown tight. It was as though she was trying to cover something revealed. "You have no idea how it is to be a woman without a man in this world."

"Jack, how could you do this to me?" Tears ran down Shirley's face. She seemed smaller, more vulnerable.

"Well, life isn't the same as before." Jack shrugged. "I like Noelle and I like her child," he said. "They fill a need in my life. I'm not giving them up."

Fred threw his hands up. "Look, you're a married man, you can't just go and have an affair with anyone you want."

"Sure and that's fine for you to say. You've got a wife and children. I don't have any children. In the past year, I can't count the number of times I've been shot at. I can die at any time. If I die, none of me survives, none. So, I'm going to live life to its fullest. And if I can, have children."

"Don't you care what people think about you?"

"Name the people you've buried in Cedar Point cemetery," Jack said. "You can't, because there's too many—all forgotten. Life may be cheap, but it's still dear to me. There are things that I want out of life. Nothing will change that."

"Well, Taylor," Fred said. "What d'you think?"

"I've got no desire to rule on private morality. I'm more concerned about survival." Taylor sighed.

"Well, what should we do about this?" Fred asked.

"We can't tell people how to live their lives, especially behind closed doors. We can only ask they live peacefully."

"Well, they were disturbing the peace."

"True." Taylor nodded. "There're penalties for that. I don't want to—and will not—set moral standards."

"You mean these two can sin without penalty?" Fred jerked his thumb toward Noelle and Jack.

"That's between them and their moral values. Whatever they do, they must do privately, without violence and without disturbing the peace." Taylor stared at them. "Shirley, if anything happens to Noelle, we know of your threats. There'll be no mercy if you resort to violence."

"But she—"

"Shirley, this is not a Clan matter unless you resort to violence. If you do, there are severe penalties. Do you understand?"

"It isn't fair." Her lower lip quivered.

"It may not be fair. The Collapse wasn't fair. Life isn't fair," Taylor said. "I can't solve every problem."

"If that's what you want," Fred said, "I guess I gotta go along with it." A frown lingered on his face.

"No more violence and no more disturbing the peace." Taylor wagged a finger at them. "Otherwise, exile. Is that clear?"

Both Shirley and Noelle nodded, their reluctance obvious.

IN THE IN-BETWEEN

The Egg-that-Flies plunged onward, a dark shape in a dark place.

It has been a long time, Bilik Pudjata thought. *And we're still only halfway to the Kota system.*

He stared at the holographic model of the Kota system he had created, piece by piece, based upon ongoing fragmentary observations. It shared certain similarities with his system: two large outer planets and at least three small inner planets. He was certain this was from where the strange creature had transmitted its image.

It wasn't possible to deploy an antenna similar to the deep space observatory on Qu'uda. At their current speed, it would erode away rapidly. Anything protruding from the surface received the punishing impact of hydrogen atoms at one-third the speed of light. Only short-life sensors worked.

Once the ship reached its maximum speed, Bilik's sensors saw a faint pinprick-sparkle of radiation outlining its nose. The tiny sprinkles of light came from atoms impacting at near relativistic velocity. The bow, once a pockmarked half-asteroid, became smooth and rounded after years of such erosion.

Within the ship, Bilik found life had a steady rhythm. There were few demands other than its passengers maintaining their physical and mental condition. At first, many focused upon the universe outside, confirming the observations of the Star-Seeker, which had been destroyed by the alien Hoo-Lii on its expedition to the Deka star system. There were no surprises. Then they turned inward, to concerns about their positions in a small society.

~

Cha KinLaat DoMar, an environmental specialist, was also the navigator and took it upon himself to chart the space about the Kota system. He needed to set a course to minimize the impacts of cosmic debris on the ship. His sensors monitored their destination and the reference stars he used to plot their course. He set the ship's course to arrive above the ecliptic of the Kota system so as to bypass much of its cometary belt and its debris.

Bilik visited the navigator, Cha KinLaat DoMar, at his station, far forward in the nose of the Egg-That-Flies. The room was full of electronic equipment, which had red symbols that flickered assurance all was well.

"Look." Cha KinLaat pointed to the holographic plot. A red line grew before them and climbed upward against the lacy green grid that was marked off in time and energy. It was a second order extrapolation showing data from the third planet in the system. "Kota's electromagnetic signals radiate at ever-growing strengths."

"Yes, I see," Bilik said. "However, I haven't seen any signals like those we received on Qu'uda."

"Maybe they've changed the format of their transmissions," Cha KinLaat said. "There're a lot of data recorded here."

"Perhaps," Bilik said. "We did postulate the signal was broadcast simultaneously from multiple points on the originating planet. Let me show you." He called up data from the original deep space observations and built a new holographic image that illustrated the infinitesimal differences in reception time.

"I didn't know that."

"It wasn't much discussed. The specialists had to rework the signal many times before they came to this hypothesis. It wasn't deemed newsworthy." Bilik highlighted the differences in orange. "You see, while working to improve the signal quality, they found they could separate the signal into multiple elements, then recombine them to eliminate the time lag." He changed the holographic image to plot time differences and distance. "If the specialists were right, we now know the size of the planet from the spread in the reception front."

"Ah, I see," Cha KinLaat said. "This says that it's about the same size as Qu'uda, maybe a little smaller."

"Yes, and that means—"

"It has to be the third planet from Kota." Cha KinLaat bobbed his head crest in triumph. "It's the only one that size that's within the probable habitable zone."

"We failed to come to a definite conclusion," Bilik said.

"Any other discoveries you forgot to tell me?"

"Not really, everything else is sheer conjecture."

"Such as?"

"Well, the third planet is further from Kota than Qu'uda is from our sun. On the other claw, Kota is a hotter star." Bilik took a deep breath before speaking. "This planet may not support life as we know it."

"What do you mean?"

"It may be colder. It may receive more short-wavelength radiation, more ultraviolet. Its chemistry could be different."

"Oh," Cha KinLaat said. "What about the image we received on Kota, didn't that tell us something?"

"The creature was obviously indoors. When we enhanced the image of the fur on its head, it appeared to have a shine or a gleam from a liquid, which we believe could be water. There was no clue as to what their external conditions were like." Bilik sighed. "There are so many things we don't know."

"Don't worry," Cha KinLaat said. "As we get closer, we'll learn more about the Kota system."

The room's ventilator sighed softly, exhaling the aroma of rotting vegetation. Bilik raised his head and sniffed. "What's going on in the environmental system? Has something failed?"

"I don't think so. I believe because it is a closed system, there's not enough atmosphere to act as a buffer."

"That doesn't explain the stink," Bilik said. "You're an environmental specialist, what's going on?"

"True, but there's a lot of plant vegetation left after the harvest is done and we can't throw it away. We have to compost it and make it into a growing medium for new crops. The mature compost is supposed to act as a bio-filter to absorb the odors, but there's not enough to do the job properly."

"Why not?" Bilik asked.

"Well, large decorative plants such as Podu trees require more growing medium," said Cha KinLaat. "They've taken a lot."

"I see," said Bilik. "More Podu trees for the Defenders' new homes. Did you see the new dwelling Mata ChaLik BuMaru created for himself in the food-growing area?"

"Not yet," Cha KinLaat said. "But I heard about it."

"It's a replica of a dwelling of our primitive predecessors who lived in the wetlands. It takes up a lot of space. He fancies himself to be fierce like them."

"Be careful what you say. He's at the center of the community." Cha KinLaat looked behind him as if to see if anyone were there. "So, new food production facilities are built in the low-gravity areas." He bobbled his headcrest. "Well, I suppose being the speaker for the Defenders-of-the-Egg has its privileges."

"I heard DalChik DuJuga thought he was taking advantage of his position. He's concerned about food production."

"He doesn't have enough support to stop Mata ChaLik from building more dwellings. Egg knows he's got more than enough."

"Rumor has it those close to the center of the community

want to build dwellings within the hydroponics gardens." Bilik sighed. "It's the Defenders' latest fashion statement."

"All that water and high humidity, just like the communal bath. And privacy to do who-knows-what."

"Hmm," Bilik said. "In reality, it doesn't affect our mission. Since our economy is closed, we still have the same resources; they're just allocated differently."

"Allocate more to me," Cha KinLaat said loudly. He softened his voice. "What are you doing with the drive system? I heard you started a new project that has something to do with it. Didn't you replace the propulsion tube earlier?"

"Yes. I gave the drive system a complete inspection after shut down. The main drive reactor had some minor wear, but not enough to affect its performance," Bilik said. "I decided to completely refurbish the whole drive reactor."

"Won't that mean going outside?" Cha KinLaat shivered.

"Yes." Bilik bobbed his head. "I'll build an excursion vehicle to handle the large parts."

"Why?"

"I like to build things and refurbishing the drive reactor will be like a refresher course." He paused. "It'll get my mind off the alien question for a while."

"That swamp's not for me," Cha KinLaat said. "I like my routine. Egg knows the navigation is complex enough."

"Look." Bilik called up an image of the exterior of the spacecraft and focused on the drive system.

The main propulsion tube rose above the rough gray surface of the section of the asteroid that formed the stern. The tube was long and glittering with rows of cooling lines snaking over the tightly wrapped magnetic coils made from shiny-black polycarbon. Below sat the fusion drive reactor, a bulbous shape surrounded by massive containment shields. The three large dish-shaped radiators dissipated heat from both the power generation reactor and the drive system. They pointed in the same direction as the propulsion tube. Between the radiators, like giant logs, lay spare propulsion tubes, enclosed in shiny metal cocoons.

"That's going to be my playground for the next year." Bilik pointed at the elliptical roof that covered the entrance to the holding pen for a Bird-that-Soars. It was almost below the stern's curved shape. "The hangar."

Cha KinLaat shook his head. "Not for me."

"I'm setting up a workshop in one of the Bird-that-Soars' hangars," Bilik said. "Would you like to see it?"

"Yes."

"Let's go."

"Oh," Cha said. "You actually mean to go there?"

"Of course."

"Why not just view it? That's too far to go. I don't like traveling through the axis corridor." He referred to the long, tube-like corridor that ran from the living quarters through the ship's enormous fuel tank to the propulsion system. "I don't like going into something where you can't see to its end, especially without gravity."

"You look through interstellar space all the time," Bilik said. "There's no comparison between the two."

"That's different. It's open and there's always something further off." Cha KinLaat swept his upper limb down in a gesture of disgust. "I've only been through that tube once when I boarded. That was enough."

Bilik set out for the hangar by himself.

Alone, within the gravity centrifuge, Bilik knew its quiet and safety had all the comforts he could expect in Qu'uda society. The low-gravity region closest to the central axis contained the storage and non-critical work areas, and even though the gravity was lower, it provided space and equipment for creative outlet. However, much of the vacant space had gone for new hydroponics beds, which compensated for the Defenders' new dwellings in the former food growing areas.

The society on the ship, small as it was, continued to have an active social life, while those with ambition jockeyed to move closer to the center. The continual tension of the silent struggle for central tendency occupied the Keepers and the Defenders. The abundance and availability of resources produced a richness of life unknown on Qu'uda. The plenitude was sufficient to satisfy most, but not all.

CIVICS

In December, Taylor hooked up the Yaesu short-wave radio he'd gotten from Alec's house to a salvaged car battery. He punched in the frequency of a station noted on a card taped on the side of the transceiver. Nothing. He turned up the gain. He heard nothing but white noise. He tried several more frequencies. Nothing.

Static wasn't the problem; there were no broadcasts from any of the powerful national stations. He scanned the frequencies, looking for a ham transmission.

"... is Sierra-Sierra-Bravo-November 739, stationed at Bangor. We have a severe trauma case. We need advice on removing an arrow from the spleen and necessary post-operative care. Is anyone out there who can help?" The voice faded out. "... sustained casualties in an attack by a large group of unidentified individuals ..." The transmission stopped.

"Sierra-Sierra-Bravo-November 739—you're four by seven in California. This is Master-Sergeant Buckley of the one-fifty-ninth infantry, California Army National Guard, in Fort Hunter-Ligget. Our medical officer will be here soon. Irregular groups, too, have attacked us, several times. Not military units, more like gangs...." The transmission faded in and out as the medical officers discussed treatment for the injured person. The National Guard sergeant relayed reports from refugees who said San Francisco had been severely damaged by the nuclear attack and the rest of the city had burned in its wake.

More transmissions like this convinced Taylor civilization had collapsed and an age of barbarism had begun. The more he thought about it, the more he feared the future. Winter had always depressed him, but this year, it was bleak.

~

The Clan celebrated the holidays with exchanges of small gifts of special foods or handmade items. The House of Worship was packed as the different faiths each used their allotted hour to celebrate the season.

Meanwhile, in front of the main residence hall, rows of Canada geese and a huge pig slowly turned golden brown over a bed of glowing coals. In the early afternoon, the succulent meat, aromatic with herbs and dripping with fat, was sliced and piled high on plates with steaming potatoes, boiled cabbage, fruit preserves and fresh bread. Within an hour, the meal was just a memory, save for the bones pets begged from their owners.

Afterwards, long-hidden spirits and wine appeared. For a while, a party atmosphere prevailed. Glasses clinked amid laughter which grew ever more raucous. Soon many, long tired from the extended regime of hard physical labor, fell asleep.

Several drunken shouting and pushing matches erupted, which Chris Kucinski's guards subdued. Couples slipped away, while others went to the House of Worship to seek solace.

Taylor joined the Del Corso family in the afternoon to share a bottle of wine and reminisce about their times together. They laughed about the fun and fell silent when they remembered those no longer with them.

As night closed in, Fred and Maria retired to their rooms, leaving Taylor and Franny alone.

"Taylor." Franny glanced up at him. "Why don't you have." She hesitated. "A lady companion?"

"Um, I do, or I did. I was married...." He drew a deep breath and looked away.

"Tell me about her."

"She's dead." Taylor took a breath. "Vivian was beautiful, and smart, and she had the greenest eyes. She loved the outdoors and kids, and me. She was in Washington DC during the nuclear strike. A part of me still hopes she's alive."

"You miss her?"

"Very much." His chest constricted and the lump in his throat grew enormous. Memories came flooding back.

Oh, Vivian, how I miss you. Without a word, he rose and left. In his room, he sat on the bed and put his head in his hands.

~

Franny stared over the cluttered table as Taylor disappeared through the dim doorway.

I should have realized something like this must have happened, she thought. *Poor guy, he must have gone off to be alone and we blundered into his life. He's sheltered and fed us. All of this time I've taken him for granted. He's never talked about his own losses. Dear God, please forgive me, I've been selfish.*

Franny pushed herself away from the table and followed him down the corridor, past the rows of tiny plywood-walled cubicles in which people lived. When she reached his room, she wasn't quite sure how to tell him how she felt.

Franny hesitated on the threshold to his room and then pushed aside the curtain. "Taylor, it's me, Franny. Please, I know what you're going through." As her eyes adjusted to the darkness, she saw him outlined against the pale bare plywood of the wall.

"I've been there, Taylor." She sat on the thin straw-filled

pallet next to him and put her hand on his shoulder barely touching him.

"You saw how it was when Stosh was killed. I've finally accepted the fact he's gone. I've let go. You've got to let her go. You've got to let the pain come out." She turned him to face her and brushed the hair back off his forehead. "Look, you've got to remember your wife for all the good things you shared, but you've got to let go because life goes on. Wouldn't she want you to?"

She put her arms around him and settled his head on her shoulder. "It's okay to cry, you can't keep it bottled up inside forever." She stroked his head. "You know, you saved my life. I've never found the words to tell you how much I owe you. Did you know my children love you? They think of you as their father."

She held him. The minutes passed slowly. Taylor's proximity stirred something inside her. Something came alive, a spark of something long forgotten.

Not quite sure what to do, she started to speak. "You've done a lot for us," she said into his ear. "When you need someone to lean on, you can lean on me, I'm here for you." Gently, she eased him backward until their heads touched the pillows. She lay down next to him and clasped his hand.

"Franny, I'm sorry. I just feel like I need to be strong for everyone."

"Shush." She put her finger on his lips. "It's all right."

Taylor sighed. "Franny—"

"Shush." She closed her eyes and held him tightly, acutely aware of his masculinity.

That distant spark came closer and closer to the surface. Sounds became sharp and clear. The cool night air made her shiver momentarily. She pulled the rough wool blanket up and felt its scratchiness against her bare arm. She could smell wine on his breath and something about him was familiar, comfortable.

She felt him stretch as his arm moved over her. She snuggled closer and could feel his breath on her face. His lips brushed her cheek briefly and then he stroked her forehead. He started to breathe more deeply.

In the darkness her lips found his. She kissed him, tentatively at first. She couldn't believe her surge of desire. She kissed him again.

His fingertips outlined her eyebrows, nose, and lips, then slowly meandered down to her throat. The tip of his tongue followed the same sinuous path. He moved.

Franny felt the roughness of his face against her cheek and found it stimulating, making her feel more alert and alive.

His hand descended to her breast, and despite his light touch, her nipples grew hard and erect. His lips found her again, to form and fit against her lips. This time it was an even more delicious sensation.

She felt him pull up her sweater and undershirt. For a moment, more than just cold air gave her goose bumps. His hand, warm and gentle, pushed her breast to his lips.

Franny sighed. *I should have known this would happen.*

At his touch, she took a deep breath and swept her fingers up and down his back. She grabbed his hair and pulled his mouth to hers to kiss him again and again, lips parted.

His hand slid over her belly, gently caressing. As she took a deep breath, it seemed so right to reach for him.

Under the coarse fabric of his trousers, she felt his hardness. *What am I doing?* Franny thought and paused.

Taylor stirred.

She lightened her touch but did not withdraw her hand.

He stirred again and made a sound.

She realized he had pushed himself against her. It was obvious he wanted her to continue. She clasped him and squeezed gently.

Franny felt his hand glide down over her belly and navel, to the inside of her thigh. Even though the denim of her jeans blunted his touch, its effect was still electrifying. His fingers rose to settle between her legs where they moved with insistent pressure.

She could feel him, but it was not enough.

"Taylor, please," Franny said. "I can't stand it like this." She moved to sit upright.

"I'm sorry." He drew his hand back. "I shouldn't have—"

"That's not what I mean. I just want it to be good for us."

She sat up and peeled off her sweater and undershirt, throwing them on the floor.

She stood and turned her back to him, loosened her jeans, slid them off her hips, and stepped out of them. She realized he was doing likewise.

Oh, my God, she thought, *it's really happening*.

For an instant, time stood still, and then he was there, close, naked against her, enfolding her in his arms.

"Franny," he whispered into her hair, his hands seeking and caressing her.

She tilted her head, turned to him, eyes closed, to kiss his chin, his neck, his chest. She inhaled his masculine scent and felt her excitement rise.

"Oh, Taylor," she said.

His lips found hers and she felt a tiny spark from their contact.

Taylor held her firmly as he lowered her to the bed, keeping himself alongside her. One hand rose against her breasts, to touch her still erect nipples. His other hand slid smoothly over her bare skin, descending lower.

For an instant, just an instant, Franny flinched as his fingers parted her, and then a warm, luscious feeling exploded in the center of her being. She felt a surge of wetness greet his questing fingers.

His lips became active, greedily sucking and pulling on her nipples in rhythm with his fingers' touch.

Franny felt as though she was floating as the pinpoint of pleasure expanded to fill the whole universe and overwhelm all conscious thought. It was not enough. She wanted him, all of him, now.

She knelt over him with her legs on both sides of his torso. She lowered herself until her nipples touched his chest.

"Franny—"

"Shush." She raised her hips and guided him deep inside her. "Ah." The sensation was overwhelming as he stretched and filled her. She rose and did it again, and again, and again. She bore down on him as she reached the pinnacle.

"Oh, Taylor," she said, filled with intense joy. She shuddered as the tension released and warmth flooded within her.

The tears that had threatened now streamed from her eyes.

"What's wrong? What is it?" he said.

"It's." Franny gasped. "It's been so long. There's been so much pain. It almost doesn't seem right." She collapsed against him and realized he'd been there for her all the time. She liked him, no; it was more than that. He made her feel whole again.

"Yes," Taylor said. "I wanted this, needed it. But—"

"Don't." Franny put her finger on his lips. "This is me, Franny, here and now. I came of my own free will to be with you. And." She paused, searching. "No regrets. Remember, it's me, Franny, I'm not a ghost."

"I'm sorry," Taylor said. "It's just that you're such a good person." He paused. "I like you, have liked you, for a long time. A lot."

"Thank you." Franny couldn't help smiling. "I've liked you, too. You've been really good to me." She kissed him and pulled the blanket over them. She snuggled closer, not speaking for a while.

"I didn't know how much I wanted you until we kissed," she whispered. "Now, dammit, you've been playing with me for the last half hour. I want more, and you're going to give it to me."

With a laugh, she pushed him back onto the pillows, and then slid down the bed to lean over him. She lowered her lips and took him into her mouth, gently sliding her tongue over it. She paused to look at his face and smiled.

Taylor's penis rose and wagged a partial salute. She pushed him back and again surrounded him with her mouth.

"Oh, Franny." Taylor closed his eyes and arched his back. "Please." He let out a small groan.

"What's the matter?" She rose up. "Don't you like it?"

"Yes, but—"

"Then let me. I want to." She took his full length into her mouth and used her hand to exert pressure at its base until he was fully aroused.

"Franny, please." He pushed against her shoulders and tried to rise. "Please, now."

She leaned back, laughed playfully and rolled over, opened her legs and beckoned with her index finger.

As he mounted her, she guided him. She wrapped her legs around him, grabbed his buttocks with her hands, and squeezed with her legs. She rocked her hips against his, forcing him deeper.

"Taylor." Her fingernails clawed his back as an orgasm seized her. He continued to thrust, hard within her. His breathing became rapid; his body grew slick with sweat.

Pleasure again swept over her with the intensity of overlapping bolts of lightning.

Taylor grunted, seeming to grow larger within her and then he shuddered. "Uh." He twitched and pushed against her in one final effort. He sighed and collapsed over her.

"Ow, roll over, you're crushing me." Franny pushed him to her side. "Ah, that's better." She felt so alive and yet relaxed; she wanted to laugh out loud.

Taylor smiled and gently squeezed her buttocks. He frowned. "I should have known better."

"What? What should you have known better?"

"I think I took advantage—"

"Spare me; I'm not a little girl. Why are you feeling guilty?"

"It just feels so right I don't believe it."

"Believe it—I sure do." She chuckled. "I should've realized what would happen as soon as I put my arms around you."

Taylor touched her nose. "You look like an angel."

"Hah, I'm neither young nor an angel." Franny sat upright, put her hands behind her head and stretched. "Not too bad for a forty year-old mom, eh?" Her small breasts stood out, nipples erect; the muscles of her shoulders and stomach clearly defined, and every bone in her rib cage visible.

"You can't be forty. You've got the body of a much younger woman." Taylor kissed the palm of her hand. "If I had to guess, I would've said you were the same age as me."

"Well, thank you. A year ago you wouldn't have said that. I've lost thirty pounds or more from tight rations and hard work. I bet I've got better muscle tone than I had before I had children. I thought I was in pretty good shape back then."

"Really? I never thought our rations were tight."

"You don't seem to have lost much weight, but then I seem to remember you were always lean. I'd guess I'm ten years older than you." She stroked his hair.

"Almost. I never really thought about it until you mentioned it." He kissed her nose and stroked her hair.

They talked awhile but soon sleep swept over them.

~

The following morning Taylor awoke and found Franny curled up within his arms. "Are you awake?" he whispered.

"Yes, sort of." Her voice was low, husky. She turned toward him. "You're still here. Good." Her eyes wrinkled into a smile. "I mean, good morning."

Taylor laughed. "A very good morning to you." As they lay in bed, they talked. Their conversation turned to the Clan's situation and its future. "I've been using a short-wave radio," he said.

"I've tried to find if there's a government anywhere, but I've heard nothing."

"Then we're really on our own." Franny frowned. "What's going to happen to us?"

"I don't know. We'll survive, somehow, and multiply."

"You mean more refugees?"

"No." Taylor smiled as he ran his hand over Franny's belly. "I mean a baby boom is imminent."

"Oh, no," she said. "Not me. I won't get pregnant."

"Oh?"

"I had my tubes tied."

"Oh." He seemed disappointed. "Most women haven't."

"Yes, I know what you mean." She laughed. "Most of the younger women on the Hill seem to be pregnant."

"I wonder why." He smiled and looked away.

"No TV," she said and laughed. "I figured we'd have a baby boom. So I got ready for it."

"Oh, how?"

"I made a roster of all the women who have any knowledge of delivering babies. You know, nurses. We've gathered supplies and prepared a birthing room."

"Good thinking." He nodded. "I wish more people would think ahead like that; it'd make our lives easier."

Taylor realized Franny dealt with problems in a pragmatic and direct way, but knew little else about her.

"I was a public accountant." Franny told him about her life before the Collapse, which entailed juggling a career and raising two children. "It was a never-ending struggle to balance the demands of my family and my profession."

They discussed plans for the Clan, things needed for survival. Taylor had focused on food, shelter, defense, and sanitation, whereas Franny saw the need for government.

"Look, if we continue to take in refugees, make them full members of the Clan, and give them housing and food, we'll become a magnet for every homeless person in Cuyahoga County, in Ohio." Franny's voice rose. "It's welfare we can't afford."

"Well, yes," Taylor said. "What d'we do about it?"

"How about making those who come here pay for that right? You know, kind of an admittance fee."

"Why?" Taylor's eyes narrowed in concentration.

"Look, we sweated our cobs off all summer long building this place. I got my trim figure back the hard way—warehouse laborer, cook, construction worker—all on short rations." She cocked her head to look at him. "So, what do you think?"

"Are you asking me about your ideas?" Taylor leaned back and smiled. "Or looking for a compliment on your trim figure?"

"You sexist pig. All you want is my body." Franny stuck her tongue out at him. "I was referring to the idea of refugees paying for the right to join the Clan." A smile crept across her face as she turned sideways, thrust her breasts forward and watched him out of the corner of her eye. "After all," she said. "They're benefiting from my past efforts."

"Yes. I can see that." Taylor smiled at her double entendre. Her breasts were firm and pert. "Yes, a payment to establish property rights and the value of Clan membership."

"We still need some form of government with the support of all Clan members."

"What?" Taylor feigned astonishment. "You don't like my benevolent dictatorship?" His eyebrows rose.

"I do. Others don't."

"You're right," Taylor said. "Sooner or later, we've got to establish some kind of government. It's time to give up the fiction the US government will reestablish law and order. It just isn't going to happen."

"What about a medium of exchange? Y'know, money?"

"It must be tied to units of labor," he said. "It's the only way we'll get it accepted. Too many people came here with nothing and have slaved to make it a reality. They won't stand for someone who's done nothing ending up on top of the heap."

"The medium of exchange has to have an absolute reference value," said Franny. "It's got to be something tangible, something everyone knows and understands."

Over the next weeks, Franny found to her surprise she had slipped into a relationship with Taylor. She felt like a teenager in love. She remembered how during the pressures of raising a family, sex was reduced to a hurried once-a-week event—at best. Now, it was all the time. She wasn't sure whether it was the hard work or being in love that made her feel younger. For the first time since the Collapse, she was happy.

Franny and Taylor proposed the Clan adopt a representative form of government. Some groups opposed the idea, because they believed it would imply they would not be going back to their former way of life. Others thought it was time.

Discussions among the Clan members pointed out the need to divide into districts based upon the existing groupings of Clan members. It was proposed that each District elect its own Clan Elder as its representative. Taylor nominated Chris Kucinski as the Elder to represent the defense forces.

"What's MacPherson doing, nominating that bimbo as an Elder?" Knobby Wilson asked. He was a recent arrival. "She's barely old enough to bleed."

"Oh, yeah?" Stolz said. "Have you risked your life fighting for the Clan the way Chris Kucinski has?"

"Well, no—."

"Then shut your damn mouth." Stolz's words came out like nails being driven. "Don't mess with her."

Knobby's face still showed doubt.

"Why me?" Chris said upon being nominated.

"You're the right person," said Taylor. "You know how to fight and lead. I'm confident you'll do a fine job."

The proposal for a single leader of the Clan, answerable only to the Council Elders, stirred up the most debate. Some feared giving that much power to one person.

"Look, let's resolve this issue by having the Clan vote on it," Taylor said. "If the majority wants it, we do it. If not, propose another system and we'll put it to a vote."

~

For the next two weeks, the bathhouse and streets of the Hill buzzed with people talking about the election and about who should represent them. In some Districts, there were active campaigns by several candidates for the position of Elder. In others, it was a foregone conclusion who would be elected.

Just before the election, Taylor called an assembly of the Clan members. "Many want to return to the way you lived before the Collapse," he said. "It's no longer possible. Civilization as we knew it has died. We must build a new life. It won't be easy. If we work hard, we'll survive. Let us preserve the democratic traditions of our nation and form a representative government. Every member has a vote."

~

The elections produced a council of Clan Elders, who in turn, elected Taylor MacPherson as the Clan leader.

He presented his proposal that all Clan members be required to contribute one day of labor each week to the Clan. He proposed compulsory military training for all able-bodied members, both male and female, using the Swiss Army as a model for the Clan. After a long and bitter debate, the Council approved.

Some wanted power; others feared it.

More refugees arrived. Crime increased, prompting calls for a justice system. Former lawyers clamored for the right to run the legal system. At a Clan meeting, many expressed the opinion—sometimes crudely—that they did not want lawyers running society. Many feared criminals would again go free on technicalities. That wasn't their idea of justice.

The Clan could not afford jails for long-term incarceration, preferring instead to make the punishment fit the crime, with restitution for the victim. If a criminal could not make payment, he or she could enter into servitude until restitution was paid. If not that, the only other punishments left were exile or death.

Franny presented her idea to the Council that refugees should pay for the right to join the Clan. She argued new Clan members benefited from the effort of past and present Clan members. Her idea hit a responsive chord in those whose relatives had died defending the Clan.

The Council issued a decree all new refugees would pay the equivalent of one year's labor to become Clan members. They also legalized the option new arrivals could "indenture" themselves to a Clan member who would pay their fee for membership. The decree set a value on Clan membership, and at the same time, chased away opportunists and freeloaders.

THE FORGE OF WINTER

"Exile is cruel." Shel Weitzman raised his hand and made a chopping motion. "How could you banish Doyle and Chandler without any means of support? That's just not humane." He leaned over the park bench they used for discussions.

"Shel." Fred wrinkled his nose. "We can't afford to build prisons and we didn't hang them. So instead, we threw them out."

"They behaved after they came back."

"True." Fred scowled. "If we allow exiles to sneak back in under new identities, where do we draw the line?"

"They're sorry for what they did," Weitzman said.

"Oh, so as long as they're sorry, it's okay to molest children?" Fred flushed. "If it had been up to me, I'd have cut their nuts off before I threw them out."

"It's certain death outside for most people. How can we judge our fellow man like this?" Weitzman's jaw had a bulldog set. It was obvious he didn't want to concede the point.

"There're some crimes for which exile is a fitting punishment." Taylor saw by the color of Fred's face he was losing his temper. "Those crimes that threaten the community's safety or those committed against women and children."

"Can you prove these are the same people we exiled?" asked Weitzman. "Are you positive of their identity? Did you check their documents? Do you have pictures of them?"

Fred's jaw dropped and his eyes opened wide. "Well, er, no, none other than the word of the molested child, no."

"Is it possible the child could have made a mistake?"

"Well, yes, it's possible, but highly unlikely."

"What if years went by and memories grew even fainter, what then?" The smile on Weitzman's face grew.

Taylor raised his hands. "Shel, you've made your point. We need to address that issue. In the case of Doyle and Chandler, there was no mistake. Case closed."

As winter tightened its grip, Phelps reported every bit of grain and hay had been removed from the horse farms. Albert's hunting parties traveled ever further afield. Without antibiotics, pneumonia killed even the strong. The most frequent services in the House of Worship were funerals.

Taylor encouraged the Edgepark people to return to their homes since the danger from attack was remote.

While there, Pat Rice collected ashes from stoves and fireplaces to extract potash. After a number of trials, he made a liquid soap from a concentrated potash solution and tallow. At first, the soap was only good for washing clothes. Later, he refined it, adding pine balsam and lemon mint to make scented bath soaps.

Taylor learned over the winter Sam Wylie had developed a bow made of laminated wood and fiberglass using an epoxy resin he'd found on a scavenging trip. He began by making bows for Albert's hunters, but soon found there was a growing demand.

The horsemen preferred rifles but there was little ammunition left. When they tried crossbows, they discovered they were difficult to draw while on horseback. Long bows were too cumbersome and there were too few compound bows to meet the demand.

Those who tried Sam's recurve bows liked them so much they were reluctant to give them back. Taylor brought this to the Council's attention, which appointed Sam Wylie as manager of the Clan bow-works. The Council decided archery would be a required part of the militia's training. It wasn't long before the bow became the militia's primary weapon.

Taylor set up a facility to make arrows next to the mill. The arrow makers cut flattened, steel highway guardrail into narrow, triangular arrowheads. They made the arrow shafts from straight-grained pine and used Canada goose feathers for the fletching. The stockpile of arrows grew.

~

"If we tattoo a criminal's face," Ted Callioux said. "He's easy to identify."

"That's for sure." Fred nodded.

"That's horrible," Weitzman said. "That's just like the Nazis. What're we turning into? A bunch of Fascists?"

"The difference," Ted said with some heat. "Is these people committed crimes. It has nothing to do with who they are."

"It defaces their body, their temple," Weitzman said. "It's sacrilegious, disgusting."

"Anyone who wants to be a part of the Clan must live the life. Anyone who commits a crime against a fellow Clan member doesn't deserve to belong." Taylor looked around the Council for any dissenting comments. "Those in favor, say aye."

There was a chorus of ayes. They all nodded agreement except for Shel Weitzman, who continued to shake his head.

"Ted, tell us how this will be done," Taylor said.

"Well, a criminal sentenced to exile will have a tattoo. I recommend the letter 'E' for exile in a visible location, such as on their forehead."

"Who's gonna do the tattooing?" asked Fred.

"It should be done under sterile conditions," Dr. Encirlik said. "We don't want to give anyone an infection from a tattoo."

"Figure it out," Taylor said. "Review it with Chris."

~

The Council room had a high ceiling and walls paneled in rough planking. It had an additional use as the court of justice. Weak winter sun came through tall windows on the south side. Spectators, muffled in heavy winter clothing, glanced at one another. Many people came to court, especially in the winter, for it provided much to gossip about.

"No, no, please, anything but that. I'm sorry, really sorry." Zack Steigerwald fell to his knees. He had been caught stealing drugs from Dr. Encirlik's office. "Don't exile me."

"Dr. Encirlik," Taylor said. "What drugs were taken?"

"Steigerwald took the last of my morphine."

"Are there any substitutes available?"

"No, not at the moment. I'm going to raise poppies this coming season to make opium. I'll need help for that."

After Taylor scribbled into a journal, he leaned back and his chair creaked. *I want to send a message*, he thought, *a strong message that we don't want anyone messing with our doctor*.

"Steigerwald, in lieu of three years exile, do you voluntarily accept three years servitude and a record of the crime tattooed on your back?"

"Yes, sir. I do." Steigerwald lowered his head and squeezed his eyes shut. Tears ran down his face. "Thank you."

"You'll work for Dr. Encirlik. If you fail to serve to her satisfaction during servitude, you'll be exiled. Is that clear?"

"Yes sir. I understand."

"Next," Taylor said. "We've got three refugees who want to join the Clan. They've got no valuables or needed skills. Are there sponsors for these people?"

"Yes." John Phelps looked at the papers in front of him. "Stolz will pay for Darryl Schwede in exchange for twelve months service as a laborer. Charlie DeGrandis will pay for Sara Schwede in exchange for twelve months as a house-servant."

"I see." Taylor nodded. "Go on."

"Yes. Max Artun will sponsor Kimberly Delzani in exchange for eighteen months as a house servant."

Taylor looked up. "Eighteen months? Isn't twelve months standard?" He frowned at Phelps. "What gives?"

"I'm not sure." Phelps shuffled his papers. "I think this woman had difficulty in finding someone to sponsor her."

"Why?" Taylor leaned forward.

"Er, I heard that she's not very appealing."

"Appealing? What d'you mean by that?"

"Well, she's not young or pretty." Phelps looked away.

"What's happening to the voluntary servitude concept?" Taylor asked. "Is this how the Clan builds unity?"

"Well." Phelps hesitated. "I've heard some of the indentured aren't treated well. Some owners abuse them, even force some of the indentured women to have sex with them. You see, there aren't any rules on how they're to be treated." He looked as though he'd sucked on something sour.

"That's slavery. We'll have to get a set of rules for you to review by next week." Taylor tightened his lips.

Some people, he thought, *will exploit anyone. Pricks*. "I'd like to believe future members of our Clan feel as though they're joining a community of equals, rather than being screwed to join."

Weitzman raised his hand. "Taylor, that's an excellent idea. If you need any help writing the rules, let me know."

"Thanks, Shel," Taylor nodded, "I could use your help. The next item. Jerry Solnik accosted and robbed Susan Hathaway. A witness saw him knock her to the ground and rob her."

"What did he take?" Phelps asked.

"A bag of potatoes," Chris Kucinski said.

"That doesn't sound too serious," Phelps said.

"It wouldn't be if food were plentiful," Chris said.

"Well, he sounds like a bully," Fred said. "He oughta be flogged and made to replace the stolen food."

"Any objections to Fred's suggestion?" Taylor saw the Council nod agreement. "Chris, you heard the verdict, do it."

"I'll see it gets done."

"Last on the agenda is a capital case. Since a verdict has been reached, we must act on a recommendation for capital punishment." Taylor looked around the Council room.

"Pamela Johnson stabbed her husband, Gary, when she caught him in bed with Ingrid Gee. Mr. Johnson died three days later. It was a painful death, since there are no painkillers left."

"What did Ms. Johnson say in her own defense?" Fred asked.

"She claimed that her husband abused her, beat her, and taunted her about his other women. Their neighbors confirmed they argued a lot, mostly about Gary seeing Ingrid. However, no one came forward to say that they saw Gary beat Pamela. Dr. Encirlik examined Ms. Johnson immediately after the assault. There were no bruises or other signs of a recent beating."

Taylor looked up from his notes. "Does anyone want to question Ms. Johnson and the witnesses?"

"Who conducted the investigation?" Fred asked.

"Dr. Encirlik and Chris." Taylor passed several papers to Fred. "These are their notes with the final report."

"I see." Fred shuffled the papers. "So, what do we do?"

"We don't have much choice," said Taylor. "This was an assault that resulted in a death; that's murder. While the victim did give provocation, his wife can't prove the allegation he beat her."

Council members avoided each other's eyes. The fading sun barely lit the room through its grimy windows. Silence settled on the room. The sound of the wood burning in the stove, popping and crackling, now seemed loud. The faint smell of wood smoke, wet wool, and unwashed bodies filled the air.

Taylor looked up. The faces around him, thin, gaunt, and gray, stared at him like birds of prey.

Pat Rice cleared his throat. "So, what're you going to do?"

"What am I going to do?" Taylor looked at each member of the Council. "I'm putting this to a vote. Do we accept the recommendations of the investigators? Those in favor, say aye."

"Aye, aye, aye."

Shel Weitzman abstained.

"Please ask Father Scaravelli to pray with Pamela Johnson tonight. Tomorrow, at dawn, she will hang."

"Taylor, we've got to set up a monetary system," Franny said as she passed a plate of food to him across the table. "There's no way that I can allocate supplies equitably anymore. The Clan is so large I can't keep track of who's working and who's not."

"What d'you think we should use for money?"

"Oh, there's lots of ideas," she said. "Those who have wads of paper money are screaming for a system that uses the existing currency. If we did that, we'd have a revolution on our hands. We need a system that ties into the value of labor. Like you said, it's the only way to keep people working hard. We need something now."

"What about using previously issued coins for money?"

"Only if it were coins the Clan issued," Franny said. "You know, money issued by the Clan treasury."

"Make our own coins?" Taylor frowned. "That's not easy."

"Well, no. Use existing coinage."

"How?" Taylor crossed his arms and cocked his head.

"What about gold, silver, copper, and composite coins, you know, copper-nickel laminates, only with a special Clan mark?"

"Sounds like you've got this already figured out."

"I've got some ideas." Franny pursed her lips.

"Okay, do you want to make a presentation to the Council when it meets next?" Taylor watched her from the corner of his eye.

"Me?" She slowly chewed a morsel of meat. "Won't people think you're showing favoritism if I do this?"

"Franny, who did this work? Who can explain it better?" He waved a fork. "No matter who presents it, there's bound to be opposition. If not from the paper money crowd, then it will come from the lawyers. Maybe someone else will try to figure out an angle so they can come out ahead. So, put on a thick skin and just do it." He got up and went behind her, putting his arms around her. "Smart and sexy, what a great combination. I'm glad I found you."

~

"One hundred dollars in US silver coins will exchange for any one ounce gold or platinum coin. This will be the basis for all currency used in the Clan." Franny looked over the long table around which the Elders sat. She paused to take a breath.

"For day-to-day transactions, copper pennies will exchange at a rate of one thousand for each silver dollar. One hundred pennies equals one composite dollar and ten dollars in composite coinage for one silver dollar is a fair rate."

"What about paper money?" Pat Rice asked, elbows on the table and head propped in his hands.

"No. There's too much out there." Franny shook her head. "Just think of the impact on those who've got none."

"Um, yes, I see what you mean." Pat Rice nodded.

"How does this tie into the value of labor?" Taylor asked.

"We set the base wage at one silver dollar per week for a laborer. That means two composite dollars pays for one day's labor, or twenty-five copper cents per hour." Franny glanced up.

"What about discoveries of coin hoards?" Weitzman asked, hands waving. "Won't that cause inflation?"

"An excellent question. The Wylies will put marks on the coins issued by the Clan." She pointed to John Wylie. "They've got some unique metal punches, which they think will make a permanent mark on coins issued by the Clan. Right, John?"

"Yes." John Wylie scratched his bearded chin. "I've got a punch set that produces textured letters. Apparently, it was made for a government contract. I've never seen another like it anywhere. To make a punch like it, well, it'd take some pretty sophisticated machining. As long as the punch bites deep into the metal, it will be very difficult for someone to reproduce the mark by hand work."

"Where do we get the coins?" Carver Washington asked.

"I gave my coin collection to the Clan, no strings attached," Taylor said. "I bought gold and silver bullion coins before the Collapse as an inflation hedge. I've got no use for them now."

"How many coins?" asked Phelps.

"Fifty one-ounce gold coins and two thousand dollars face amount in silver coins, mainly quarters and dimes. That should be enough to get started, anyway."

"Do we accept these coins?" Fred asked, looking at the Council. "All in favor, say aye."

Taylor abstained from the vote.

The Council agreed with a roll of ayes.

"John, when can you start marking the coins?" Taylor said.

"Well, Sam and I talked about it. We figure it'll take about three or four days to get ready, but I'm not sure how long it will take to actually mark up the coins."

"Does this involve building a machine?" Taylor asked.

"Yes, it'll be a simple punch press, hand operated."

"Better find a safe place to keep it, because it's going to be a real money-maker." Taylor smiled before a frown creased his face. "We're going to need a safe place to keep the Clan treasury, too."

"Get Stolz involved," said Phelps. "He knows the details of every building on the hill, especially those underground."

"I'll talk to him," Fred said.

~

"Taylor, the Council has awarded you three one-tenth acre tracts of land within the boundary of the old river bed," said Fred. "It's in recognition of your efforts on behalf of the Clan. One is on the Hill and the rest are in the Lower Hill."

"I don't need it—" Taylor began to say.

"Yeah," Fred said. "We discussed it before we voted. The land's yours. Don't look a gift horse in the teeth."

~

The news the Council had given Taylor land within the boundaries of the Hill caused complaints. Opposition coalesced around Pepperdine, a former lawyer, who demanded time in front of the Council.

"The Clan does not have title to any of these lands, and as such, you have no legal right to give it away."

"You may be right, Mr. Pepperdine," said Fred. "Perhaps you should file a suit in the court of Common Pleas in Cleveland."

"Well, since that court isn't functioning at the moment, I believe all legal transfers should be held in abeyance until a court of proper jurisdiction is established." Pepperdine smiled. "In lieu of that, I propose a pro-tempore system to maintain quasi-legal records and descriptions of all property transfers, notarized by an officer of the court until legal authority is duly organized. I'm happy to offer my services as an officer of the court so you avoid legal pitfalls."

"Remember, the alternatives to Clan law are found elsewhere," Phelps said. "If you don't like our decisions, you're free to leave."

"What you're doing is not legal—"

"We'll even give you a ride into Cleveland if you want. You could take up residence there." Phelps smiled. "The choice is yours, accept our law or leave."

"This is highly irregular, you have no legal basis—"

"Mr. Pepperdine, do you want to live within the Clan?"

"Well, yes, but—" Pepperdine's face grew red.

"Accept our law, or leave," Fred said loudly. "Next."

Franny solved the problem of getting money into circulation by having the Clan pay the militia when on duty and hiring construction workers to build the common facilities. At her recommendation, the Council instituted a tax system whereby all adults paid the Clan one day's labor per week, either in kind or at the going rate for labor. Franny monitored the receipts and expenditures. She recommended changes to bring spending into balance with the tax receipts.

The ease of administering the tax system earned its grudging acceptance. The budgeting process evolved into a pie-slicing exercise, because either resources were available for what was needed, or it did not get done.

Agriculture became an individual effort controlled by supply and demand. Still, the Clan bought a large part of the harvest, which maintained price stability. The standard workweek became four days, with the fifth day used to pay the Clan tax.

As Franny lay next to Taylor, she traced a pattern with her finger on his chest, "Taylor, do you love me?" She worried about their relationship because it had no formal basis. She loved him deeply and enjoyed the recognition of being the companion of the Clan's leader. She was aware there were more women than men, many younger than her. She worried about the attention shown him by attractive, unattached, and nubile women.

Taylor had started to doze. As his eyes opened, they slowly focused on her. "No, I lust for you." He reached for her.

She pushed him away with a trace of a frown. "I'm being serious." His answer had put her off.

The smile faded from Taylor's face. "Franny, you're the medicine that cured my broken heart. Of course I love you. You brought me back to life. I haven't felt this alive since I was with Vivian. In my heart I still love Vivian; I guess I always will. Now you're my love."

"Really?" Her spirits rose. She wanted to ask him why he had not formalized their relationship, but realized it might be confrontational. She snuggled close to him. "Tell me more." She reached for his hand, separating his fingers with hers.

"It's strange how we came together. You helped me come to grips with my sorrow. You make me see things to which I'm blind. You know, the social and political issues of the Clan. We complement each other. You're an effective foil for my ideas. You're not afraid to tell me when you think I'm screwing up. You're many people: My lover—ah yes, no doubt about that—a friend, an intellectual peer."

"Yes?" Franny waited for him to continue, enjoying a warm, happy glow.

His eyes took on a far-away look. "And," Taylor frowned slightly. "Almost like my mother."

Franny sat up. "What? Your mother?"

"Let me explain," Taylor said. "You treat me the same way my mother did. She guided me and forced me to defend my ideas. She was always there when I needed support. In many ways, she was my companion. You see, I had no brothers or sisters. In some ways, I missed a lot of the things normal children experience as the result of sibling rivalry. My childhood frame of reference was, in many ways, quite adult." He looked up and smiled. "You fill a big need in my life. You brought me back to life emotionally. Don't you see?" he held out his arms. He beckoned with his fingertips for her to come to him. "Of course I love you. Do you love me?"

Franny folded into his arms. "I love you more than you'll ever know." She held him tightly to hide the tears that crept into her eyes.

As the days grew longer and the maple sap began to flow, Phelps pressed tanks and tubs into service as evaporators over hot fires. The sugar shack soon became the most active building in the Lower Hill. The workers sealed the excess syrup in sterilized jars and stored it in the underground food warehouses.

The river rose several times during late-winter thaws, topping the dams. The first time, tree trunks and branches clogged the old river course and caused flooding in the low-lying areas. When the river rose in flood the second time, it vomited out the debris and flushed the old river course clean.

The river rose for a third time after a late-winter downpour. It became a turbulent, scouring current, which devoured the embankment of the old river course near the main entrance and washed away a section of the palisade. When the water subsided, Higgins made stopgap repairs with large stones to restore a continuous wall on the riverbank around the Hill. However, he could not replace the dirt embankment near the main entrance because the ground was too wet to work.

As the winter faded, Phelps prepared forty acres of land for a vegetable garden as well as another eighty acres for grain. He'd saved seed for the spring planting, but there was not enough for the expanded farm area.

He sent scouts out to farm areas to trade gasoline and maple syrup for seed. The scouts started a communications network in the rural areas, which brought news and manufactured supplies to wary farmers.

THE OFFICE OF MAYOR

"Pretty nice digs, eh, Knuckles?" Skid put his feet, clad in engineer boots, on the mahogany desk and puffed on a cigar.

Once the office of the Mayor, the wood paneled room in Cleveland City Hall had survived the Collapse virtually unscathed.

"Uh, sure, Skid, it suits you," Knuckles said.

"I kinda like this set-up. In fact, I should be Mayor. No one else keeps order around here 'cept us, right?"

"That's fer sure." Knuckles went on automatic agreement when Skid started on a rave. "Everyone's doin' what we say."

"You know, this is a chance to take care of business, legit-like. I'm the Mayor and the boys are my administration. Get it, Knuckles? You can't fight City Hall. Heh-heh."

"Uh, do we hafta clean the streets, pick up the garbage an' the rest of that shit?" Knuckles' eyebrows knitted together.

Skid paused. "Hell, no. The citizens gotta keep their own neighborhood clean and tidy. No welfare for the chumps. It's against my political philosophy, heh-heh."

"Uh." Knuckles nodded. "Yeah."

"The more I think about the idea of me being Mayor, the

more I like it. I deputize the boys as cops and we collect taxes. That's a good one, the citizens paying me taxes."

"Uh, why's that Skid?"

"There's only two things that go down for sure—death and taxes. An' in my administration, if the citizens don't pay their taxes, they're dead."

Skid was on a roll. "Knuckles. This's for real, I gotta do it. Come on, man, look for the, y'know, the thing that makes it legit. Aw, what's it called? The Mayor's official seal. Understand?"

"Uh, oh, er, sure." Knuckles chewed on his fingernail as he wandered into the anteroom next to the mayor's office, with a large mahogany conference table and credenza. A stack of papers caught his attention.

"Yo, Skid, I got it. I got paper, an' all kinds of stuff with the Mayor dude's name. In color, too." He held up a sheaf of paper.

Skid grabbed the stationery, took one glance, and threw it into the air. "Man, is my name Alijah Moohamed Brown?" He rolled his eyes heavenward. "Is that my name?"

"Uh, no, er, yer name's Skid."

"Do I look like a fuckin' melon? You see me tellin' the boys my name is now Alijah fuckin' Moohamed Brown so I can be Mayor?" Skid said. "No fuckin' way. I ain't gonna change my name into a fuckin' watermelon name like that." Flecks of spittle flew in all directions. "Understand?"

"Uh, I'm sorry." Knuckles backed away. "I thought that was what you was lookin' fer." His lower lip quivered.

"Man, this shit's no good, I want something to make me Mayor. I'm not gonna pretend to be someone else, especially a fuckin' watermelon. It's gotta be a seal I can put on a piece of paper after I've signed my name." He glared at Knuckles.

"Uh, I see." Knuckles lowered his eyes. "I'm sorry, I din't know that's what you wanted." As he turned away, he put his hand to his mouth and started to suck his thumb.

"Aw, cut that out," Skid said. "It isn't the end of the world."

In the storage room off the anteroom, he emptied a filing

cabinet. “Knuckles, lookit! Shit, I’ve got it.” Skid waved an embossing tool over his head. “I’m gonna be Mayor.”

“Uh, right on, Skid.” Knuckles slapped his hand and finished with a high-five handshake.

“I’m gonna run this city for real. My orders are gonna be signed and sealed with the authority of the Mayor of Cleveland.”

“What kinda orders?”

“I’m gonna make laws so I can tax the chumps, er, the citizens, deputize the boys and take anything I want, all legit-like. There’s nothing I can’t do, ’cause I’m now the law in Cleveland, the law.” Skid’s voice rose an octave. His eyes took on a bright gleam.

Skid recalled how the winter in Berea had started off okay until those Park assholes fucked with him. They’d pay for that, he vowed. In a way, the move had worked out, for after he’d incorporated the Diablos into the Deacons, they were still below their earlier strength. They’d taken over the Rodina Gang, those crazy Russians. The way the Rods’ leaders had trusted him and had come unarmed to a “Summit” meeting made him laugh.

It had been so easy to ambush and waste them. The rest of the Rods joined up with the Deacons soon enough. Still, for a while things had been tough. Good thing that “Fast Eddy” MacArthur and his Rubber City Road Warriors joined up and increased his gang to more than two hundred men.

It was also a lucky thing Stubby Knox had been a laborer on the construction of a false wall in the basement of the gun store. He didn’t believe Stubby at first when he swore the basement had another room. When they broke in, the owner had tried to shoot it out with them.

He chuckled. He was just like a cornered rat, ’cept more fun. He didn’t last any longer than a rat, either.

There were a hundred SKS semi-auto rifles, which proved to

be a useful addition. But the ammo—twelve full cases—twelve thousand rounds, that was the ace of spades. There'd been other guns too, UZIs, MAC-10s, some nine-millimeter stuff.

Skid preferred the high-velocity assault rifles. In a rumble, he liked to back off out of a nine-millimeter's effective range and pick 'em off. He fingered the bulletproof jacket that was his personal memento from the gun store. He wore it all the time—just another edge.

He'd used the nine-millimeter guns to make deals with the black gangs, but kept them short on ammo to ensure their cooperation. It wasn't a real solid alliance, but the ammo helped. He wasn't gonna tell the melons how to run their turf. When he needed them, they'd better pony up. Besides, downtown and the West Side were more comfortable. His kind of ethnics.

I've gotta move the Deacons into City Hall right away. We've lived in that hotel all winter and it's gotten to be a real mess. My ol' lady keeps complaining about the smell. Skid vowed he'd keep City Hall clean and use it solely as his headquarters. "Heh-heh, this is way cool." He laughed out loud.

~

George C. "Skid" Vukovitch, leader of the Cleveland chapter of the Devil's Deacons, held his inauguration as Mayor of Cleveland by rounding up a group of citizens, who, confronted with the choice of electing him or dying, elected him by acclamation.

"Hey, Skid," Fast Eddy MacArthur said. "You gonna lighten up a little, now you're Mayor?"

"What d'you mean?" Skid narrowed his eyes. He wondered what had come over his ally. "Lighten up a little?"

"Aw, man, you've been riding our asses all winter."

"Oh yeah? Well, winter's been one long pain in the ass. What with the Rods, the Venoms, and those other melons, the Tombs, trying to push me around, an' having to fight back, understand?" He took a deep breath. "Now I'm Mayor, I'm gonna get some real respect. Anyone who gets outa line is gonna go down, but good."

"Easy, man," Fast Eddy said. "We're blood brothers, remember? There ain't no need to go all crazy on us."

"When I take care of business, I don't let anythin' get in my way." Skid whistled the refrain from "Pachebel's Canon."

"Cool," Fast Eddy said. "Me an' the boys are on your side."

"This is what we're gonna do...." Skid waved his hand over the heads of the assembled gang and explained how they would collect taxes. "If you don't do good as tax collectors, me and Knuckles will give you a job-performance review, understand?"

"What's our turf?" Fast Eddy spat on the ground.

"Lemme see." Skid frowned. "Well, out to the 'burbs, but there isn't any law out there, is there?"

"Naw. So, that's our turf?"

"No, not really. You see, it isn't legit to collect taxes from an area where we don't have jurisdiction." Skid paused and scratched his head. "Hey, hey, wait, that gives me an idea. Call the council into session."

"What d'you mean?" Fast Eddy's eyes widened.

"Listen. I'm gonna incorporate all of Cuyahoga County into the City of Cleveland, 'cause it doesn't have any government. Since we're the only surviving government, we're it. Understand?"

"Sure, Skid." Knuckles' words filled the silence. "Er, why do we wanna do that?"

"We have the whole county as our turf so we got more citizens to pay taxes. If they don't do as we say, then they're the ones breaking the law." Skid clapped his hands. "Got it?"

"Sure, man." Fast Eddy rolled his eyes.

~

John Phelps went straight from church to his fields. Overnight, spring's gray, cold, and wet days had changed to warm, windy weather, drying the fields quickly. Green stems waved in the breeze.

"Taylor, what're you doing here?" Phelps asked.

"Hi, John. I'm enjoying the day. It's a beauty, isn't it?"

"See how the winter wheat is coming along? It'll be ready for harvest in no time."

"It looks fine, you've done well." Taylor looked at the field. "When did you plant this?"

"We sowed eighty acres last fall." Phelps paused. "I'm amazed at how self-sufficient we've become." His face grew serious. "The only thing that scares me, is getting injured or sick. Sure, Encirlik and Weitzman work miracles with what little they have, but if someone is really sick, it's curtains. The thought of another battle scares the daylights out of me."

Taylor's gut knotted at the memory of the rows of bodies: both close friends and anonymous faces.

Oh, God, he thought, *please, not again*.

~

Taylor took a sip of water. The Council room was warm, even with its tall windows open. The public section was filled, the rustle of clothing and shuffle of feet forcing him to raise his voice.

"Next item. We got a letter from the Cleveland Mayor's office." He held up a sheet of paper with an ornate seal on top. "It states that Cleveland has annexed all the communities in Cuyahoga County, pursuant to ordinance so and so."

"And?" A frown crossed Fred's face.

"The letter goes on to say we must pay taxes to Cleveland based upon food inventories and agricultural output. Included is a survey form for us to list what we have." Taylor passed the letter to the Elders sitting at the long table.

"Who delivered this letter?" Weitzman asked.

"It was a person dressed like a cop." Chris paused. "The

guards escorted him in from the perimeter. When I got a good look at him, the tattoos on the back of his hands and the fact his uniform didn't fit, well, his claim to be from the Cleveland Tax Collectors Office just didn't ring true."

"The present Mayor of Cleveland," Ted Colagrossi called out in a loud voice. "Is that scumbag Vukovitch. He's the leader of the Devil's Deacons gang in Berea we thrashed last year. Either he's crazy, smoking too much dope, or both. Even his own guys—the scouts overheard them talking—they wonder which planet Vukovitch is on."

"So, what d'we do about this? Ignore it?" Taylor asked. "Send back a funny reply?" He tried to gauge the Council's mood.

"Maybe we should ask them for a copy of their ordinance," Weitzman twisted his hands. "Then we could send them a copy of our own incorporation or some other fantasy document that shows we're not subject to their rule."

"Rule? That scumbag rules us?" Fred's voice cut through the rising tide of voices. "No fricking way."

"Those, those bastards." Shirley O'Connor's brassy voice rang out. "You're not serious, are you?"

"Tell 'em to pound salt." a voice called from the audience.

Taylor rapped the gavel on the table for quiet. "Okay, okay, I hear you. That's enough. If what Ted tells us is correct—and I've got no reason to doubt his word—this is the same group who gave us trouble last summer."

"So, what d'you intend to do about it, Mr. MacPherson?" Pat Rice asked in an icy tone.

"I have to assume these demands will lead to a fight."

"I hope you're wrong," Weitzman said. "We lost many fine young people last time. I don't want to see that happen again."

"Being prepared for a fight doesn't mean we'll have one. However, if we're not ready—"

"Won't our preparations send the wrong message?"

"Well, Shel," Taylor said. "Why don't you draft the letter you mentioned, the one with the phony ordinance?"

"I'll do it." Weitzman picked up the letter and studied it.

"Good. Best case they leave us alone for a while. All it will cost is some paper." Taylor slapped Shel on his shoulder. "We need time to get our defenses ready. Sam Wylie, how's our bow production coming along?"

"Well." Sam cleared his throat. "I've got a problem. There just isn't enough seasoned Osage Orange available."

"Aren't there other woods that will produce the same result?"

"Good, yes, but not the best. That Callioux hasn't brought me the Dacron twine I've been asking for. What's he doing on those jaunts?" Sam's voice quavered. "Sight-seeing?"

"Sam." Taylor lowered his voice. "You've done a super job under difficult circumstances. I really wish we could get everything you need, but under the current conditions, we're grateful for anything we can get."

"Well, if those scouts would just look a little harder."

"Sam, how many bows do you make in a week? Not counting those made for children?" Taylor realized that Sam had aged significantly over the winter. He looked frail.

"Well, last week," Sam said. "I finished twenty-four bows. They're the standard sixty-five pound draw weight recurve bows, which take a standard thirty-two-inch arrow."

"Is that your normal production?" Taylor narrowed his eyes.

"Are you asking me if I'm working as hard as I can?"

Taylor flinched. "I want to know how many bows we have."

"Well, let me see now." Sam stared into the distance. "In the past twenty weeks, give or take a day or two, I've made three-hundred and thirty-eight bows, more or less. All have my lifetime unconditional warranty." He smiled without warmth. "If you're gonna break them, you'd better do it soon."

"We really appreciate your efforts," Taylor said. "With the threat of attack, we need more bows."

"Well, I'm working as hard as I can, so you're out of luck."

"We need another one hundred bows." Taylor forced a smile

onto his face. "Let's talk after the meeting, I'm sure that we'll find a way. Next item."

~

"Taylor." Ted Colagrossi ran into Taylor's cluttered office, out of breath. "There was a raid on the Oxbow."

"What happened? Was anyone injured?" Taylor clenched his teeth in anticipation of bad news.

"There's four people hurt, none of them seriously. It looked like a mob, a band of refugees backed up by a few gang members."

"How many?" Taylor asked, scribbling notes.

"We're not sure. The ones wearing colors held back and were hard to see in the woods. I'd guess that there were about sixty. The militia held them off at the entrance."

"Something feels wrong about this." Taylor looked up as Chris came in the door. "What d'you think it was?"

"It was a probe of our defenses. The City gang has got a lot of guns. I've seen them. Most of those guys in the attack just threw rocks."

"If that's the case, then we'd better assume an attack is imminent. Every night, everyone inside the walls."

"The wheat harvest will be ready soon." Phelps had silently joined the group. "We'll have to harvest it by hand."

"We'll just have to take our chances on the grain harvest when it's time." Taylor made a wry face. "I hope the gangs don't know anything about farming."

~

Skid stared at seven leather-clad men standing in front of his desk in the former mayor's office. They were his gang lieutenants, whom he'd appointed to his City Council. "Those assholes in the Park won't take any more refugees. We can't get our people inside," he said.

His men listened silently.

"They refused to let us inspect their food supplies. They won't pay their taxes. They're defying the law. We've got to do something about that. Understand?"

"Sure. Like what?" Knuckles asked.

"They wanna play hardball with me, fine. I've got the law on my side." Skid stared into the distance for a few moments. He jumped up. "I'm gonna raise a citizens' army and restore order."

"Now just a minute, Skid," Fast Eddy MacArthur said. "What's this shit about a citizens' army? You gonna open recruiting offices or something like that?"

"You think I'm a dumb-fuck?" Skid's face began to twitch.

"No, I didn't mean it that way." Fast Eddy held up his hand. "You ain't gonna give the citizens guns, are you?"

"I'm gonna raise an army. You know, round up citizens and tell 'em they're in the City's army. Understand?"

Fast Eddy's face remained blank.

"I'm gonna use them as our front-line troops. You know, give them clubs, whatever. They're gonna be the ones who'll march in front and use up those Park assholes' ammo." Skid waved his hands. "A human tide, to wash away their defenses in a sea of blood. It's gonna be beautiful."

"We don't do no fighting?" Fast Eddy's face brightened. "We don't hafta bust our asses enforcing the law?"

"You'll have to fight. Most of all, I want you to keep the citizens in line. Make sure they do what I want."

"Uh, Skid," Knuckles asked. "Do I get to kill anyone?"

"As many of those assholes in the park as you can."

DAY ONE

"What a beautiful day." Franny linked her arm through Taylor's and smiled up at him, eyes bright in the afternoon sun.

The sky was intensely blue and the new leaves—lush and vividly green—fluttered in the breeze. The road down the Hill to the main entrance was now wide and smooth, made from compacted stone. It was time for their afternoon walk.

Taylor smiled. "You make it even more beautiful."

"Oh, Taylor." Franny said.

She stopped and pointed over the wall. Three horses had come into view. Two of the horses cantered awkwardly—they had bloodstained bodies draped over them. "Look."

"It's Colagrossi. Someone's hurt. Get Encirlik and Weitzman." Taylor ran toward the bridge crossing the river, which functioned as a moat for the Hill. Franny headed back up to the Hill. He reached it as the horsemen clattered across.

"The gang's on the move," Colagrossi yelled. "They're coming. There are thousands of them."

"How far away are they?" As Taylor spoke, Weitzman arrived on the run, puffing and panting.

"Three, maybe four miles," Colagrossi said.

"Taylor," Weitzman called. "Give me a hand with these men." He began cutting the straps that held the men on the horses.

"Shel, I've got to mobilize our defenses. Get someone else." Taylor ran for the guardhouse. "You, with the hat," Taylor called to a guard. "Ring the alarm. Move it."

"Yes, sir."

"You." Taylor pointed to a young Clan soldier. "Tell Kucinski, Phelps, Del Corso, and O'Connor to meet me at Lookout Point. You." He beckoned to a short, stocky blond man. "Send runners to the gates and tell them to keep them open for our people only until the gang's army arrives."

"Yes, sir." The young blond-haired guard ran.

A bell boomed across the valley. Its sonorous voice—the tocsin of war—imposed a moment of silence. Soon, hundreds of shouting people, prodding livestock, streamed across the bridge and through the gates.

Within an hour, only solitary stragglers remained outside the walls, dragging crying children and driving bawling cattle toward the gates.

From the lookout point on the Hill, Taylor saw the leading edge of the on-coming army.

Thousands of ragged men, many wearing bandannas pirate-style, flowed like an angry river in flood stage down Cedar Point Road into the valley. As they closed, they made a savage roar like that of an angry animal, deep and primal.

"Damn," Taylor muttered. "They're here." He shifted his binoculars to the main gates. In the periphery of his vision, he saw a family running for the gate. "It's too late, run away," he urged. It was impossible for them to hear him.

The family continued to run toward the main entrance more than two hundred yards away, dragging children by the hand. A brief crackle of gunfire sounded. The man and woman staggered and fell. The couple was still moving when a wave of ragged men overran them. Clubs rose and fell in a bloody rhythm.

"Sweet Jesus." Taylor took a deep breath. "That was awful."

He glanced toward the main entrance where the gates remained motionless, open. "What? Get those gates closed, now."

After what seemed an eternity, they began to move but the mob flowed ever closer.

"Get a squad to the main entrance," Taylor said to Chris. "Right away." He watched the mob approach the gate and held his breath. *It'll be close. God help us if they get in.*

The bridge was still down and there was no time to raise it. The river, deepened over winter, was deep and flowed slowly under the bridge to the main entrance. The mob formed into untidy ranks to march across the bridge. As they started across the bridge to the entrance, the gates clanged shut.

~

"I almost got them. If you'd nailed those pricks on the horses who'd been shadowing us, I'd have had the drop on them," Skid's voice held an accusatory tone.

"Aw, man," Fast Eddy MacArthur said. "We killed three of 'em. I'm sure we winged at least a couple more." He spat on the ground. "I figure my boys did some pretty good shooting."

Skid took a deep breath. *Fast Eddy sure fucked-up security on this job*, he thought. *An' the loud mouth son-of-a-bitch pisses me off all the time. But he's Deacon through and through, and that means I gotta trust him.*

"Eddy, if your boys had picked off those Park assholes like I told ya, we could've walked right in. Understand?"

"Yeah, well, mebbe." Fast Eddy spat on the ground.

Skid glowered at Fast Eddy. "Okay, now I've got to figure out how to get past the gate and over the wall. First, I'm gonna give them a chance to submit to the law of the land." Skid stared into the distance. "You're gonna be the official messenger from my office, the Mayor's office, and tell 'em to comply with the law. Understand?"

"Er, you'd better run that by me again," Fast Eddy said.

"If they don't obey the law, I can seize their property."

"Sure, anything you say, Skid," Fast Eddy said. He looked at one of his lieutenants and rolled his eyes.

"Look," Skid said. "We're gonna do this legit-like, so those citizens, the draftees, can't object when called to do their duty. Understand?"

"Legit-like." Fast Eddy stared at Skid and a smile slowly grew on his face. "Yeah, cool."

~

Three men in black leather clothing, emblazoned with the red and yellow death's head emblem of the Diablos, advanced with a white flag. Twenty-five yards from the moat, they stopped and huddled to confer. A large muscular man with a beer-belly emerged and came forward alone as the others retreated.

"The Honorable Mr. George C. Vukovitch, Mayor of the City of Cleveland, advises you the City of Cleveland has legally incorporated the entire Cuyahoga County into one corporate entity, namely the reorganized City of Cleveland, pursuant to Ordinance 2035.507b, duly enacted by the City Council and signed into law," Fast Eddy bellowed.

"We demand you open the gates and submit to our tax inspection as required by the above referenced incorporation ordinance. You've been notified. This is your last warning." He looked up from the sheet of paper. "You gonna obey the law?"

From top of the wall, Taylor stepped to the edge of the palisade. He cupped his hands to his mouth. "For your information, the Clan of Rocky River incorporated itself and this territory last November," he yelled. "Sorry, but you're just a little too late." He held back a smile.

"Our incorporation of Cuyahoga County into Cleveland counts more than yours. You're in our area now. Under our law." Fast Eddy stumbled over his words. "Get it?"

"Can't be," Taylor called. "It hasn't been put to a vote."

"Look," Fast Eddy yelled. "Our ordinance is superior to yours, 'cause we're bigger than you, an' you know it. If you accept our conditions, no one's gonna get hurt."

"Oh, and just what are your conditions?"

"We're the law in Cuyahoga County." Fast Eddy's words sounded rehearsed. "Our jurisdiction. Because you refused our authority, judgment has been passed, and you forfeited the right to own property in Cuyahoga County. You must vacate this property immediately. If you comply, you can leave without penalty."

"Taylor," Franny whispered in Taylor's ear. "That's them."

"Who?"

"The men who killed Stosh."

"Where?"

"The two men standing behind the speaker; they're the bastards who raped Cathy and me." Her face was pale. She gripped Taylor's arm tightly. "Don't trust them."

Taylor raised his voice. "Let me get this straight. You want us to give up our homes and walk away from everything we own, just because you want to claim the whole county. Is that right?"

"If you'd complied with the law an' submitted to a tax audit, you wouldn't have made this problem for yourselves. We're only enforcing the duly enacted ordinances of the City of Cleveland—"

"We don't accept your authority," Taylor yelled. "We don't want representation on your City Council. Remember, one of the founding principles of this country is: No taxation without representation."

"If you don't comply with the law, you'll be the one responsible for the consequences," Fast Eddy yelled. His face had become red. "You'll make us use force."

"Force? You're threatening us with force?" Taylor called. "Let me make you an offer. If you don't leave us alone, we'll hunt you down and kill you, all of you. That's a promise." His voice rang across the now-silent valley.

Fast Eddy threw his hands up and walked back to the other

men. Five minutes later, he returned to the edge of the moat.

"Hey, asshole," Fast Eddy yelled. "The City's got an army. We're the law around here. If you force us to use it, you're gonna get wasted. Understand?" Fast Eddy clenched his fists, arms stiff. A deep flush suffused his face.

"I hear you," Taylor yelled. "We have no intention of complying with your law. This is our valley and we'll defend it. We're free people and we intend to remain free. Until something better comes along, we'll stay with what we've got."

Cheers broke out along the wall.

Fast Eddy held up an index finger and waited. Slowly, silence descended. "Look, shithead," his voice cracked with anger as it boomed over the valley. "If you don't surrender, I'm personally gonna tear you a new asshole after I stomp you into the ground. Got it? You've had your warning." He spat, turned on his heel, and rejoined the army with the other leather-clad men.

Without warning, the leading edge of the army surged forward to cross the wooden bridge and mass before the gate. The rear ranks continued to press forward and spread along the banks of the river.

The men on the bridge fired at the Clan defenders on the towers above the gateway. A phalanx of men in gang colors pushed forward toward the gate. Gunfire from the army was continuous.

"Get a battering ram. Break the fuckin' gate down," yelled the scar-faced man pointing with his gun. "Get something to knock this stupid gate down."

"Uh, yeah, get a log," called the big man at the side of scar-faced man. "Quit using yer hands, they ain't gonna do no good."

"Boys, shoot 'em if they stick their heads up." The scar-faced man pointed toward the Hill.

"Hey, hey, make way." A dozen men staggered across the bridge toward the gate with a long, mud-stained log. The scar-faced man pointed to the men carrying the log. "Break that gate down." His voice rose to a scream. "Now."

The battering ram's blow made the entire entrance structure vibrate. "Harder, hit it harder." The scar-faced man yelled. He paused and stared at the walls above on each side of the entrance.

He backed up. "Hey, Zits," he called. "Take over. I want that gate down. Understand?"

"Ooh, sure." Zits was a pock-faced man with a strong Russian accent. "Okay, you fookers, bash that fooking gate down." He kicked a man on the battering ram. "Harder, fook-head."

"Me and my administration gotta plan strategy," the scar-faced man said. "Let's go." He retreated from the bridge.

~

"Chris, move those people onto the Hill." Taylor pointed to the new arrivals milling behind the main entrance. "Then put a squad at the gate. Use those carts to barricade the gate."

"Ammo?"

"Distribute thirty rounds per person." Taylor frowned. He knew they had very little left. "Use it wisely."

Chris nodded. Thirty rounds was a generous ammo ration.

"If the gang breaks through, slow them, and then retreat to the Hill. We need time to get our people and livestock to the Hill. If they break through," Taylor said. "We'll cover you."

"Got it." Chris turned and sprinted to the main entrance.

Each blow from the battering ram shook the gates. The tough white oak drawbar cracked. It wouldn't last much longer.

"Listen up, form a semi-circle around the gate," Chris yelled. "Not so close." The squads moved into formation. "Frank, you're in charge."

"Okay." Frank's eyes lit up at the command. "Right away."

From above, Taylor waved to get the militia leaders' attention. "Del Corso, Phelps, Washington, Rice. Put your men on the palisade. Get ready with the bows."

Taylor turned to Wylie. “Move the catapults to the edge of the Hill. Load them with fire pots and wait for my signal.”

“Got it,” Wylie said as he hurried off.

“Taylor,” Chris Kucinski said. “We’re positioned and ready.” A line of militia snaked its way onto the palisade. “We’d better do something; those gates won’t last much longer.”

“I need a few more minutes.” Taylor scanned the scene.

“How many are out there?” Chris asked.

“Maybe two hundred wearing colors, y’know, hard-core gang members. There’re ten times that number who don’t have guns, only clubs or whatever.” Taylor panned his glasses over the Clan positions. “Ready.” He got a thumbs-up gesture from a figure on the palisade. He made a stabbing gesture toward the enemy.

A flock of arrows lofted over the palisade to drop on the army clustered about the main entrance. A chorus of screams rose. The battering-ram crew staggered and dropped the ram. They struggled to pick it up. A skinny, pimply-faced man in gang colors yelled and waved at the battering ram crew.

Another flight of arrows arrived.

The battering ram again slammed down onto the wood planks. The screams got louder. Bodies cluttered the bridge, with arrows sticking out at odd angles. Some of the bodies still moved but most lay motionless. Half of the original attacking force remained standing on the bridge.

A third volley of arrows arrived.

The survivors on the bridge fled, tripping over bodies, pushing those who didn’t move fast enough. Some jumped off the bridge to wade or swim away. Another flight of silent death fell from the sky. Blood ran off the bridge, forming a dark tongue in the slow-moving water. The metallic smell of blood and the stink of torn guts drifted to the Hill.

“That’s better.” Taylor watched through binoculars. The army had moved away from the entrance and out of range. On the palisade, the militia stood jeering at the retreating army.

In the distance, Taylor saw that the gang members had their

rifles raised. "Look out," he yelled. "Get down."

Automatic weapons erupted into a sustained, booming yammer. Half-a-dozen Clan archers toppled, some into the waters of the moat. More collapsed backward onto the catwalk. As the firing ceased, screaming started inside the Clan's walls.

~

The cries of the wounded were a constant backdrop for the rest of the day. Shots occasionally rang out. Taylor could see the army had set up camp in the pastures below the Hill, adjacent to the Rocky River. Like a dirty stain, they slowly spread out around to the south and east sides of the fort.

As the day waned, a steady stream of wagons and carts filled with supplies and equipment arrived. All, he saw, were guarded by gun-toting men. The army settled in and built campfires.

A line of troops surrounded the Hill. Darkness closed in. Isolated screams, raucous laughter, and shouts punctuated the quiet. Campfires flickered fitfully; slowly fading into a sea of dull, red glows that stretched around the Hill.

The Hill was under siege.

~

"I want their numbers, their armaments, where they're camped, and their security." Taylor stared intently at the squad and militia leaders. From the lookout point on the south side of the Hill, the gang's campfires below seemed almost endless. Overhead, through the gaps in the foliage, stars sparkled with a hard brilliance. "I want scouts outside to see if there's any gap in their encirclement. Ted, handle it."

"Gotcha." Callioux turned to leave.

"Before you go, there's something everyone must hear." Taylor took a deep breath. "I'm not going to tolerate a repetition of today's performance on the palisades." He made eye contact with each squad leader. "Becoming a target is stupid. Yes, stupid. You, as leaders, are responsible for preventing this type of useless sacrifice. You read me?"

Phelps's militia group had suffered ten dead and fifteen wounded on the wall this afternoon.

"Do all of you understand this?" Taylor asked.

Each leader nodded. None spoke.

"We have to destroy the army's leadership, the hard-core gang members who have the automatic weapons, the ones wearing colors. Once they're taken out, the rest will be easy."

At some level, Taylor welcomed this conflict as a means to get rid of the gang. Even if it meant sacrificing some of his own. For just the briefest moment, the face of Vivian appeared in his mind's eye. He focused on the group before him as guilt nagged. Soon, some of those faces will be stiff, cold, and lifeless. *More are going to die*.

For an instant, he had a vision of a field of endless bleached skeletons and grinning skulls. He shook his head and the vision disappeared. "I've got an idea how to do this," he said. "It goes like this...."

At dawn, a thin fog lay over the valley below the Hill. The gang's army stirred to life with a rumble of massed voices. As the sun emerged, it burned off the mist to reveal the encamped army that looked like a dark, squirming mass filling the valley.

The smell of cooked meat wafted over the Hill and reminded the Clan farmers it was their livestock they had left behind. The hours passed and the army still did not move.

Within the Hill, Stolz's crew braced the main entrance gate by the river with a mound of dirt. They'd also stocked the palisade walls with stones, boulders, and bundles of arrows. An ant-like stream of children carried water and forage up the Hill.

Wylie's people armored two large dump trucks with planking, mounting a catapult on each. Mechanics had reduced the trucks' exhaust systems to a whisper.

Throughout the day, the sound of hammering came from the valley below. Scouts went out, but none got close without encountering guards. The gang was up to something.

Scouts came back with word the gang's army had gaps in their cordon of guards around the swamp on the north side of the old river. Jack O'Connor and thirty armed men with horses waded through the swamp and then climbed the steep side of the valley to the ridge above. On a bluff overlooking the valley, they hid in a patch of scrubby crabapple trees surrounded by briars and waited for nightfall.

The tri-axle trucks moved from the Hill to the northwest gate. Whatever sound the trucks made was drowned out by the noise from the army. When the trucks reached the northwest gate by Shepherd Road, they disappeared under the dense foliage. By late afternoon, the pace of activity slowed. Even the Hill became quiet. A pall of smoke rose over the army's encampment; it was time for the evening meal.

O'Connor flashed a mirror at the Hill. A brief series of flashes replied. He listened carefully, but heard neither the sound of trucks or gunfire. Ten minutes later, the trucks rolled to stop by the briar patch to join Chris's group.

O'Connor said quietly, "How did it go?"

"No problem." Chris gave a thumbs-up gesture. "Callioux's people took out the guards near the river ford. They were like silent death, dropping them one by one. The others never saw us, never heard us. They don't know we're here," she said.

"Stubby," Skid called. "I've got a special job for you."

Stubby raised his head at the summons. "Sure thing, Skid."

"See that house up there?" Skid pointed. "The one that's got a deck sticking out over the valley?"

Stubby squinted at the top of the hillside. "Yeah."

"Okay, grab some supplies and take those boys up there before dark." He pointed to a group of men. "Understand?"

"Sure thing, Skid," Stubby said. "Whatcha want us to do?"

"I want you there tomorrow. When we attack, you're gonna blow away those assholes on the wall. When I give you this signal." Skid raised his hand and made a downward sweeping gesture. "You let 'em have it. Y'understand?"

"Sure thing, Skid."

"Keep your binoculars on me." Skid glared at him. "If you shoot at the wrong time, I'll kill you."

"Sure, sure, I got the picture." Stubby nodded. "As soon as the boys are ready, we'll motor on up."

"Stubby, go the back way, on foot, quiet-like. I don't want those assholes to know you're there. Understand?"

"Sure thing, Skid." Stubby had a grin on his face.

"Stubby." Skid smiled without warmth.

"Yeah?"

"No drinkin' or smokin' dope. An' forget about taking a chick for a gang-bang. I want you sharp in the morning. Understand?"

"Yeah, sure, Skid." The corners of Stubby's mouth turned down.

"I'm gonna send Knuckles to check you're comfortable. Understand?" A smile spread across Skid's face.

"Yeah, sure, Skid." It was well known Stubby didn't like Knuckles and had once lost a fight with him, too.

Skid put the citizens to work, preparing for the day of reckoning. They filled the night with the sounds of coming and going, axes ringing as they bit into wood. Occasionally came the sound of branches breaking and the thud of a falling tree. Smoky torches along the palisade wall reflected off the moat.

Coughs and distant muttered curses punctuated the darkness. As the night deepened, the army's campfires gradually faded from flickering orange circles to barely visible dots of glowing embers. Eventually, the valley became quiet.

DAY TWO

A blood-red sun climbed above the trees into a brassy sky.

The air was still, warm and humid. In the valley below, the army came to life with a sullen murmur, chasing away the quiet of early morning. The clamor of metal on metal began and grew loud, and then fell silent. The rhythmic sound of marching started.

At the lookout point on the south side of the Hill, Taylor raised his binoculars and viewed the scene below. Through the leafy trees, he saw a collage of whites and yellow with an occasional red octagonal shape flowing from a distant paddock. It was the front ranks of the gang's army.

Ah, Taylor thought. *They've made shields from road signs and other sheet metal. It's their answer to our bows.* At the rear came battered U-Haul trailers, many with ladders. The metallic clanking sound of thousands of pieces of equipment and the rhythmic thud of marching feet grew louder as the army got closer.

"Look at all those people." Weitzman put his left hand to his mouth as he pointed with his right. "Shouldn't we negotiate with them? We can't stand up to a force that large."

"They're hoodlums. They won't push us out of here. We'll

fight until we win or die. If you're going to leave, you'd better hurry." Taylor hesitated. "Shel, I need you, the Clan needs you. We all need you."

Shel Weitzman did not move.

A hundred yards from the moat surrounding the Hill, the army stopped and formed up into three untidy blocks. A man clad in shiny black leather that bore the bright red and yellow death's head emblem of the Diablos strode to the front. He raised an arm. For a moment the army was still, quiet.

He dropped his arm.

In unison, the troops in the army beat on their shields and yelled. The noise rolled through the valley like a tidal wave.

Birds rose up in clouds, fleeing.

The man raised his arm.

The army became still. The valley was silent, absent even of the sounds of nature. Again, he dropped his hand. Another wave of noise exploded.

~

For a third time, Skid raised his hand and swept it down. The army again erupted into a percussive chorus. He pranced around, waving his arms, urging the army on. The volume swelled, like a giant savage beast roaring out a challenge to its foe.

All at once, Skid thought of Wagner's Flight of the Valkyries, the part that swelled to a triumphant chorus. It was an omen; he knew he would be victorious. Enough.

He raised his hand. Quiet descended.

"Remember your orders," he yelled. He dropped his hand and moved to the rear of his army.

A voice rang out, and in unison, the center block of the army raised their shields to form a protective layer—like the scales of a serpent—covering those below.

Skid raised and dropped his hand. The two outside blocks of the army beat upon their shields. The center section advanced toward the palisade. Gang members wearing the Diablos' colors, those with guns, began to shoot at the defenders on the wall.

Two U-Haul trailers—laden with ladders and pushed by men protected by raised shields—advanced to the edge of the moat. The Diablos continued shooting their guns at any Clan members who showed themselves.

The writhing serpent of shields slithered through the moat's water to reach the base of the wall, heads barely above the water. Clusters of troops raised individual ladders. Strings of troops snaked up the ladders with shields held overhead. As the first troops clawed ever closer to the top of the wall, the army cheered.

From behind the wall, half a dozen containers swished through the air to crash into the moat and burst. Iridescent fluid streamed out over the surface of the water. A moment later, two plastic jugs trailing smoke, arced into the water. Fire erupted with a dull thump and raced across the surface of the water. Clouds of thick, black smoke rose, obscuring the palisade.

In unison, a line of archers rose above the top of the wall. Bows flexed and a cloud of arrows sliced into the men who were between the wall and the flames in the moat. The archers disappeared below the top of the palisade.

More plastic jugs filled with gasoline—large Molotov cocktails—dropped into the water, spreading the flames wider. More arrows streaked into the men below. The cries of pain grew louder.

"Ah, gotcha." Skid smiled and glanced at the house high on the edge of the valley. He waved and pointed to the walls of the Hill with a downward sweeping gesture.

The ripping sound of automatic weapons cut through the noise of battle. The line of archers on top of the wall collapsed. The gunfire slowed to a popcorn-popping pace. Voices in pain screamed without stop.

The flames on the water flickered out. Blackened bodies

drifted downstream amid the flotsam of broken ladders and arrows. Floating bodies contorted, slowly and without hope.

"Again." Skid pointed to the left wing of his army, which began to move forward. This time the snake-like procession crossed the moat without opposition.

Another cloud of flaming pots arced through the air into the moat. Eruptions of flame made holes in the army's ranks, but they continued to advance. Troops clambered up the ladders like streams of ants seeking something sweet, reaching the top of the wall in ever-increasing numbers.

Within the palisade, a thin line of brown-clad defenders faced the wall. They fired steadily at the intruders as they came over the wall. More men appeared on top of the wall, replacing those that dropped.

The chatter of automatic weapons started again. One after another of the defenders within the palisade fell. The thin, brown line became ragged, which then broke and ran. More of the gang's army flowed over the wall in ever-increasing numbers. Slowly, they assembled into ranks and started toward the Hill.

From the lookout point, Taylor stared through the binoculars. "Ah, now I understand," he said. He saw a swath through the woods up the side of the valley leading to a house with an overhanging deck that had a clear view of the main entrance. Pale blue smoke drifted from the deck. He estimated that there were at least ten marksmen with automatic weapons positioned there. "That was the noise we heard last night. They cut down trees to get a clear shot at our defenses."

Franny nudged him and pointed to Ted Callioux, who had just arrived.

"What do we do now?" Ted Callioux asked. His eyebrows split by a deep furrow.

"Fall back to the Hill." Taylor frowned.

"I sent a squad down to reinforce them," Ted said.

"Recall them," Taylor said. "The snipers will get them."

Callioux sprinted off.

The sound of gunfire started anew. Taylor pointed to a messenger. "Tell Sam Wylie it's time."

Minutes later, a gasoline motor coughed into life and then revved-up. It was for a generator. The engine changed tone and slowed, becoming louder and more resonant.

Taylor watched the gang's army climb in formation up the road leading to the main entrance of the Hill. Before them fled the few survivors of the squad that had tried to stem their assault over the wall. He could see more and more of the gang's army flow over the outer wall. They too, began to move toward the Hill.

"Sir," a messenger said, gasping for air. "The gang's army has reached the entrance to the Hill."

"So?" Taylor had a feeling that something was wrong.

"It's not closed."

"What?" Taylor bit his lip to control his anger.

"Our people waited for the squad to get back. They didn't realize the people coming up the road were the gang's army."

"Who's in charge?"

"Well, Callioux is now in charge. Before, it was Dr. Weitzman. He wanted to keep the entrance open for our people."

"Go and get me an update." He hesitated, "Tell Callioux to do his duty."

Dear Lord, he thought. *A favor, please.*

"Taylor." Franny handed him his bulletproof vest. "Please, put it on. Shouldn't you take charge?"

"No. They'll get it closed. They have to." He gave her the binoculars as he put on the bulletproof vest.

More large Molotov cocktails arced over the wall, landing among the attackers at the almost-closed entrance and bursting into flame. Archers on the walls above popped up in groups, each firing a volley of arrows. Three men pushed a large boulder off the tower by the gate. It bounced once and began to roll down the road through the army's ranks, its passage marked by a trail of scattered bodies and dark stains. Another cloud of arrows rained down on the gang's army below the Hill.

A metal drum dropped from the entrance tower and exploded. A ball of fire rose above the towers that guarded the entrance. Smoke billowed around the entrance to the Hill, a black cloud rising in a mushroom shape. Flames again erupted in front of the gate.

Blackened figures ran screaming down the hill.

The gang's army wavered, backing away from the entrance.

Franny pointed. "They're near the outer palisade."

"Yes, I expected that. I don't think they can get past the electric fence on the north side. That's keeping them confined."

"You've got something planned, haven't you?"

"Let's go to the other look-out point."

~

"Uh, Skid, I ain't getting to kill no one," Knuckles said. "It ain't fair."

"Go up the hill." Skid absently pointed to the promontory formed by the two branches of the Rocky River. He continued to watch the battle unfold through binoculars.

"Uh, how am I gonna get to kill someone up the hill? There ain't no fighting goin' on up there."

"You oughta be able to get a clear shot at the hill from there." Skid pointed. "There's always some asshole stickin' his head up, understand?"

Knuckles enjoyed killing almost as much as sex. He didn't care who or how he killed, just as long as he got to kill. "Uh, okay. I'll be up the hill if you need me."

He climbed the hill until he found a clear view across the valley. He leaned against a tree and peered through the telescopic sight on his SKS rifle. He panned the walls of the Hill.

Wait, he thought. He had overshot a face. He brought the scope back to where he'd seen the face. *Nothing*, he thought and waited patiently. A woman's head popped up. She glanced briefly toward him.

Hey, I've seen that bitch before, Knuckles thought. *Lemme see, it was last year, yeah, when we got the new van at the Nature Center an' we got our rocks off. So, she's here now*, he thought. *She'll do*.

At that moment another face came into view. *Well, fuck me*, he thought. *If it ain't the mouthy asshole who gave Fast Eddy a buncha lip. If I blow him away, Eddy'll owe me*.

The two people moved along behind the wall, heads bobbing in and out of view. Patiently, Knuckles waited for a clear shot. They came to a standstill and waved as though signaling. The woman was slightly in front of the skinny dude. He aimed at her heart.

You're mine, he thought.

Blam! He fired the rifle just as the woman started to duck down. She staggered and disappeared below the wall.

Gotcha, he thought. He felt a rush and a warm, almost sexual glow of satisfaction creep over him—it was just the fix that he needed. *Now*, he thought. *Lemme get the skinny fucker*.

If I go higher, I can get a better shot. Knuckles climbed to the top of the escarpment. *Wow, the view is great. Now, I can see the mouthy asshole*. He braced his rifle against a tree and sighted in on the wall. After what seemed like a long time, the skinny dude finally stood up and waved his arms. He was still just long enough to line up a heart shot.

Blam! The man went down like he'd been jerked over. Again, Knuckles got that warm, pleasant-all-over feeling.

He looked around. Something had happened. *Our boys and the conscripts are on the move*. There was a lot of shooting going on. There were two giant boxes moving down the valley, followed by two groups of camo-clad men firing automatic weapons. And there was a bunch of men on horses.

"Oh, shit," Knuckles said. *Where's Skid?* He thought. *There ain't no one there to protect him*. He ran down the hill in leaps and bounds, slipping and sliding, to get back to where he had left Skid.

Gunshots intensified into a chorus, coming closer.

~

Chris moved the trucks and the horse-mounted militia to the west entrance above the valley. A scout brought the news of the slaughter on the palisade from the house on the hill.

"Okay, listen up," Chris said. "We've got to get every single one of them." She pointed to the squad leaders. "You and you, take your men to the south, and you to the west side. Wait until you hear the first shot, then move in, quick." She knew her father's killer led this gang. She wouldn't rest until she found him.

Silently, they moved into positions where they could see the snipers on the deck.

"Open fire," Chris said.

The opening volley lasted thirty seconds.

"Cease fire," she yelled.

No one on the deck moved. They were all dead.

Several shots rang out from inside the house. Chris's men charged into the house, firing continuously. Moments later, silence fell. Two militia died and four were wounded in the assault. Cautiously, the militia searched the house. Inside were two dead gang members ripped apart from multiple bullet shots.

"Hey, will you come and take a look at this?" O'Connor called from the doorway.

"What is it, Jack?"

"It's a whole box of ammo. At least a thousand rounds." He cracked the barest trace of a grim smile. "This could make things a lot more fun. Now we've got ammo to burn."

"It won't be fun." Chris's face was like a slab of gray stone. "Let's go."

The squad boarded the trucks, released the brakes, and without the engines running, coasted down Cedar Point Road. O'Connor's horse mounted militia followed behind. At the bottom of the valley, Chris stopped and pointed. "Listen up. We'll take the road to the bridge, and then push north. The trucks will lead and provide cover for the two squads. Use the fire pots on those with rifles. Remember, the ones we really want are those wearing colors, the gang members. Show them no mercy."

She turned to O'Connor. "Take six rifles and half of the ammo for your horsemen. Push the army east and north."

Side by side, the two trucks advanced, their catapults throwing large Molotov cocktails into the army. Flames blossomed within the confined ranks of the army and human torches ran screaming through the ranks. Each time, like a giant amoebae, the army surged away from the flames.

From the armored boxes on the trucks, the militia fired continuously at the gang members wearing colors.

The army nearest to the trucks retreated and swung south.

O'Connor's horsemen charged at the advancing army, guns on full auto. The army wavered as its front ranks collapsed. The hail of lead from O'Connor's men drove them back, north toward the trucks. More flames erupted from Molotov cocktails.

The army broke. As the gang members ran, sharpshooters on the trucks picked them off.

Gunfire from the house on the hill stopped. Taylor knew the trap was set. As he climbed up on the wall, Franny joined him to catch a glimpse of conditions below their line of view. "You shouldn't be here." As he jumped down, he heard a distant shot.

Franny yelped, staggered, and fell onto her back. Blood gushed from her neck. She twitched twice and went still.

Taylor tried to stem the blood flowing from her throat with

his hands, but it pulsed out between his fingers. As the flow of blood slowed, she stopped breathing.

He laid his head on her chest. She had no heartbeat. "Franny," he said. "No, not you, Franny." He stared at the blood oozing from her neck and the blood dripping from his fingers.

It's on my hands. I caused this. His heart lurched and sank like lead. *I caused this to happen.*

A rattle of gunfire made him raise his head. It had become much louder.

Already, he realized. *A river of blood has flowed, and before the day ended, more will flow*. Something stirred inside him, a rage that consumed him to the point of not caring whether he lived or died. He felt an urge to kill, to kill as many of those responsible for this attack as he knew how.

He left Franny where she lay. He peered over the wall. He saw the Clan's forces had caught half the army between Wylie's electric fence and the Hill's defenses behind the palisade. The trucks drew close. Smoking trails arced away from the back of the trucks, splashing fire on the army. Guns fired steadily from the trucks. The gang's army continued its retreat.

The horse-mounted militia charged.

The army, now more like a mob, fled. The swirling mass of the army's remnants swept the gang's leaders closer and closer to the walls of the Hill.

It's time, Taylor thought. He climbed onto the wall and waved to the archers. "Now," he yelled. "Kill them, kill all of them."

Rows of bows moved in unison. Every Clan member who could use a bow joined the barrage, men, women, and children. A huge flock of arrows rose and fell like a rain of gray death onto the writhing mass of color.

A mighty force struck Taylor in the chest, spinning him around. As he fell, his world faded into a blue haze.

~

The steel-tipped arrows fell from the sky in droves, killing dozens of gang members. The army scattered and ran. More arrows and unceasing gunfire followed. Control disappeared; armed gang members fought as individuals.

The trucks with men firing guns pressed ever closer.

"Where were ya?" Skid yelled. "We gotta get outa here."

"Oh, man." Knuckles was breathless from his breakneck run down the hill. "I nailed that skinny asshole who mouthed-off at us. I got him but good. An' that bitch—"

"Gimme a fuckin' break." Skid's face was contorted with rage. "Tell me your life story later. We gotta get the fuck outa here. Those bastards have trucks and a shit-load of guns. An' those spineless shits in the army turned tail. There ain't any of our boys left. Let's go." They headed south.

~

Chris saw two Deacons run south, away from the battle. She recognized them—they were her father's killers. They were the scar-faced man and his gorilla-like companion.

"Jack, I just spotted the men who killed my father. I need a horse to go after them." Chris felt her heart pound.

"What're you going to do?"

"I've got a score to settle with those two." Chris raised her voice. "Jack, it's important." Unwanted, images of her father's death crept into her mind. Again, for a moment she saw her mother's and sister's desecration. *I must avenge them, I must!*

"Give me a minute."

"Hurry."

A messenger ran up to O'Connor, waving his arms. O'Connor hurried over to Chris. "Uh, that was bad news." He cleared his throat. "It's real bad. Your mom's dead and Taylor is wounded, bad, real bad. He may not live. Someone shot them."

Chris went cold inside. She felt her jaw muscle work. *Oh, God, not them too*. Rage filled her.

"Chris?" O'Connor asked. "You still want to go?"

Chris clenched her jaw tightly before speaking. "Yes. Now more than ever. They killed my dad. Now my mom is dead. And Taylor may be dead. I've got to do it. I must."

"Okay, Chris. Here, take my horse. There's a rifle in the scabbard. There's ammo in the pouch on the opposite side."

As Chris climbed onto the horse, six horse-mounted militia joined her, insisting they go with her. She spurred her horse to a gentle trot and headed south. The horsemen followed.

As she left, the Clan demanded the army caught behind the outer perimeter and the electric fence surrender. They didn't respond until several more volleys of arrows fell upon them. Over a thousand lay down their weapons and put their hands on their heads.

The battle was over.

~

"Uh, Skid, what do we do now?"

"Wait until it's dark, then we make a break for it," Skid said. They crouched behind boulders with a steep cliff behind them. They were in an abandoned sandstone quarry. In front was low scrub. He peered over the edge of a boulder.

A horse whinnied.

A shot rang out and a bullet whined off a boulder. "What the fuck? How did they find us?" Skid ducked low.

"I dunno." Knuckles put his gun above the boulder and snapped off a couple of shots. Nothing moved. Quiet returned.

"Take off anything that makes any kind of noise when you move, understand?" Skid said.

"Uh, Skid, what're they doin' out there?" Knuckles asked.

"I've got no fuckin' idea."

Why do I keep him around? Skid wondered. He heard a noise above. He looked up, just in time to see a man on the cliff heave a Molotov cocktail toward them.

Skid fired almost reflexively. The man toppled off the cliff. The Molotov cocktail arced down and struck the boulder in front of him. It exploded and a flash of flame washed away from him. Its heat made him jump behind another boulder.

Another Molotov cocktail landed. It was just behind Skid and showered both of them with flaming gasoline. Screaming, they both rolled about on the ground to extinguish the flames.

It took a few moments to extinguish the flames. He sat up.

"Hello, Mr. Vukovitch."

Skid looked up at the sound of a woman's voice. It was a tall, thin woman dressed in camo. Off to one side, three men in similar clothing pointed assault rifles at him.

Knuckles's hand inched toward the gun tucked in his belt.

"Don't, unless you want your hand shot off," a voice said. It was man behind them, who had a rifle aimed at Knuckles.

Shit, another asshole, Skid thought.

"D'you know who I am?" the woman asked. "I'm Chris Kucinski. That mean anything to you?"

Skid said nothing, eyes moving, scoping out the scene.

"I thought not." The woman's mouth tightened and turned down at the corners. "You know, I've had fantasies about what I would do with you when I caught you. I've changed my mind," she said. "If I did anything except kill you, I'd sully myself with your dirt."

Shithead, Skid thought. *The bitch did look familiar*.

"This is for my father, my mother, and my sister." The woman raised the rifle and aimed it at him. As the muzzle flashed, the gun boomed.

For just an instant, as pain exploded in his thigh, Skid realized where he had seen the young woman before. Another slug slammed into him and tore a hole in his crotch. It was in the Nature Center where he got a blow ...

THE FRUITS OF VICTORY

Around the Hill, the moans of the wounded mingled with the wails of the bereaved. Clouds of flies filled the air. The smell of blood mixed with the foulness of spilled guts. The sun rose higher and brought heat without mercy. Overhead, crows and buzzards circled endlessly.

Taylor regained consciousness. Even though the bullet had penetrated his bulletproof vest and cracked a rib, it had been slowed, thus sparing him. He moved like a zombie, numb and overwhelmed with grief, pain a constant companion. Burdened by his loss but driven by sense of duty, he made hard decisions as he allocated medical care. The Clan had won, but at what cost?

Chris Kucinski and the horse-mounted militia hounded the remnants of the army that had attacked the Clan. Remnants of the gang fought fiercely, but by day's end, they were gone from the Rocky River Valley. The militia questioned the prisoners to identify the various gangs—their hangouts, weapons, and manpower.

Chris's militia hung those prisoners wearing colors or decorated with gang tattoos. Every day for a week, bodies swung from a large sycamore tree at the point above the two rivers on the edge of the cemetery.

The horse militia moved east and sought out the gangs exploiting the general populace in the shattered remains of Cleveland. They cornered a joint force of the Tombs' and Vipers' gangs in a brick warehouse and set the building on fire with Molotov cocktails. As the gang fled, the militia pursued them and killed them, one by one, without mercy.

Those who opposed the Clan felt Chris's anger. Her militia scoured the land around Rocky River for the distance of a day's ride in all directions. She freed those held in servitude by the gangs and negotiated loose alliances with the groups and communities that respected freedom of the individual.

By fall, Chris's militia had freed northeast Ohio from the grip of gangs and petty warlords. Few people remained in the ruins of the former Cleveland metropolitan area; it had become the badlands for solitary bandits and crazed individuals. Broken by roads and shells of houses filled with bodies and bitter memories, it was poor land for farming.

The summer was warm and the harvest good. Stolz's men raised the height of the dams in the Rocky River and increased the water supply. At the same time, Taylor built a water mill at the base of the Hill.

The mill provided forced air to a cupola that melted steel to cast items no longer available. At the same time, the mill powered a drop hammer to forge items too large for a smith to shape with a hammer.

Scavenging parties found lathes, drill presses, and other metal working equipment, which they brought back for the machine shop. The forge's furnace now heated the water for the community's expanded laundry and public baths.

During the night, the mill drove a piston pump that lifted a steady stream of water to the cisterns, which met the Hill's needs. On weekends, the mill processed grains and fruit throughout the harvest season. It even made small amounts of flour for a newly established bakery.

~

Over the summer, Taylor, consumed with grief, became thin and gaunt. Even his clothes grew shabby. He became withdrawn and didn't participate in any social activities. He stopped shaving and didn't bathe often. Since the battle, he'd driven everyone hard, demanding more and more, working without a break. Many believed it was a means of distraction so he would have no time to think about Franny's death.

~

Fred built Taylor a new house in the upper Hill and worried about Taylor. His wife Maria did too.

"Look," said Maria. "He needs help. You've got do something for him. Franny would want you to."

"Well, yeah, but what am I supposed to do? Tell him to snap out of it?" Fred spread his hands. "That'd be like talking to a stone wall. You know how hard-headed he is."

"*Va bene*." Maria's shrug reversed the meaning of the Neapolitan words for okay. "What would Franny tell you to do?"

"I dunno. What?"

"Persuade him to take another woman."

"C'mon, gimme a break."

"The quickest way to mend a broken heart is in the arms of another. He needs a woman."

"You think so?" Fred pulled at his lower lip.

"Think about it." She touched his arm and pulled him close. "Look, he ran away to the woods after his wife died in Washington. When he took up with Franny he became quite human, a nice guy. Since she was killed, well, he's not so nice."

"You're right. He's been a regular slave driver this summer. He pushes himself harder than anyone else."

"Think what it'll be like for him when winter sets in and there's less to do. You know how it depresses him. I wouldn't be surprised if he went off into the woods and never came back."

"Yeah, you're right and we still need him." Fred sighed and looked away. "Have you been in his new house lately?"

"No, what's it like?"

"It's kind of ..." He struggled for words. "Well, a mess, not like a real home. When I go there, I never smell food. I know he's not eating right."

"What did I tell you?" Maria put her hands on her hips. "He needs a woman. He needs someone to look after him, his home, his heart, and his body."

"So, how do I go about that?"

"Get him a housekeeper." She smiled. "A good looking woman who'll take care of him. You know, in every way, as only a woman can do."

"Aw, Maria, y'know what they call guys who do that?"

"I didn't mean it that way. He needs someone to see he eats right, cleans his house, and washes his clothes." She looked up and smiled. "And takes care of him, like I take care of you."

"Where do I find one of those?"

"Fred, you must be blind." She slapped his hand without anger. "There's dozens of widows who'd jump at the chance to take care of Taylor. They're desperate to get out of the common rooms. He's the most powerful man in the Clan, and probably the wealthiest. That makes him sexy, very sexy to a lot of women. Believe me."

"Look, you find the woman and I'll twist Taylor's arm about taking a housekeeper." Fred rolled his eyes heavenward. "Don't mention a word about these other things that we talked about."

"Fred, I'm not a *stupidone*." Maria slipped a hand around his waist. "I'm so glad I've got you."

"Noelle Smith?" Taylor ran his eye over Noelle like he was sizing up a spavined horse.

Noelle had cut her brown hair short, bathed, and washed her only dress. Her child clung to her long dress, which was becoming threadbare. She was bone weary and her hands were cracked and raw from swinging a hoe in the fields.

"Is this your child?" His voice was softer.

"Yes, sir," Noelle said. "This is Martha, my baby." Life had not been kind. She remembered how angry her parents back in Iowa had been when she'd become pregnant, left college, and moved in with Al, her boyfriend. It was after her second child, the Collapse came and her boyfriend disappeared.

Even though she had killed to get insulin for her eldest, little Howie, he'd died when it ran out and that still hurt. Her relationship with Mick O'Connor had ended when she'd refused to bear his children. He lived only for the moment, which meant there was no security with him. Alone, far from her family, she had no one to whom she could turn. It had seemed hopeless until Maria Del Corso had asked if she'd be interested in being Taylor MacPherson's housekeeper. She remembered him as a hard man from the time of her run-in with Sally O'Connor.

Desperate, she agreed to an interview.

"Where d'you live?" Taylor's face revealed nothing.

"In the Clan dormitory, in the common room," Noelle said. "It's difficult to find someone to look after Martha while I'm working in the fields. I worry about her all the time."

"What can you do?" His voice was brusque, almost to the point of being harsh. "I mean, what skills do you have?"

"I, er, I don't have any special skills." Noelle felt her face begin to burn. She desperately needed this job. By now, she'd do almost anything to find a home in which to raise Martha. "I think I know how to keep house."

"Oh, you think so? Can you cook?"

"Yes, sir. I helped my mother in the kitchen from the time I was small. Y'see, we lived on a farm. We butchered our own meat, and during hunting season I dressed game, too." Questions about food were safe. "If there's anything special you like, ask and I'll tell you if I know how to make it."

"Hmm." Taylor sniffed. "So, you want to be a housekeeper?" He fixed a stare upon her. "What makes you think that you can do a good job of housekeeping? Can you clean?"

"Yes, I know how to keep house. I can clean, wash clothes and I know how to cook. My mother also taught me how to sew and mend. We were a very traditional family."

Noelle was afraid she wouldn't get the job and have to look elsewhere. Positions that offered accommodations for a woman with a child were hard to find. She'd found from experience most men looking for a mistress didn't want a child around; they had other things in mind.

His eyes ran over her again. "Well, there's only one room available for a housekeeper." He frowned. "There's only one sink in the house. There'll be a probationary period of one month to prove competence."

"Yes, sir." Compared to her current living conditions, his house seemed luxurious. "I understand. It would be fine." She breathed deeply.

Dear God, please let me get this job, please.

"It's one silver dollar per week plus food and lodgings," he said. "What d'you say to that?"

"Are you offering me the position?" She held her breath. He was offering a man's wage, and lodgings, too.

"Yes, subject to the probationary period."

"Yes, oh yes, Mr. MacPherson, I'll take it. Thank you so much." Noelle felt a tremendous sense of relief. "I'll do the best

I can. I promise you won't be disappointed." She dropped to one knee, grasped his hand, and kissed it.

He withdrew his hand quickly. "There's no need for that. It's a job, not slavery."

"Yes, sir." She lowered her eyes. "When do I start?"

"Today. D'you have things that need moving?" His voice had become softer. "Can I send a man with a cart to help you?"

"That would help." Noelle was surprised. It was a simple thing, but it would ease the problem of bringing her few possessions here, especially with Martha at hand. "Thank you, sir. As soon as I get back, I'll get right to work." Her heart soared. It was the first good thing that had happened in months and months.

~

At first, it was awkward to have someone around, for Taylor had become accustomed to living alone, doing things in his own minimalist fashion. His home was a mess, for he had neither the time nor the inclination to do housework.

Each night the first week, Taylor came home and found changes; clean linens brightening the dining table and freshly cut evergreen branches giving the air a pleasant fragrance.

He realized that Noelle was a good cook. Somehow, she prepared foods he liked and did it well. As his living conditions and diet improved, Taylor realized how much his appearance had deteriorated. On Saturday, he got a haircut, a shave, and replaced most of his clothing.

"Hey," Fred said. "I almost didn't recognize you."

"Oh, really?" Taylor said. "How's it going?"

"Fine. How're you and the little lady doing?" Fred nudged him and grinned. "Is she taking good care of you?"

"She seems to know how to keep house." Taylor saw no reason to discuss his personal life when there wasn't much to discuss. "Say, how's the development of the lower Hill going?"

"I'm giving an update at the next Council meeting. It's on the agenda." Fred's eyes never stopped moving. "New threads, too. Your social life must be looking up these days."

"If you'll excuse me," Taylor said. "I'll see you later."

~

"This Saturday will be one month since I started working for him," Noelle said. "I should do something special."

"Look," Maria said. "Taylor likes roast duck served with a fruit compote or a spicy cream sauce."

"That sounds good. Can I use your roaster? D'you know what sauces he particularly likes? My family used to make an orange sauce to go with duck." She laughed. "We used orange marmalade as its base. I don't have anything like that now."

"I've got recipes for sauces," Maria said. "Another thing, he's quite the wine connoisseur. Ask Minotti, the spirits man, I believe he has a few bottles of good wine hidden away."

"D'you think Taylor will notice?" Noelle sighed. "He hasn't said a word about my work." She twisted her handkerchief.

"Don't be silly. I know how Franny kept house. You're doing just fine." Maria smiled and patted her hand.

"That was different. They were, you know—"

"Yes, yes, I know. You just have to be patient. His wife died in Washington, DC, in the attack. It was sad, so sad. Then Franny was killed just six months ago, right next to him. He loved her, too. He's had his heart broken twice. It'll take time, but you can do it."

Maria wagged a finger at Noelle. "Look, take care of him and treat him well. It's up to you, as a woman, to heal his heart, only the way a woman can. D'you understand what I mean?"

"Oh." That took Noelle aback. "I think so." She smiled. *Well*, she thought. *That would make it a permanent relationship, wouldn't it?*

"So, start with the meal. So you don't have any distractions, I'll take care of little Martha for you."

"Thanks," Noelle said. "That's really nice of you."

"If Minotti gives you any crap about the wine, tell him you know me and Fred. Tell him to charge it to me." She gave Noelle a hug. "I'll find those recipes and drop them off tomorrow."

"Thank you, Maria. I don't know what I'd do without you."

"Just take care of Taylor. Make him a happy man."

"Yes, I'll try. 'Bye, Maria."

~

She got a wine from Minotti who swore a connoisseur would rave over it. On Friday, she went to the market and bought the best food she could find; two plump mallards, Brussels sprouts, carrots, new potatoes, sweet butter, herbs, and charcoal for the roaster.

Later, she did the laundry and cleaned the house. It was difficult not saying anything, but Maria had assured her nothing would keep Taylor away that day.

On Saturday, she bruised fresh cedar branches to make the house fragrant and polished the dishes and glasses until they were spotless. By late afternoon, after the ducks had been put in the roaster, Noelle took Martha over to Maria for the evening. After bathing, she put on her nicest clothes and tied a ribbon in her hair. As a final touch, she used the perfume and makeup that Maria had given her.

~

Noelle poked the duck with a fork. Fat-laden juices oozed from the meat and the bone wiggled easily in its joint. It was perfect. She brought the ducks in from the roaster.

The vegetables on the wood stove were done. She took them off the heat. "Mr. MacPherson," she called. "Supper will be served in five minutes." She juggled the pans. It was more difficult cooking on a wood stove than with gas.

"Hm, okay." Taylor looked up from a stack of papers. "Something smells good. What's for supper?"

"Duck, it's in season. I hope you like it." Noelle carved the ducks and arranged them on the platter.

The sauces, she thought and quickly stirred them. "Darn," she said to herself. "I wish I had another pair of hands."

"Here, let me help with that." Taylor took the spoon from her hand. "This looks like quite a production."

"Oh, I didn't hear you coming." She released the spoon into his cool fingers. "They go in those two gravy boats." She pointed with the fork she was using to put meat on the platter.

Taylor transferred the sauces to the serving dishes. "Your table setting looks good." He held up the two gravy boats looking for a place on the crowded table. "Where to?"

"Next to the meat platter," Noelle said as she carried dishes to the table. "Leave some room for the potatoes."

"All right. Now what?"

"Sit down and eat before it gets cold." Noelle mentally crossed her fingers as she looked the table over.

The cut-up duck—skin golden—was neatly arranged on the platter. The redskin potatoes had a light sprinkling of parsley, the carrots glistened from a maple syrup glaze and butter slowly melted on the Brussels sprouts. The sauces, one a tangy plum and the other, hot peppers in cream, steamed in their gravy boats. Wineglasses sparkled in the flickering candlelight on freshly pressed linen.

Well, everything looks all right, she thought. She took her first bite. *Doesn't taste bad, either*.

"Hmm." Taylor's eyes were closed, his mouth moving. He swallowed. "This duck is perfect." He sniffed the plate. "The sauces are great. I haven't had anything like this in a long time." He hesitated and a frown clouded his face.

Noelle's heart leapt into her mouth. "Is something wrong?"

"No. No, it's not the food. It was a memory from another time, another place." His smile was forced.

"How about some wine?" Noelle hurried to hand him the wine bottle. "This is supposed to go well with duck."

"Wine?" He seemed surprised as he took the bottle. "Well, well, an Oregon pinot noir, an excellent choice." He poured some into the glass, swirled it around, and sniffed it deeply. "Nice nose." He took a sip, aspirated it between his teeth, and swallowed. "Hmm, this is the best pinot I've tasted in years. Where did you get it?"

"Minotti's recommended it when I said I was preparing roast duck for you."

"It goes very well with this meal, which is excellent."

Noelle's spirits soared. She knew that one of the paths to a man's heart was through his stomach. The other, she was certain, was found in bed.

Maybe tonight's the night. She felt a smile cross her face. *I did it*. Relaxing somewhat, she tried everything, even the wine, which quickly went to her head.

Taylor ate his food slowly, obviously savoring it.

"Noelle." He paused. "I don't quite know how to say this, but this is the best meal I've had in a long time. I guess I'm saying you're all you claimed to be." He leaned back in his chair and smiled.

Noelle returned his smile. "Do I get to keep the job? It is a month since I started."

"Certainly. You've made a big difference in my life."

"Well, thank you. I aim to please." She lowered her eyes. "And, I like it here." She looked at him out of the corner of her eye.

Really, she thought, *even though he's on the thin side, he isn't at all bad looking*.

~

In the flickering candlelight, the room somehow took on a different appearance. Its soft light, the sound of wood burning in the stove combined with the smell of the food in an almost magical fashion. It had that strange undefined amalgam that made it special, yet familiar—home.

Taylor was full of good food and fine wine. The room was warm and comfortable. "You know," he said. "For the first time since I've moved in here, this feels like home." He stretched, moved his chair away from the table, and picked up the wine glass, swirled it, and sniffed.

He glanced at Noelle.

He'd remembered she'd come before him over some domestic disturbance last winter involving the O'Connors. Apparently, the relationship she'd had with Jack O'Connor was over. She looked a lot different now. Something was different about her current appearance from when she had applied for the position. She no longer looked as worn out and her clothes were new. *She's really quite good looking. Ah, she's wearing some makeup.*

"You have such a nice home." Noelle twisted her napkin and said, "I like it here."

"Well, it's not much, at least compared to the way we used to live. It is a big improvement over the first year we spent on the Hill." He drained the wineglass and sighed. "Noelle, that was a great meal. Thank you."

"You're welcome." She started gathering the plates. "I'd better get the dishes done. The water's heating on the stove."

"Here, let me help." He picked up several dishes. "You must've worked all day to get this meal ready."

"Please, Mr. MacPherson, I can take care of the dishes. Really, it's no problem."

"Try Taylor." He carried a stack of dishes into the kitchen. "And I'm going to do my part."

"You don't have to—"

"I know." He smiled. "I want to."

In the kitchen Taylor scraped dishes and placed them on the sideboard.

Noelle ladled steaming water from the pot, splashing it onto the dishes in the sink. Scrubbing and rinsing the dishes, she quickly moved them to the drying rack.

Taylor wiped and put them away. In the close confines, they kept bumping into each other.

Each time, she smiled.

Taylor realized that Noelle was enjoying the physical contact and was perhaps making the contact deliberately. He found he liked it, too. As she reached up to put away the last plate, he slipped his arms around her waist, holding her loosely.

"Noelle, this is the best evening I've had in a long, long time. Thank you so much." He really meant it.

She leaned back and moved her head slightly to one side so her face was against his. "It can get better," she said in a voice barely over a whisper. She pulled his hands up onto her breasts.

"Really?" His arousal was instant and tight against his trousers. He eased away from her.

She guided his fingers to her erect nipples. "Yes." She turned her face up to him, lips moist and eyes closed.

Taylor kissed her, barely touching her lips.

Noelle turned to him, wrapped her arms around him, and pulled him close. She lifted her head, eyes closed.

Desire surging, Taylor put his hand to the back of her head to hold her while he kissed her again, more firmly.

"My reward for making the meal," she said, "is you have to kiss me again."

While kissing, his hands moved to her small, firm buttocks. He squeezed gently.

Noelle's hands slid down inside his trousers, her fingers insistently seeking, reaching, and then finding him.

He broke their kiss. "Do you want to?" he asked.

"Yes."

He broke their embrace. "Let's go to bed," he said.

"Yes." She took his hand. "Let's do it."

~

Noelle stretched across the bed after Taylor left. *My, my, it wasn't so difficult*. She thought about the previous night and the time again this morning. *He doesn't move me like Al, my old boyfriend, but he is gentle. Well, I'll get used to it. It's got me a home for Martha and me.*

Noelle was convinced she was on the path that led to Taylor's heart. *I've just got to get him to the point where he can't do without me, and then he'll ask me to be his wife. Then we'll be secure*.

~

Over the next week, she came to his bed every night. The day she mentioned the possibility of becoming pregnant, Taylor felt a surge of feelings.

A child, he thought, *my own flesh and blood*. At first the idea seemed wonderful. As he searched his feelings and examined those he'd had for Vivian and Franny, it wasn't the same.

What if something happens to the child? Oh, God, he thought, *I couldn't take that*. The immensity of the loss and pain rose up and choked him. He almost cried.

The fear of loving and losing again paralyzed him. *I can't face this*, he thought. He shut down his feelings and his heart became cold, cold as a winter's night. *I'm afraid to love, afraid of losing again*.

...

As for Noelle, do I love her? he asked himself. *Am I ready?* He already knew the answer. *Do I owe it to her?* He thought about them being together and realized the physical aspect of their relationship was all that they really shared.

He smiled. *Yes, it was good, but love is more than that. Something more like the easy affection Noelle shares with Martha, her child. The shared challenges he'd faced with Franny and how they'd grown to ease each other's burdens. However, Noelle's affection toward me seems forced.* That convinced Taylor she really didn't love him.

She's nowhere the equal of either Vivian or Franny—she doesn't have ... He struggled for a moment before he realized that it was sophistication. *She's not smart and knowledgeable about the world, and sex cannot be the only basis of our relationship. It could become difficult*, he thought. *She's a good housekeeper, and as long as she does her work, she'll have a position. As for a formal relationship, no.*

Taylor felt a bond of gratitude to Noelle, for she had brought him back from the edge of the precipice. Again able to view life as a whole, he asserted his leadership of the Clan. He renewed honing the Clan's military skills, instituted regular drills and practice in the arts of war.

It is, he thought, *our only assurance of peace.*

A ONE WAY TICKET

We're over halfway to Kota, Cha KinLaat thought. Even at one-third the speed of light, the Egg-that-Flies seemed motionless. *After I compensate for the distance, the planet's electromagnetic output continues to grow. I've never been able to resolve a signal and obtain another image. If that's a society, he thought, it must be growing rapidly.*

Cha KinLaat glanced around the navigation center. View screens stared back, their red icons glowing without change, indicating normal operating parameters. The small room at the front-most position of the Egg-that-Flies was in the rotation center of the living quarters' centrifuge, which meant there was no up, nor down. Handles protruded between view screens, useful for maneuvering within the navigation center.

He'd just reset the time-elapsed counter to indicate the time remaining to reach Kota, the home of the strange mammalian alien.

The coasting phase was a time of unchanging routine, so much so he wished for something to happen. Anything.

Cha KinLaat DoMar yawned. Against a myriad of multi-colored stars scattered upon the black sky, nothing ever seemed to move. Cha KinLaat felt tempted to look up Bilik Pudjata, to see what he was doing. Bilik, the alien specialist who had a knack for drive system engineering, talked little about what he was doing. Even though Bilik appeared regularly at the navigation station, they had drifted apart.

Perhaps I should have shown more interest in his project to rebuild the drive system. Bilik never quite seemed to fit in, even though he was close to the center and worked hard.

Cha KinLaat yawned again as he glanced at the displays once more. Time for a break. *Maybe I need some time in that new replica of a prehistoric swamp with those fantastic holograms of the fierce denizens of the past. That'll get my heart moving.*

"Ping." The deep space monitoring system's emergency alarm went off with an out-of-parameter signal.

"Great Egg." Cha KinLaat looked up quickly. The force of his movement made him float toward the ceiling—low gravity was the main disadvantage of being so close to the center of rotation. The size of the electronic pulse shown on the deep-space sensors was enormous. The overload saturated the instruments' readouts and they dropped down close to zero input.

"Mata ChaLik," he called. "Something strange just happened."

"Describe what happened." Mata ChaLik's voice was calm and strong as it boomed through the comm-net.

"We've picked up a very powerful electromagnetic pulse that seems to come from—"

"Ping." the audio monitor screeched. The visual displays washed out into whiteness. All readouts went to maximum input capacity, icons glowing.

"Great Egg."

"What's going on?"

"It was another pulse," said Cha KinLaat. "Its energy is orders of magnitude greater than anything seen before from Kota."

Mata ChaLik's voice took on a hard edge. "Is it an attack?"

"No, I don't think so." Cha KinLaat tried to bring another set of sensors on line, something more suited to this signal.

"Then what is it?"

"Let me explain." Cha KinLaat unconsciously bobbed his head to acknowledge an order from one who was at the center. "The sensors monitoring Kota detected an enormous signal." He paused. "Well, the actual strength of the pulse is quite weak. It's totally harmless to us."

"You're sure it came from Kota?"

Cha KinLaat hesitated. "I'm not sure." It was possible it could have come from somewhere else. "You see, a signal of this strength overwhelms our sensors—"

"Isn't that an attack?"

"Oh, no. It's too weak. The sensors are very sensitive."

"Then what is it?"

"I don't know, but compared to the electromagnetic signature of Kota, it's vastly more powerful."

"Yes, yes, I understand. What or who caused them?"

"I don't know."

"Then I suggest you find out," Mata ChaLik's voice dripped with scorn. "And soon."

"I'll analyze the data to find what's responsible." Cha KinLaat struggled to find the right words.

He'd just failed to make a good impression with Mata ChaLik, the Defender at the center of the ship, one who held Cha KinLaat's fate in his claws.

"Do that," Mata ChaLik said. "Especially if it comes from Kota," he said with a note of sarcasm in his voice. "Which, I find I need to remind you, is where we're going."

Cha KinLaat worked furiously to analyze the powerful electromagnetic signals. Another pulse lit up the equipment. He ran the signals through the algorithm on the original signal detected on Qu'uda. There was no trace of video information.

After several more analyses, he had to conclude the pulses

had no data content. The longer he studied them, the more he realized there was something frightening about them. He needed confirmation.

He contacted DuKlaat YataBu who had studied radio astronomy extensively and asked him to review the signals. After much discussion, they both came to the same conclusion.

"Mata ChaLik," Cha KinLaat called over the comm-net. "The pulses definitely came from the proximity of Kota." He stopped.

"Are you sure?"

"Yes, absolutely."

"Well?"

"Well, the only thing that these pulses look like, is, well, a star exploding," Cha KinLaat paused. "Or a fusion explosion."

"Has Kota gone nova?" Mata ChaLik asked.

"No."

"Are you sure about this?"

"You mean—"

"Are you sure that it was a fusion explosion?"

"Not absolutely, but they certainly look like it."

"They? How many?"

"Three big ones so far and many smaller ones."

"Have you any way of estimating their size?"

"No, but the initial pulses were orders of magnitude larger than the subsequent pulses."

"Is there another source for these electromagnetic pulses?"

"I consulted with DuKlaat YataBu. We both agree with this analysis. Nothing else looks close. We believe a whole series of fusion explosions took place in the Kota system."

"Swamp fire." Mata ChaLik's voice was heavy.

Cha KinLaat knew the history of Qu'uda. In a remote time, fusion explosives had been a weapon option. At that time, the only difference between "treachery" and "diplomacy" was in the way the word was inflected. That period of their history was now viewed as one of group insanity—something of which they were ashamed.

Cha KinLaat realized the entire crew might have heard his words. He silently swore. For a moment he wished he were on the private comm-net. *Fusion explosives? What kind of species would use fusion explosives? Especially in such numbers?* He knew the Egg-that-Flies could not withstand an attack of fusion explosives.

"Cha KinLaat." Mata ChaLik's voice was low, vibrating in a manner that suggested great emotion, fear, or perhaps, anger.

"Yes?"

"Review options for aborting the mission."

"There are no options to abort our mission."

"What?"

"The mag-sail will not cancel our velocity in absence of wind from a star, so that means we must use the fusion drive to slow down, saving enough fuel to maneuver. That will take most of the fuel in our tank, so we would need to refuel. If there were a gravitational body large enough, we could use it to change our course and return to Qu'uda." Cha KinLaat paused. "However, there are none between here and Kota. Our mission was designed to use Kota's star to reduce our velocity, and use its gas giant planet as a source of fuel for the return trip."

"What about the star of the Kota system?"

"It's large enough, but we'll be there."

"Egg," Mata ChaLik's voice took on an angry edge.

Cha KinLaat was puzzled. Mata ChaLik should have known the answer to that question before it was given. He realized Mata ChaLik had just demonstrated he didn't have every fact at the tip of his claws. His focus on matters military must have left him no time to understand the technical aspects of their voyage. That realization gave him a bitter sense of satisfaction.

"Mata ChaLik, what are we going to do?"

"We cannot alter our course, therefore, we continue."

The radio transmissions from Kota stopped. Cha KinLaat worried his equipment had malfunctioned. He disassembled the equipment and rebuilt it to be even more sensitive than before. He checked it thoroughly, calibrating it against known stellar bodies. When he pointed it toward their destination, he only heard the hiss of empty space. It no longer emitted its former noisy electromagnetic babble.

The Kota system was silent.

Something terrible must have happened.

To Be Continued ...
The next novel in the series is *Stranger*.

DRAMATIS PERSONAE

Note: * indicates major characters
Founding Clan Members

***Taylor MacPherson:** Engineer and first leader of the Clan.

***Chris Kucinski:** The first recruit to the Clan. Becomes a fierce fighter.

***Franny Kucinski:** An early member of the clan.

***Fred Del Corso:** Construction man, early Clan member.

Maria Del Corso: Wife of Fred Del Corso.

Albert Del Corso: 2nd Son of Fred Del Corso.

John Wylie: Millwright, Spokesman for Master Rd. neighborhood.

Sam Wylie: Father of John Wylie, retired, bow maker.

Dr. Shel Weitzman: Dentist, spokesman for the Horse people.

Klaus Stolz: Construction equipment owner-operator, one of the Horse people.

Jim Higgins: One of Klaus Stolz's workers, equipment operator.

John Phelps: Horse farmer freed by Taylor MacPherson.

Jack O'Connor: One of the Horse people, cunning fighter.

Shirley O'Connor: Hot-tempered wife of Jack O'Connor.

Ted Callioux: Berea Resident freed by Taylor MacPherson; former college professor.

Patterson Rice: Spokesperson and driving force behind the River Park community, former NASA scientist.

Dr. Meltem Encirlik: Medical doctor who joins the Clan.

Noelle Smith: Refugee who becomes Taylor's housekeeper.

GANG MEMBERS

Bart Thompson: Ill-fated first leader of the Warehouse gang.

Dave Luken: Second leader of the Warehouse gang.

Armando Diaz Velasquez: *"Jefe"* or Chief of El Diablos Gang, also known as "Blade."

Enrique Maquinez: A Capitan and enforcer in El Diablos.

Skid Vukovitch: The leader of the Cleveland chapter of the Devil's Deacons.

Knuckles Milano: A Devil's Deacon; strong right hand to Skid.

Fast Eddy MacArthur: Leader of Rubber City Devil's Deacons; joins the Cleveland Deacons' alliance.

ALIENS (THE QU'UDA) AND THEIR EQUIPMENT

***Bilik Pudjata:** The discoverer of life on the Kota system (solar system of Earth) and alien specialist on expedition.

***Mata ChaLik BuMaru:** Spokesperson and leader of the Defenders of Qu'uda on the Egg-that-Flies.

Cha KinLaat DoMar: Pilot-navigator for the Egg-that-Flies.

DalChik DuJuga: The head of the Investigator-on-Interstellar-Life; later the head archivist on the Egg-that-Flies.

PiRup: The Prime Communicator on Qu'uda.

DuKlaat YataBu: Principal analyst for the Keepers-of-the-Egg.

DeKah NahBu: Pilot on the Bird-that-Soars.

Egg-that-Flies: The Deli Qu'uda fusion powered interstellar spacecraft which is a massive, self-contained system made from an asteroid; mainly a fuel tank.

Bird-that-Soars: The Qu'uda's fusion powered surface-to-space shuttle; also capable of interplanetary travel.

THE QU'UDA SOCIETY

A hermaphroditic egg-laying race inhabiting the Qu'uda planet and star system (also known as Epsilon Eridiani). Their planet is the second from a variable yellow star with several moons in orbit. It is a watery world given to fierce storms that roar in from the polar oceans across the small continents encircling the equatorial zone. The Qu'uda are an ancient civilization that has long had space travel capabilities. The race, once war-like, is very long-lived and has strict population controls and is strongly oriented to conformity. Their government is by consensus; personal biocomputers link with the center of the community for real-time feedback. Uses fusion as the principal source of power and mines the outer asteroids for scarce metals.

ABOUT THE AUTHOR

Malcolm Wood, born in England, came to the USA at age fourteen and graduated from Aurora, Ohio High School and Kent State University with a degree in chemistry while working full-time. Three years later, he fulfilled a self-made promise and spent two years traveling around the world. After resuming a career in chemistry, he obtained a MA in economics. About thirty years ago, he became a registered professional engineer in two disciplines (petroleum and environmental engineering), leading to a career in finance, and later, environmental consulting.

It was about this time he resumed writing fiction while working for a company that prepared economic analyses on specific industry sectors. Since these publications contained a significant amoung of estimating, it motivated him to start writing fiction. He attended numerous writing workshops and joined the Cleveland Science Fiction Critiquing group (also known as the Cajun Sushi Hamsters from Hell), which had such writers as Geoff Landis, S. Andrew Swann, Charles Oberndorf, and Maureen McHugh. Their critiques and comments pushed Malcolm hard to improve his craft. Almost twenty years ago, he formed the West Side Writers Fiction critiquing group, dedicated to writing at a professional level. During this time, he finished twelve novels and a biography of his travels.

His activities include obtaining a private pilot's license and a competition driver's license. In addition to writing, he has found time to ski, hunt, taste wine, and enjoy gourmet food.

IF YOU LIKED ...

If you liked Collapse, you might also enjoy:

Gamearth Trilogy Omnibus
by Kevin J. Anderson

Racers of the Night
by Brad R. Torgersen

Shadow Warriors
by Nathan B. Dodge

Our list of other WordFire Press authors and titles is always growing. To find out more and to see our selection of titles, visit us at:
wordfirepress.com